Winter's Reckoning

Lela Markham

Published by Breakwater Harbor Books

A Word from Lela Markham

Thank you for reading my book. If you enjoyed it, please take a moment to leave me a review at your favorite retailer. Only with your help can independent writers like me reach more readers. I appreciate it!

Wow, when I foreshadowed the virus that is sweeping through the Transformation Project universe, I had no idea Covid19 would be front-page news as I completed this book. Go back to *Day's End* and you can see that I was way ahead of the curve. I'm not a prophet. I just read the news and let my imagination run free. When a government can't keep personal information from being hacked, but holds stores of bioweapons, sooner or later some of them will get out. When better for that to happen than during a massive terrorist attack when everyone's attention is somewhere else?

Way back in *Life As We Knew It*, I had riots as a precursor to the attacks – part of the transformation process that would change the world my characters knew into something different. I did not foresee the racial component of the riots that are also front-page news as I finished *Winter's Reckoning*. Afterall, the white citizens of Emmaus don't think twice about the skin color of Vint and

Lila Barrett or of the Ramirez family. Shane's views on race are very similar to what my offspring hold – skin color is an identifying feature like eye and hair color or height. It doesn't tell them anything about who you on the inside because we're all pink there. Still I couldn't resist touching on the current racial unrest since my virus seems so prescient.

The Republic of Afrika is a real dream of some people who believe the color of our skin is the most important feature of our being. Will it come about because of the current unrest? I don't know. I do think there's a dark heart in some people who wouldn't object to a "winnowing" and I pray it is just fiction.

I might gore someone's ox with JT Delaney's prologue blaming military-adjacent service for Shane's PTSD. Let's be frank. Yes, Shane was a mercenary, which is a real thing, but the US military doesn't work any harder at trying to repair the psychological damage done by the wars they send Americans to. I live right next door to a military base and I'm within an hour's drive of two others. I literally have known hundreds of soldiers in my life and thousands of vets, including my own brother, my stepfather, two uncles, and at least one cousin. While what goes on in Shane's head during his PTSD-induced major depressive episode is a work of fiction, it's based on the reality of many of those that I have known.

Transformation Project started in the days when American politics still looked "normal" – if you can define normal as a president promising to "fundamentally change the country … our history, the way we talk and our traditions." (Okay, I'm melding Barack and Michelle Obama, but you don't think she gave an unauthorized speech, do you?). I never anticipated the election of Donald Trump or the clearly-evident mental decline of Joe Biden. Although I envisioned some sort of fire-sale scenario as part of the coordinated terrorism afflicting the Transformation Project universe, I never expected US leaders to shut down the majority of the economy over a strain of the common cold. I have no idea where things are going in the real world. It'll be interesting to look back on the outcome of this election and what I suspect will be a hard winter when the next book "A Death in Jericho" comes out. Let's hope people can still afford to buy books then.

I still strongly believe that centrally-managed societies are failures in the making. Central planners just can't know everything – especially not the future and I'm afraid we're going to learn some tough lessons about that as we try to "restart" the economy. Ever try to push start a 2-ton truck by hand?

The political winds of change currently sweeping our nation have not altered my opinion that we're headed in a wrong direction and that the danger to all comes from those who would be our "leaders". Some of them mean well, but the belief that they are more qualified than ordinary people to "lead" us is the primary problem.

I don't believe politics – choosing who will be in charge this year or next – will save us. If there is any salvation coming our way, it will be from the actions of ordinary people living their everyday lives – milking cows and harvesting apples, inventing the next world-changing technology (more about that in coming books). I know the propaganda machines of today insist politics is the center of all power, but it's really just swapping one crazy train for another at periodic intervals. If insanity is doing the same thing over and over again expecting different results, elections are absolutely delusional. Until we start doing something differently, we cannot expect different results.

Power corrupts and absolute power corrupts absolutely. The White House is as close to absolute power as you will ever find. Remember that as we head into the 2020 Presidential election. Look at all who are running and ask yourself – are any of these people "incorruptible"? Then why would you want to make him or her ruler over you, even on a temporary basis? There has got to be a better way to govern society than what we are doing now. If you fully intend to vote this fall, may I suggest Jo Jorgensen of the Libertarian Party appears sane and maybe a third-party can set something right that the major parties appear to have lost track of in their zeal to stay in power. Truthfully, what have we got to lose by trying something different? The Crazy Train is leaving the station regardless. Might as well get a new conductor at the controls and see what she does. Just a thought.

Or we could just stop voting altogether and delegitimize the entire system. What would that accomplish? It's got to be better than the mess we have now.

Lela Markham

Thanks!

This book is dedicated to Bernard Sliney who plays an important role in one scene of *Winter's Reckoning*. His invention of the WERC-U Heat Recovery Vat may revolutionize woodstove technology in the near-future. I liked it so much I installed it in my house and my novel.

No book is the work of a single individual. The author gets all the glory but standing behind every published writer is a host of support personnel. Thank you to visitors to my Facebook conversations for, often unknowingly, giving me many of the ideas presented in my novels. Rather than risking leaving anyone out, I'll just say "Thank you!"

Once again, I owe a huge debt to the composers of hymns. Bill and Gloria Gaither for *Because He Lives*, John Newton (and the unknown composer of the tune) for *Amazing Grace*, Marian Wright Edelman for *My Boar Is So Small* (which I've said before is the only song I know in Inupiat, thanks to Harley Shields), and especially whoever wrote *Wayfaring Stranger*. If you're unfamiliar with these songs, google them. They're well-worth the exploration. You may not expect to find faith in a graveyard, but I couldn't send Jacob Israel Delaney off without a few of his favorite songs.

Table of Contents

"In war, the damage you inflict on the enemy might be immediately apparent. The damage you inflict on yourself in doing so will only become apparent later."

—Stewart Stafford

Winter's Reckoning

Book 6

Transformation Project

Prologue

Americans had always seen war as something foreign. It happened in other countries. We sent soldiers to pound on the bad guys and then we sat back smug in the knowledge that we'd made the world a better place.

The harm we did to those countries might have been outside of our view, but the harm we did to ourselves came home with those soldiers. Maybe they could hide the pain when the world was alive, and the distractions were many. They covered the wounds with Netflix and Monday night football, parades and frisbee in the park. And then the world as they knew it died. With winter encroaching, and hunger growing, some began to feel the scars they'd borne silently for so long.

Death comes to all of us, especially during the Apocalypse. Death came for more of us as the days grew shorter and the food grew scarcer. What little we knew of the outside world reminded us that we were among the lucky ones, but luck can run out and then you're left with only stubborn optimism and Midwestern hardiness. That can run out too.

JT Delaney

Sky Dance

Black Friday

Emmaus, Kansas

Jacob Delaney never wanted a whole lot of fuss made over his passing from this world's realm into paradise, but when you died in November during the Apocalypse, just burying your body required a good deal of fuss.

Rob Delaney pulled his truck over on the side of the road at the bottom of Beulah Drive. A light dusting of snow had covered everything in the night, making navigating the unlighted roads a bit easier since headlights reflected off the ice. The unplowed road to the old Jericho township lay silent in the chill night. The sky had cleared, revealing a black velvet carpet sprayed with silver diamonds. Rob's breath fogged as he stepped from the truck.

The cemetery marched up Beulah Ridge in plateaus carved in its gentle slopes. The switchback road hadn't seen a plow all winter. The town had been fortunate not to need the cemetery much since a hundred people died in the City Hall bomb shelter air-filter disaster in early October. Fuel was tight, so nobody plowed out roads that didn't need to be plowed. That meant you couldn't drive to Beulah Cemetery and Jacob's pallbearers would have a hike ahead of them.

Rob started the long climb toward the distant glow of a bonfire where he knew his younger son thawed the ground for his grandfather's final resting place. Someone had to do it and Shane didn't want to be around people right now, so he'd volunteered. Rob doubted his son was unable to hear his breathing as he approached, but Shane leaned over the bonfire and only lifted his head just before Rob entered the fire's glow. He blinked into the darkness like he expected wraiths to appear any moment. Maybe he had already been visited by wraiths. Were his nightmares dreams or visitations?

Rob removed his baseball cap as he approached to assure Shane knew who walked up on him. The boy was always armed and when he'd come to the house a few hours ago, he'd been less than sane.

"Who's with Grandpa?" Shane turned a log over with a long-handled pike. The grave was nearly deep enough, but it took most of Thanksgiving Day to get there.

"Ed Greyeyes showed up. I figured I'd give him and his boys some time. They'll bear the casket."

Shane cranked off the cup on the thermos and filled it three-quarters. He topped it off with bourbon. Ordinarily he respected Rob enough to be covert about drinking, but apparently the rules for private wakes were in force.

"The Rez and some Army guys stormed the Wyandot Lake facility day before yesterday." Shane's gaze steadied on him. He'd been out of town, collecting a friend's wife in

Santa Fe. "They lost the Army guy walking point and John Swaim broke his hand somehow, but they got all the supplies that were left. There was just one guy guarding, so that was quite a bit." Shane muttered swear words under his breath. He'd previously turned down a siege of the Department of Agriculture facility because he'd calculated Emmaus would lose too many men. The boy wasn't psychic, just the best trained mercenary available right now.

"Was it Packard?" Shane was on record that he considered Dick Vance's death on Packard's head and, though he had never met this man, he would kill him if he had the opportunity.

"No. Just some young kid. They killed him so we'll never know how he was connected to Packard, if he was being relieved regularly, any of that. Ed was headed this way with the Army guys because Cai made a deal with them – shelter in exchange for coming onto our border patrol."

Shane scowled.

"He might have wanted to tell me about that."

"Yeah. You were in Santa Fe and, frankly, you two can argue that later. Whatever you arranged is none of my concern." Shane gave him a narrow-eyed glare. Rob decided not to push his luck. "When Ed learned about Pa's passing, he wanted to send Uncle Israel off with an Indian flair. I'm never comfortable with that." Rob's mother, Jacob's wife, had been a Wyandot Indian, but Vi hadn't truly raised her boys in the culture, focusing instead on the girls, who now lived far from Kansas.

"Why do we have to bring God into this fucking mess?" Shane's normally deep drawl spat like machine-gun fire into the crisp pre-dawn air. Rob could argue Jacob loved God, but he decided to address the real issue.

"When was the last time you slept?"

"Through the night? Never. Your point?"

Rob never liked to discuss emotional issues with his kids. He'd somehow managed to avoid the dating ethics talk with both boys, leaving it up to Jill. Stu Mackler told them both about sex and how not to get a girl pregnant, somehow couched in a conversation about horses. Alex's father bought Shane his first box of condoms before Rob even knew how close the kid was to having sex with his girlfriend. Rob had preferred taking them fishing and teaching them about the natural world. *I was a good father, but I wasn't a great father.* Jacob treaded Shane's stormy waters better than anyone, but now the job fell to Rob, who knew it should always have been his.

"You're not a mystery to me. I haven't had a good night's sleep since this whole mess started. Pa understood that you never really leave the suck behind. You get better, but there's always something going to happen that'll trigger it. Yours was already close to the surface and Pa's death has triggered it."

Shane swallowed the hot coffee, wincing from the pain.

"Did you get a letter from him too?"

Rob frowned at him, then shrugged.

"Hell, I got a whole binder." Shane's forehead wrinkled with confusion. "I'll tell you about it later. That's a nice bottle of booze – not the one that's been kicking around in your closet the last few weeks."

Rob snooping in his closet might have mattered to Shane any other day, but today he didn't even seem to question it.

"Jason."

"Oh, that man! I will never see what Pa saw in him."

Jason Breen was actually a relative now – father of Rob's daughter-in-law Marnie – but for many years he'd been a thorn in Rob's side. As mayor, you were supposed to care about the semi-legal doings of the people living in your town, but it was hard to take a strong stance when your own father encouraged those doings. It was a paradox about Jacob's character, that he could love Jesus and Jason Breen at the same time.

Shane shrugged. Like his grandfather, he appreciated something in Jason that escaped Rob. The younger man poured more bourbon into the cup and moved to put the cap on the bottle. Rob could smell it from across the firepit.

"You want some?"

Rob snorted, shook his head.

"Every day, all day, especially on days like today."

"Toast Grandpa with me."

Shane straddled a corner of the pit to hold the cup out toward him. The desire for oblivion roaring through him, Rob sighed and took it, staring deep into the dark amber depths with temptation's claws waited to get its hooks in him. Irish coffee was the fastest way he knew to not feeling.

"He was the best person I ever knew." Shane nodded agreement. "Always up for a challenge and wise – oh, so wise."

"Passionate and consistent." Shane gestured with the bottle.

"Matter-of-fact and to the point, but never bossy. I wish I'd learned that trick from him."

"There's a lot of stuff I wish I'd learned from him." Something dark and scary moved behind Shane's eyes as his gaze flickered toward a gravestone to Rob's left. He looked. Shadows – moving, swirling, taking shape. He'd seen the photo. He expected an Indian woman in a gingham dress, wielding a long buck knife. He blinked at the Vietnamese woman in a silk *ao dai* of dark blue over light grey. Her long black hair moved in a breeze he couldn't feel, and she carried an SKS in her hands. "You see her too, don't you?" Shane's awed whisper sighed across the crackle of the fire

Rob wrenched his gaze back to his son and raised the cup in toast.

"We became Death and there's a price for that. Here's to Pa understanding that for the both of us."

Shane wiped tears away and raised the bottle to his lips, the expression in his eyes daring Rob to choose.

Pour it on the ground.

The cup wavered its way up toward his mouth as Rob's arm took on a life of its own. It never minded how many years you'd successfully controlled it. Addiction wanted its own way. The delightful aroma of bourbon filled his nasal passages and his tongue went dry as every cell in his body screamed "Drink it!" The Vietnamese woman, now standing at the end of Pa's grave, pointed her SKS at him as if to enforce compliance.

8

And then that quiet Midwestern twang. "Son, what do you think that'll accomplish?"

He had no answer for Jacob, who had known him so well. Thirty-three years of sobriety and he still couldn't answer what a drink of bourbon would accomplish. He didn't even like bourbon. He'd been a Johnnie Walker man.

The fire near his feet flickered up at the introduction of 100 proof. He looked up from the fiery depths to stare in awe as an auroral display danced above the ridge line to the north. Shane lowered the bottle from his lips and turned to watch a trail of folks coming up the cemetery road with a simple wooden coffin on broad shoulders. Ed Greyeyes and his two boys, Cai, Alex and Andrew Bennett bore the weight while Brad Snow led the procession and a hundred people followed behind. The path proved slick with snow and ice, but they couldn't get a truck up the road without plows, so this was all they had -- a proud procession in the black and white world of winter in defiance of the apocalypse.

For many years, Jacob told people he didn't want anyone sad at his funeral. People remembered, dressing in the brightest cold-weather clothes they owned. Others tied bright bandanas and ribbons on their dark coats.

"I'll be getting an upgrade," Jacob assured. *"Don't weep for me. Dance. Sing. Shout to the Lord."*

You need air to sing and the folks coming up Beulah Drive were winded. Rob tossed the cup at Shane and filled his lungs with air so he could send the notes of *Because He Lives* boldly into the cold night air. Jazz's surprisingly deep alto, a little ragged with the exertion of the climb, echoed back. Others picked it up, breathless. Shane dropped into the pit to scoop out the coals and finish the grave. Danny Hughes left Sharon McLaughlin's side to help Shane. Jacob righteously championed his redemption and Rob thanked God he'd listened and not hung the boy with the USDA cow cops.

"Pa didn't want mourners." Rob thought he'd cry, but he didn't feel it. He smiled as Ed Greyeyes straightened from setting the coffin beside the open hole. Jacob and Ed built two simple pine coffins when Vi died and stored the longer of the two for this day. There had to be a hundred people quietly filing into the spaces between the surrounding headstones.

"We sent him off with laughter." Ed looked at his boys who wore tribal regalia, as if they'd somehow known what they find in Emmaus. Rob wouldn't scoff if they said they did. "Your ma's waiting." Ed indicated the dancing lights – mostly green, but with flickers of blue and lavender, sweeping in ribbons against the black of the sky. While they stared, the single ribbon split into two, pulsing rapidly across the sky like lines of dancers chasing each other across the top of the ridge – one mostly green and the other almost red.

"We should finish with music." Rob watched as more people straggled up the hill.

"And funny stories." Cai took Marnie's hand as she arrived. Jill moved in beside Rob. Shane retreated to a headstone on the far side of the pit, his eyes dark slits in the lantern light.

"I was a boy when I met Uncle Israel." Ed's voice echoed over the gathered crowd. "And such a young fool." The tall man with the wavy raven-black hair and Fu Manchu beard launched into a story of meeting his aunt and uncle at his father Lai's funeral. He'd been young – maybe eight, no nine – and hot-headed and angry that he'd never known his father and now never would. Jacob took him under his wing, taught him to be a man. All those years and Rob just heard this story now. Pa wasn't much for tooting his own horn. The Wyandot had a historical funeral ritual that involved lengthy story-telling and an exchange of potlatch gifts, but folks didn't have a lot to give these days and most folks were up before dawn and would have to get back to milk the cows or stock the fire.

Cai started them all singing *My Boat is So Small*, which had been Vi's favorite song and one Jacob knew many versions of on the fiddle. Who would play the fiddle now that both Stu Mackler and Pa had gone to their reward? Alex told a story about meeting Jacob – a briefer version of the one he'd told over Thanksgiving dinner. Cai told one about getting tossed by the horse when his grandfather was teaching him to ride.

Unexpectedly, Shane's clear baritone rang out across the hillside in the haunting tune of *Wayfaring Stranger*, vibrating with pain on the high notes and resonating like thunder when it dropped into the bass range.

"I'm just a poor wayfaring stranger, traveling through this world below, there's no sickness, no toil, nor danger, in that bright land to which I go."

Cai picked it up at the chorus, his higher tenor-baritone inviting others to join. The two leads – one higher, the other lower wove together like a choir, riding above any other voices. Meanwhile, the lightshow pulsed as if in counterpoint.

"I'm going there to see my Father, and all my loved ones gathered there, I'm just going over Jordan, I'm just going over home."

Of course, Shane, that inveterate agnostic, knew the words to his grandfather's favorite hymn.

"I know dark clouds will gather 'round me, I know my way is hard and steep, But beauteous fields arise before me, where God's redeemed, their vigils keep."

Now Keri and Alex carried the tune, their voices weaving together as if they'd sung together all their lives. Shane automatically lowered his volume to let them lead.

"I'm going there to see my loved ones passed beyond the veil before me. I'm going over Jordan, I'm just going over home."

Now Rob and Ed took lead. They were near the same register, but Ed's voice echoed with passion Rob never quite grasped.

"I'll soon be free of earthly trials, my body rest in the old church yard. I'll drop this cross of self-defeat and I'll go singing home to God."

It was customary for whoever started to complete the song, but Shane slid off the headstone and disappeared into the cemetery, so Cai finished, joined by Rob, Ed, Alex, Keri, and Jazz.

"I'm going there to meet my Savior, dwell with Him and never roam. I'm just going over Jordan. I'm just going over home." As the last notes trailed out on the wind, the aurora ribbons joined, pulsed, and started to fade.

The funeral gathering sang a couple more songs and then Rob said it was time. Shane's grief notwithstanding, Jacob didn't want a lot of fuss made over his passing to a better world.

"When my mother died, she left me a note asking me to take care of my father and explaining that she'd try to wait just over Jordan, but he shouldn't be surprised to find her picking daisies in her bare feet with her hair loose."

The crowd laughed. Danny, Cai, Dell and Kix Conopher, Mace Kettridge and Alex made short work of filling in the hole. Rob indicated the single dulling ribbon of light that had replaced the two.

"I guess the Wyandot would say she's chasing her man."

Ed grinned.

"We'd say she caught him."

The crowd laughed. Rob opened his mouth, took in a deep breath of icy air and started.

"Amazing Grace, how sweet the sound, that saved a wretch like me …."

The last shovelful of dirt fell, and the funeral crowd turned toward the road, singing as they went in a send-off worthy of Jacob's final wishes.

Contract Offer

Seattle, Washington

Geo Tully flicked the blinds in the former craft room, staring out at the street. Not much moved, which itself felt creepy. His calendar said it was Black Friday. People should have been heading for shopping centers and putting up Christmas lights. None of that happened this year because an EMP had rendered shopping centers and Christmas lights obsolete.

Thirty-five hours since Liam Carson left him to consider B&W's offer. Join the Knights Industries security force here in Seattle or be put on a truck headed east. He and his skills weren't welcome here as a free agent, but nobody wanted to kill him.

Why did he doubt that?

"You've been trained to distrust private industry," Liam had said. "As far as you're concerned Knights Industries are mercenaries. Surely you've noticed that we're not abusing the local population."

He'd noticed. He just didn't believe it.

"We could use your help, but it has to be voluntary. We're not slavers." Carson sighed. "This is a nice set up and that radio tower would come in handy as well. It's been here so long your neighbors don't even notice it. But my superiors worry about men like you inside the city possibly causing trouble."

"So. what does that mean for me if I say 'no'?"

"You've got family in Kansas, right?"

Everyone's information resided online these days so even though Geo's stomach tightened, he knew he shouldn't be surprised at what Carson knew. The Knights still had access to the Cloud, even as everyone else lived without electricity.

"I do."

"We could provide transportation as far east as our network goes currently. Winter in the Plains has cut us off somewhat."

"No trains?"

"You ever take a train through the Cascades?"

"No, but I've seen the hanging bridges in photos."

"It's impassable until we reinvent the older technologies. But there's trucks until the passes close by spring avalanche."

"Dropping me off in the middle of nowhere in the dead of winter?"

"You're not our problem if you choose not to join us."

That seemed fair. Geo wished he knew what his answer would be when Carson returned. If they knew he could monitor their radio chatter with the tower, they'd done nothing to stop his spying. He'd only heard benign conversations – techs and security personnel going about ordinary business. What sort of help would they need from a trained Navy Seal? Was it possible they were seeding the radio transmissions so he wouldn't know what was going on? The wisest choice might be to go along and observe, to infiltrate the enemy camp so to speak. It wasn't like Mara Wells needed him. He didn't know how to farm and that was all Kansas was good for. He wondered if Bunnell & Wilson, parent company of Knights Industries, had the means to communicate with Kansas. He'd like to know his folks were safe.

Duke the Labrador retriever tick-ticked up behind him and settled his big head against Geo's muscular thigh.

They hadn't searched the house – hadn't even asked to. Somehow, they knew his tower was active, though. He stared harder at the street, still not sure what he'd say when Carson arrived. Thirty-five hours and five minutes. He sat down on the floor and massaged Duke's floppy black ears.

"What do you think, boy?"

Dogs never had the answers, but Labs managed to look deeply wise while thinking of chasing a frisbee. Maybe he should have just got in the old truck in the garage and headed east as soon as Carson left the house. The Knights Industry supervisor had assured him nobody would stop him. So why did he feel like he was under house arrest?

Half an hour. A rumbling through the house's frame got him up on the window seat, peeking through the blinds, but the Knights truck just stopped a few houses down, let off a couple of people and picked up three more. As a bus system it worked okay on a dry day. It wouldn't be dry for much longer today. Clouds piled up against the fabled Seattle emerald hills. The truck drove away. Geo opened the blinds enough to let the weak morning sun into the attic room so he could reread the contract. He'd signed a contract with the US Navy a few times and this seemed pretty straightforward and a whole lot less dictatorial. He had actual rights under this contract. He could get out of it at periodic intervals. He could refuse some orders he'd always wanted to refuse as a SEAL. The Knights didn't court-martial you for disobedience. They claimed to just release you from service if an arbitrator agreed you were wrong to disobey.

Fifteen minutes.

He'd joined the service for the honor and glory. His father had said he'd find neither and, truthfully, if he were honest with himself, he hadn't. He'd dropped into a compound in Kandahar and killed some guy who might or might not have been Al Qaeda. A team member had shot a woman who might have been the guy's wife. Three kids under the age of 12 watched while their parents died and then were taken into custody and delivered to an undisclosed location. The thought of kids in a black site sickened him. Honor and glory? Not bloody likely, though he had a medal that said so.

After President Meyer had been killed by a ground-to-air missile taking out Airforce One, and Dotson had risen to power, Geo had almost not signed his contract last year, but he'd been convinced men with his skillset were needed to combat the rising threat in Miristan. Except US regular troops weren't even deployed to most of Miristan. Most of the work was done by Knights Industries contractors. Was that why he distrusted this offer so much?

Five minutes.

Duke moaned and opened a sleepy brown eye to stare at him.

"Yeah, boy, I don't know either."

Geo pushed himself up from the floor and closed Duke up in the basement in case a firefight ensued. He'd just slid his service weapon into the back waistband of his jeans when a knock sounded on the door. This time there were no guards at the back door, though he figured they were watching the alley.

Carson was about 35, fit, medium height with blond hair shot with caramel streaks. His business casual clothes looked slightly damp from the misty rain starting to coat the street.

"Where's your partner?" he asked after they shook hands. There were no Knights standing behind him on the porch.

"Duke?" Carson nodded. "Just got him out of the way in case we had some unpleasantry."

"Labs are not dogs of war ordinarily, but you needn't worry about that. I told you. We won't force you to do anything you don't want to do."

"What's this paragraph – special duties as assigned?"

"You know what that is, Geo. You're a Navy SEAL and we need your skills. We'll pay you for it and we won't blow smoke up your ass and tell you it's for God and country."

"Who do you want me to kill?"

"That's what I like about you Special Forces types. Bluntly honest."

Geo leaned against the dining room table and waited. Carson's smile flickered.

"You monitor radio frequencies. You know we have a problem on our eastern border."

"I know you have a *military* problem on your eastern border. Are you asking me to go up against my former teammates?"

"No. I'm asking you to give us a chance and then decide if you want to go up against them. And hopefully, in the meantime, we'll figure out a way to halt hostilities. We're only enemies because they were abusing people – and I think you know that."

Geo remembered the mother and children who walked into the front of the command trailer at the market and never came out again. He tried not to shiver as gooseflesh rose on his forearms.

"They don't know that we've broken their digital codes. Do you understand what they're saying?"

"I'm Navy, not Army and I can't usually hear them at all." Wes could finesse far more from the radio than Geo could. Geo's real skills lay in knowing when to shoot someone in the face.

Being careful not to make Geo suspicious, Carson drew a crisp piece of paper out of his inside breast pocket.

"Try those codes and there's a possible translation matrix. It's only partial, but you know – maybe if you hear what they're up to and you compare it to what we're up to – I'll be back in a week. You should know, though, that we're watching you and monitoring you. As long as you're squatting here as a solo, that's fine, but you start meeting up with people and you're going to have to leave town. Right?"

Geo nodded. Carson seemed on the up and up and he wasn't demanding Geo sign a contract just yet, but trust wasn't something they trained into you in SEAL training. Carson jotted something down on the back of the paper.

"If you make up your mind before the end of the week, you can pull up this frequency and use this code and I will appear at your door to collect the contract. We really need guys like you, but we really will not force you to take our side against your former coworkers."

Geo nodded, still unwilling to commit.

"How are you fixed for food here?"

"I'm not starving." He'd kill for some fresh meat and vegetables, but he had plenty of calories to live on.

"I've got a box of fresh out in the truck. Yours as a goodwill gesture." Geo's gut tightened. "You can select one item, make me eat it, if you need to test my sincerity."

"Why do I get the feeling I'm not the first one you've encountered who wasn't sure of this offer?"

"You're not." Carson spoke quietly into his radio and a Knights mercenary carried a box to Geo's door. Apples. Oranges. Celery. Tomatoes. "Which do you want me to choose?"

"I'm going to trust you."

"Good. I'm not hungry anyway. If it helps any, after we identified your friend's body, we notified his family."

"I didn't know how to get hold of them. His aunt must have had all her numbers in her phone and that probably perished with her."

"Yeah." Carson seemed appropriately sad. "Apparently, they knew you were staying here, and it never occurred to them not to say anything. They're okay with you being here."

"Didn't even really think about that. Do they want Duke?"

"It isn't in the file, so I'm guessing not. You keep trying to give him away, but then you put him out of harm's way."

"I like him well enough that I don't want him to starve or get shot. He deserves to have a good home."

"Like I said, he has one. You can stay here with him if you take our job offer or you can take him with you when you go. When I come back, you're going to need to make a decision."

Geo walked Carson to the door and thanked him for the food. He actually thought he liked the man … except he was not ready to trust him.

Soup

December 7
Wichita, Kansas

The bowl felt cold to the touch as he spewed his life into it. His forehead burned while a chill ran up his back, sending a shudder through his dehydrated body. Ren collapsed back onto his pillows, coughing. The ceiling blurred and warped as the door to his room opened and closed.

"I've brought you some soup." Eden came forward with another bowl that steamed, wafting mist into her face, causing her hair to curl slightly.

Now that he'd emptied his guts, he thought he could eat, and he pushed up against the back of the sofa his bed pulled from. She offered him the spoon, but he shook too hard to get the soup from the bowl to his mouth.

"Let me." She took the spoon and brought up a spoonful that he could sip. After five of them, he stopped shaking, though his muscles ached like he'd been stomped on by an elephant. He indicated he needed to rest.

"What day is it?" His voice cracked.

"Tuesday."

"The date?"

"December 7."

He'd been five days at this. The first two hadn't been bad. He'd just been uncomfortable. The last three had made him wish he'd die.

"What's going on out there?"

"Phil says he and Crispin have it under control and you should concentrate on getting well."

The girl looked scarcely more than a teenager, though he knew she was 21. Her cheekbones were her strongest feature, probably from her father's people, although her mother had a strong bone structure too. Her jawline was more delicate. Her skull reminded him more of Asians than Indians, indicative of her Eskimo blood. Her amber eyes were almond-shaped, fringed with lashes darker than her medium-brown hair which had no ash tones in it. He'd seen photos of her siblings and knew she was the lightest of them and her elder brother the darkest.

"Since when do you call him Phil?"

"Since I started calling you Ren. After you've held a bowl for each other's vomit, it's time to be friends." Ren chuckled. It was belly-laugh funny, but he didn't have the energy for that.

"Eden, know that I mean to get you back to your family as soon as possible."

"I appreciate that, sir, even though I know it's not possible now."

"It will be. I need sleep. You might want to bring me a fresh puke bucket."

"Yes, sir. You know, don't you?"

"Who your mother is?" She nodded as he settled his pillows. "Yes."

"How?"

"You use her maiden name and you look a bit like her. And probably I saw you during the campaign. She wasn't the reason he lost, you know. He was just a bad candidate for a party that was fed up with lying progressives pretending to be conservatives of which he was the poster child."

She giggled.

"I don't think the country was ready for her. Alaska was though. When Don Young stepped down, she took his seat and then won reelection with more of the vote than Don had."

"How'd she pull off being Speaker of the House?"

"I don't think she knows. She didn't even want to be. Dad told her he thought it was a bad idea. That's why he decided to spend most of the year in Alaska with Hannah, Michal and Jeph."

"Some people thought they were having marital trouble."

"Not that they've shared with us kids. It was like he sensed this was coming. I wonder if they're okay. She flew home because he was hurt in an accident. I wish I knew."

She gathered the puke bowl and put another one in its place. She really managed his affairs efficiently, not at all like a young girl caught up in a world she knew nothing about, but like a woman who had been raised in an environment

where life and death decisions were commonplace. Shoot
the bear or get eaten by the bear. Shoot the caribou or
watch it run over the mountain and go hungry this winter.
Judge the jump across the creek right or swim to your
death. They didn't raise them delicate in Alaska and Eden
Maracal was a strong Alaskan.

"I'll come check on you in an hour – bring you more of
that soup."

"Thank you." He could scarcely produce a whisper
from his raw throat. He dozed off considering his
granddaughter. Had her parents made it home to Emmaus
yet? If not, was she as strong as Eden Maracal?

Cost of Living

December 22

Emmaus, Kansas

Dell Conopher squatted in front of the coal stove, working the bellows, watching the glow slowly build. Coal stoves were hard. You could build a fire in a wood stove in a matter of several minutes, but coal took a long time to reignite if you'd let it burn too low. His callused hands ached with the cold and his view out the side window tightened his stomach. Snow had drifted up against the barn door overnight and he'd need to shovel before he could get in to collect the eggs and milk the goats. Winter came early, and most days flakes fell from the sky. When the wind picked up, that snow piled up in inconvenient places, and the wind always blew in northwest Kansas. Without mechanical devices to clear the snow away, it meant time taken from vital chores just to access vital chores. He'd known 25 years ago when he'd decided to follow his father into farming that it was a hard life, but he'd not expected to be doing it all by hand. On the other hand, he didn't envy his brother Rafe, trying to eke a living out of mechanicking with no food in the pantry.

Dell closed the stove and headed upstairs, wondering where Leisha had gotten herself to. When he'd woke up at the first blush of light and found her not in bed, he'd expected to find her making breakfast, but the kitchen had been cold and empty, no food pulled out on the counter. He'd concentrated on building up the fire before going to look for her. At the top of the stairs, he bent his head under the lintel. He always felt like Paul Bunyan on this second floor. His father had been an inch shorter than him, but his grandfather would have only come to his shoulder. Life had been hard before World War II. Even on a farm, you didn't always eat regular. History was cyclical.

When he reached the top of the stairs, he paused to listen. Leisha's low voice filtered out from the boys' room. Dell pushed open the half-closed door to see Leisha checking their oldest boy's temperature.

"I thought he'd gotten over the flu. I wouldn't have had him working this week if he were still sick."

She looked over her shoulder at him. A small woman with a braid that fell almost to her knees, she still looked nice in jeans after five children.

"Can you close the blinds?" She pointed to the window. "He's complaining of a headache and he's running a fever."

Dell stepped over to the window, meaning to pull down the blinds, but ended up staring down the front driveway as twenty people came struggling through the snow toward his house.

"Leisha, go get a gun and get the kids up and armed. We've got company and they ain't bringing pie."

Dell grabbed his AR15 from the rack above the coatrack and stepped out on to the porch. He heard the window above his head open. Kix might be sick, but the kid knew the stakes. A mob had stripped the church's refugee center of every scrap of food a week ago and beat Brad Snow when he and some of the refugees tried to resist.

"What can I do for you?" Mace Kettridge led the vanguard, but others struggled along behind in the knee-deep snow. Dell figured Mace as the instigator of this train of trouble headed his way.

"We've come for your stores."

Dell's rifle had been across his back, but now he brought it forward. People recoiled.

"I don't want to shoot my neighbors, but I've got nothing for you. I've got seven mouths to feed and just enough calories to make it to spring."

"And we're already out of food, so you need to share."

"Get off my land." Dell thumbed off the safety. "You and I have known each other a long time and I don't want to kill anyone, but I'm not giving up my kids' food, so get going."

Mace leveled his own rifle at Dell. A shot rang out, a round splatted the snow beside Mace's foot. Dell heard Leisha chamber the next round in her Remington.

"You lower that gun, Mace, or the next one goes through your head." Leisha sounded certain of her aim. She *was* a better shot than Dell.

Dell heard two more windows open above the porch. That had to be Kix and Geneva, his oldest daughter. He'd told them after the raid at the church that they needed to be ready to defend the property and the all-important food stores.

"You can't keep food from starving people," someone shouted. The dozen neighbors gathered on his drive all looked fairly well-fed at this point, but that might change in a day or so if they were out already. Before Dell could say anything in response, a bullet tore through the siding beside where he stood. He dropped behind the porch wall and sent an AR round in Mace's direction. He heard more weapons fire over his head, and he knew several rounds punctured the siding he stood behind. His father had lined the inside of the porch with siding too and apparently AR rounds couldn't go through both layers.

The firing ceased and Dell risked a peek. Mace hid behind Dell's truck and some of the mob seemed to have disappeared.

"Mace, I don't want to kill you, man, but you can't have my children's food."

"My children are starving *now*, Dell. You can find more food, but my kids are going to die before I can do that."

"I don't know that. If you take my food now, we could be starving in two weeks."

"If you don't share, we starve now."

"And how is that our problem, Mace? None of us were prepared for this, but some of us were less unprepared. I'm sorry, but I can't starve my own children so yours live. I wish I could create food, but I –."

A bullet ricocheted off the porch light, creating a sharp report, followed by a barrage of shots from above. Dell couldn't do anything but stay hunkered down until the shooting slowed. He was just about to try again when he heard the roar of a truck engine and the blast of an air horn and dared a peek to see a City maintenance vehicle fishtailing up the driveway. Rob Delaney bellowed at the top of his lungs, sitting in the open passenger window, an AR15 of his own propped across the windshield. People scattered, some of them no doubt remembering that Rob served three tours in Vietnam. Chief Joe Kelly rode in the back, his own rifle out while Cai Delaney handled the slippery push up the driveway.

Leisha missed Mace's head, but his blood darkened the snow beneath him. Two others lay screaming with grazes and the others hightailed it into the brush.

"God dammit, Mace," Dell screamed as he closed the gap between them. "We were friends!"

Mace's eyes grew wild with fear as he realized he'd been shot.

"My kids are starving."

"That's no excuse for making *my* kids starve." Dell opened Mace's coat and tried not to gasp. Leisha's Remington was for deer, not men.

Police Chief Joe Kelly and Mayor Rob Delaney knelt by the other injured men now.

"Leisha, bring the first aid kit," Dell yelled. She came out of the house way too quickly to be obeying him. She must have gone for the kit as soon as the shooting slowed. Tears and snot ran down her face.

"I'm sorry, Mace, but you can't shoot at my husband," she said as she knelt in the red snow. Her hands shook so hard she couldn't pick up the first aid supplies. Dell grabbed some gauze to shove into the hole she'd made. Mace screamed in pain. "We need to check to see if the bullet went through."

"Woman, the bullet went through," Dell assured her. "It's a hunting rifle. Of course, it went through."

The amount of blood in the snow provided a secondary clue to just how bad it was. Cai Delaney came with a backboard.

"We need to load him in the truck, see if Marnie can stop the bleeding."

A sheen of sweat covered Mace's white face and his eyes rapidly grew unfocused. Dell could feel his own throat choking up, but then he heard glass breaking and Kix shouting. Dell and Cai both ran toward the house. Kix's AR reported three times followed by silence. Two men lay still on the kitchen floor as Kix leaned on the countertop, shaking like a leaf in a high wind. Geneva called down from above, begging for Kix to tell her what was going on.

"I got them." The boy's voice wavered with weakness; color drained away with the shock of what he'd just done. "We know them," he whispered.

Leisha appeared beside him.

"Oh, god. Oh, my god."

Cai checked the vitals of the two men, shaking his head, swallowing convulsively. Kix vomited on the counter and Leisha pulled herself together to get her boy back to bed. He left the AR on the counter and walked out leaning heavily on his mother.

"I don't believe this," Dell whispered. It would have been so much worse if the Delaneys hadn't shown up. Could they have held off an entire mob with just four rifles? Lace could shoot too, but she was only 11. Her job was to take the two younger ones into the knee wall closet and be prepared to shoot whoever opened the doors who weren't her parents or older siblings.

"Neighbor turning against neighbor," Cai whispered. Rob's oldest son, he wore a black watch cap pulled down over his sandy hair, several days of reddish scruff blurring his jaw line, and he looked like he hadn't slept in a week.

"How did you know?"

"We were out patrolling, saw the crowd headed up your driveway, then we heard shots."

"It would have been so much --." Dell cut off as Rob came to the door. "Mace?"

"There's nothing we could have done." Rob scanned the two bodies, casting a questioning look at Cai, who shook his head. "We need to get the other two to town, let Marnie patch them up before we banish them."

"Banish them? They'll starve out there."

"They're starving now, Dell. There's nothing any of us can do about it. My family has maybe a month left before we're that desperate."

"We'll figure it out, Dad. Shane said he might stalk those deer Andrew Bennett saw yesterday." Cai Delaney was an inveterate optimist.

"I better check my salt licks." How quickly you could forget about the dead men lying on your kitchen floor. "I got one last week, gave it to Janna Thomas. She's trying to keep her kids fed and she's not out raiding other people's pantries."

He wiped cold sweat off his forehead as the shakes suddenly hit him.

"Dad, take them back to the med center. I'll stay here and clean up."

Rob nodded at Cai's suggestive gaze shift and turned toward the door, then paused.

"Dell, there's no shame in protecting your family. If you could loan Cai a vehicle to get these bodies to Beulah." Dell cast off shock enough to nod. "We've got Sharon's foster kid digging graves as fast as he can."

"I'd send Kix, but the boy's got the flu."

Rob nodded like he understood and kept on through the front of the house.

"Still?" Cai asked. "That's like three weeks."

Cai had come over and helped Dell and his younger boy with some chores when Kix first got sick.

"I don't know," Dell admitted as another shudder ran through him. He'd need to board up that broken window. Another chore, another slide toward third world status. It wasn't right that a man had to shoot three neighbors just so his kids could eat.

Dell told Cai he'd be right back with a truck. He needed the break from the house. Quakes wavered through his body and he puked in the snow as he went. Tears spilled down his cheeks as he backed the Chevy half-ton up to the back door. Cai already had dragged one body out to the porch and now brought the second one. Norm Watson was a family man too. Terry Smith had been a fine auto mechanic.

"I just can't believe times are coming to this," Cai said.

"I believed it *could*, but I never really thought it *would* happen."

"Could and would are two different things." They loaded the bodies silently, Dell crying some more. "I hate it, but Shane's right. Some of us survive separately or we all starve together."

"Thanks for taking care of this. I got some millet I can give you in payment."

A month ago, Cai would have said "no", but realism had finally reached even the eternal optimist.

"I'll gladly take it. Thank you. These guys ain't going anywhere. You want help boarding up that window?" A cold breeze swirled through the shattered glass of the back door.

"I'd appreciate it. Silver's only 10 and Rafe won't be out until afternoon."

"Rafe helping you here on the farm?"

"They're moving out here today. It ain't safe for people in the town anymore – obviously. I'm surprised you haven't deserted your place for Alex's."

"Marnie needs to be in town and, I don't know. I'm not willing to give up on our community."

"What community?" Dell stared at the two bodies in the bed of his pickup. Cai looked off across the fields, blue eyes haunted. Hearing no counter to his assertion, Dell moved on.

"I've got some plywood in the barn. Thanks for helping."

Cai nodded. What more was there to say?

"I'll go clean up that vomit while you get that and then I'll help you with the blood."

Real tears rolled down Dell's cheeks now.

"This is not right."

"I know, but it's our reality right now."

"My wife and son had to kill people – men I played softball with."

Cai hugged him.

"I know. I know. It's horrible and there's no solution for it. And, you're going to feel it for a good long while, even though you had no choice."

Dell wiped his tears and steeled his backbone.

"I'll go get that plywood. Thank you for helping."

Cai nodded, wiping some tears of his own. They'd never forget this day and yet neighbor could be as nice to neighbor as they could be as cruel.

Overwatch

Seattle, Washington

Geo wearied of the Seattle rain. In Kansas, there'd be crisp white snow by now instead of this sodden grayness that sucked the vitality from life. Beyond the rain were the emerald hills of Seattle, shrouded in fog so you couldn't see them. Geo straightened his shoulders and patted Duke on the head before getting out of the old truck to cross the street. He glanced back to see Duke watching him with an incredibly intense look.

The area around Seattle Center had months ago been transformed into an adjunct compound for Knights Industries because Bunnell & Wilson's headquarters in Columbia City would not hold all the troops they'd absorbed into their security forces. Geo paused at the gate to be wanded. The screening guard noted his service weapon, checked his identification, and then wished him a good day.

The collection of ATCO trailers provided a complex maze to figure out as he walked to Carson's command center. Geo'd talked to him last night after he sent in his latest data package. He'd awakened this morning to his officially-issued phone vibrating with a text message.

CARSON - I need to see you first thing.

Nobody stopped him as he stepped into the command trailer. The Knights on duty here glanced his way, but as usual, nobody seemed especially paranoid. Geo himself still expected to be discovered as a fraud and arrested.

"Go on in. He's waiting for you." There were female Knights and some of them even did clerical work. Jillanne seemed to work directly for Carson as some type of secretary, but the service pistol under her left arm assured Geo that she was also there as security. He didn't doubt she was a dead shot who would surprise him if he went hand-to-hand with her. He'd still win, but she'd leave bruises. The Knights didn't spend months in training their operatives as the US military did. They let the US military train and reject them and then scarfed them up like a sale on overstocked items. Training after that was more in serving in hotspots all around the world.

Carson leaned over a table where an actual paper map rested. He glanced over his shoulder when Geo entered. On the far side of the table stood a uniformed Knight. So far, nobody had told Geo to wear the official uniform.

"Geo, meet Juan Carlindo. Juan, Geo is a Navy Seal."

"Good." Juan held out a hand to shake. "You know why you're here?"

"I was the source of last night's transmission."

"The crypto guys think your analysis is correct."
Carson moved to a cart with coffee in poly pots and silently asked Geo if he wanted some. Geo nodded. He liked real coffee. "If it's correct, then this is what we think is about to come about."

They moved back to the table with their coffee. Geo surreptitiously scanned Carlindo, trying to note mannerisms and even his scent, ready to have his suspicions confirmed. Meanwhile, Carson pointed to a section of the map.

"We think they're in this area. If your analysis is correct, they're hitting a power substation in this area sometime in the next two weeks. We're re-tasking a communications satellite to scan the area, but it can't pick up visuals."

"My group is trying to expand our camera UAV system without invading the privacy of individuals." Carlindo paused to sip coffee. "Unfortunately, we were under severe restrictions from the FAA before the Pulse, so the program languished in its infancy. Now it is vital we get it up and running, but we are just getting started. Your intel allows us to guess at the area of search. If we can pinpoint it, we can narrow the target area to a substation or two and hopefully prevent the attack before it happens."

"That's where you come in, Geo." Carson hadn't moved his finger from the map. "When we narrow the field, I want you to co-lead an interception unit."

"This is where you tell me who I'm supposed to kill."

Carlindo frowned and Carson straightened from the map.

"We're not the military, Geo. We prefer not to kill people."

Geo stared at Carson.

"You know I ran across mercs in the Box and the Mirage, right?"

"Yes. I'm sure you did. We were hired to do a job in Miristan. We're writing our own contracts here and it doesn't include subjugating American citizens."

Geo kept his face as impassive as he could manage, but Carlindo continued to frown at him.

"Lee, how about Geo and I go for a walk, see if we can find a way to work together?"

Carson cast a questioning look at Geo and Geo nodded. Carlindo didn't say anything until they cleared the end of the trailer headed for the base of the Space Needle.

"If it helps any, I served in the Army for four years. Never really left the States, but I was honorably discharged."

"What was your assignment?"

"MP at Fort Lewis. My wife had a complicated pregnancy and died when my daughter was four months old, so I chose to leave the service after my first tour. I got hired as a mall guard for a company that later was bought out by another company that was later bought out by Knight Industries. I recognized the opportunity. By that time, I was remarried and could afford to work remotely for a few weeks at a time. I did my time as a merc, mostly guarding dignitaries. Worked my way up to supervisor and then they asked me what I thought of UAVs. I started training a fleet of pilots for package delivery."

"So you're re-tasking these people for surveillance?"

"That's what I've been asked to do. Like you, I was raised to believe the US military protects us." Carlindo only thought he knew how Geo had been raised, but that was okay. He'd come to believe what his father taught only after he was in the service. "When we got our UAV fleet aloft after the bombs, we started seeing behavior that wasn't protective. We started hearing from people that the Army was pushing people around. We heard rumors of people shipped to camps. We haven't found the camps yet. UAVs have limited flight times. We're retrofitting a few of the package bots for extended batteries. It could be we're wrong. It could be we're right. We just don't know right now. We don't want you to kill your former colleagues *unless* they're enslaving people and, even then, we'd prefer they be taken alive and adjudicated based on their actual abuses."

"They should be judged by a military tribunal."

"Ideally, but I have yet to speak to an officer willing to cooperate with us. A lot of the non-coms like yourself have come over, but the officers – we have a fair number of them in custody."

"And this group east of the lake?"

"There's still plenty we haven't found yet and I suspect that's where they are." They had reached the base of the Space Needle and Carlindo nodded to a Knight guard before punching the elevator button. Geo visited the observation deck but had never gone to the restaurant, now converted to a second observation deck. Geo wasn't afraid of heights, but the glass floor messed with his depth perception as they crossed to a bank of computer stations where serious and mostly young people were typing quietly on keyboards. Carlindo grinned at him

Rain obscured the legendary view through the near-seamless window, just like it did the day Geo brought Jazz up here when she visited in the summer. He immediately fought the feeling of skydiving without a parachute. He breathed out and looked up at the windows that faced the Cascades.

"We thought that wasting the high-ground advantage would be foolish, but yeah, the floor takes some getting used to."

"What are they doing?" Geo indicated the computer jockeys.

"UAV pilots are providing surveillance for the area."

"You don't have access to military satellites?"

"We've got some of our best hackers on that task. The bots keep scrambling codes before we can acquire control."

"Not a computer guy. Can bots do that?"

"Not indefinitely. We suspect either Cheyenne Mountain or Utah Data Center is also working against us. The few times we've gotten images it's been a broad area and we haven't been able to focus in before the unit is recaptured."

"So, you're down to old-fashioned means – radio scanning and plane spotting?" Carlindo nodded.

"Sir?" One of the young techs raised his hand. He dressed casually in jeans and a UW sweatshirt.

"What can I do for you, Reisser?"

"Take a look at this. I hacked the brain of a low-altitude military drone that was under repair at Boeing. Wanted to see if I could actually acquire visuals with it."

"And?"

"I'm still learning, but -- ." He pointed to his screen. "This is Lake Washington. This is Inglewood. And then there's this image of that area six months ago." Reisser threw up a split-screen. "That should be Kenmore College, but it's not there today. Look, I'm not trained in all this stuff, so I'm not sure what that means except that it looks like someone is playing hide-n-seek."

Carlindo raised his eyebrows at Geo.

"What do you think?"

"Someone's camouflaging the area. It's pretty sophisticated. Either that or you're not using the drone's heat registration."

"No, I am. Figured that out pretty quick." Reisser pointed to some icons on the right of the screen.

"Again – what do you think?" Carlindo never turned his gaze from Geo.

"That's where I'd look, yes."

"Will you?"

Fish or cut bait? Geo rubbed a hand over his hair. His high-and-tight was no more. He probably needed a trim.

"Introduce me to my squad leader."

"Well, that'll be easy." Geo frowned, perplexed. "We think you'd be an excellent sergeant."

43

Geo's heart somersaulted before pogo-sticking a few times. He ran a callused hand over his jaw.

"Show me my potential squad and I'll let you know."

Carlindo didn't smile, but Geo knew that twinkle in his eye meant he thought he'd landed the big fish. Geo hoped he hadn't.

Brother Against Brother

Emmaus, Kansas

Marnie Callahan Delaney, MD, pulled the AR round out of Sherwin Reese's leg as he bellowed swear words at her and thrashed against the restraints. She couldn't afford painkillers for so minor a wound and she was out of xylocaine, so she had to just not care that he was in pain.

"Clean the wound, stitch him up and bandage him." Jill Delaney, her mother-in-law and nurse, nodded. "I'm going to let Rob know what's going on."

She washed her hands and went out to the lobby where Rob waited.

"Joe back on patrol?"

"He's headed back to get Cai. Dell said he'd deliver the bodies to Beulah himself. He feels it's the least he can do."

Marnie sighed. The morality of mobs tearing into people's homes or people defending what little they had left baffled her. She chose to ignore it and concentrate on medical ethics.

"Sherwin's not walking anywhere for a few days and Paul has not had a meal in a good long while. His injury is

45

minor, but I don't put his odds high for surviving it without proper medical care and some food."

"So, you're saying I can't banish them?"

"Sure, you can, but they've got no chance of survival out on those roads."

"They've got no chance of survival here, either," Rob countered. Lila looked up from the charts she was updating and then away. More and more went unsaid every day. Rob growled. "I'm sorry, I don't know what to say and my options for dealing with this are limited. Three people are dead. If I let Paul and Win stay, I'm sending a message that marauding is okay when it's not, so we end up with more dead bodies."

Banishment or death – what a horrendous choice and not just for the neighbors turned criminals by hunger but for Rob as well. Plus both men had families who were as hungry as they were. What to do about all that? The door opened and Shane came in, stomping snow off his boots and stripping off his mittens. They all wore coats indoors now because of the inadequacy of interior heating these days. It worked well to hide the weapons Shane no doubt carried.

"You wanted me, Dad?"

Shane looked exhausted, dark circles under his eyes, several days' scruff darkening his chin. Unlike her husband Cai, his brother Shane needed to shave every day and had always made it a personal discipline to do so. But now shaving had gone the way of showering and eating regular meals. Shane and Cai voluntarily cut themselves to two meals a day to assure that she and Alicia Sanchez got adequate calories for their pregnancies. Neither man carried spare weight, so the reduced calories showed. None of that concerned her as much as the fevered look in her brother-in-law's eyes.

"We had another mob at Dell Conapher's this morning."

Shane let forth with a single scatological swear word. He no longer tried to control his tongue around his parents, and they had given up being bothered by it.

"And I'm supposed to do what about that?" he asked after his outburst.

As he asked the question, Cai came in the door amid a swirl of wind.

"I need manpower. The threat on the borders is almost non-existent now. We need those men inside the wire."

Shane toed the floor with a heavy boot. Marnie backed up to get out of the blast radius. Shane didn't have a long fuse these days and two of his primary sparks were right here in the room now. She knew better than to stay in a free-fire zone.

"No." He barely whispered. Such a simple understated way to throw a bomb.

"Shane, we've got people having to shoot their neighbors to keep them from stealing what little food they have left." Rob sounded reasonable, but Marnie doubted that mattered anymore.

"I know that." Shane's striking green eyes came up to meet Rob's gaze now. "I'm not a jailer. I can't ask my crews to patrol the streets. That's not what any of us signed up for."

"You're going to prevent your crews from protecting their neighbors?" Cai didn't know when not to poke a bear. He never had and he didn't seem to be getting any wiser on that topic.

"Not preventing anyone. They're welcome to join you and Joe if they want, but *I* am not going to be part of it."

"Shane, this is just to calm the tension and keep everybody safe," Rob reasoned.

"Safe? Dad, we've had this discussion. I'm anything but safe." As if to prove his point, Shane's gaze followed something that wasn't there at a point behind his father. What did he see? With a supreme act of will, he pulled himself back into the conversation. "Neither is Murphy or the Army guys Cai brought in. We're killers who were trained to push people around in Third World countries." Another flicker toward the specter no one else could see and then back to Rob. "We can't be trusted to control people inside the wire. We might start with the best of intentions, but we will turn our guns on anyone who opposes us and become tyrants."

"Men are being killed for trying to feed their families and you're worried about pushing people around?" Cai drew himself up to his full height, strengthened by righteous indignation. "You can't refuse to take care of the community."

"Like hell, I can't. Don't tell me what I can and cannot do." Marnie swore she smelled sulfur.

"I'm asking you, son, for your help," Rob interjected. "Starvation and illness are taking enough of us. We don't need more dying, bleeding in the snow because they have lost all sense of boundaries."

"Then create a volunteer force to do it. Don't include those of us who are killers. If some of my non-military folks want to join you, that's fine, but leave me out of it."

"I can't believe you!" Cai exploded. In an instant, brothers were chest to chest, flinging spit at one another. "You didn't see what I saw out at Conophers. We have got to put an end to this before something worse happens."

"Back off!" Shane shoved and Cai shoved back. "You think I haven't fucking seen what hungry people will resort to? Are you stupid?"

"Then why are you refusing to do your duty? What the hell is wrong with you?"

Instead of intervening, Rob turned away muttering under his breath. Marnie knew taking sides wouldn't help. Rob could end up hurt trying to pull them apart. Lila stood up as if she might, but Jill came running down the corridor and imposed her petite body between her two tall and angry sons.

"Stop it!" she bellowed. "Stop it!"

They both shifted their attention from each other to their mother.

"I've had enough of this to last a lifetime. Just stop!" she repeated.

Shane turned on his heel and stalked out the door. Cai groaned and turned to Marnie.

"You're both right and so incredibly wrong," she replied to his unanswered question.

Rob sighed heavily and looked Jill in the eye.

"I don't know what to do." Tears glistened in his blue eyes. "My neighbors are starving. We're headed that way. Dell Conopher shouldn't have had to shoot people in his yard today. And I don't know what to do to stop any of it." He wiped his eyes.

"Shane could do his job," Cai muttered.

"That's not Shane's job," Lila spoke up from where she'd been working. "Isn't there a difference between the people outside the wire and those in?" They all stared at her. "We hired him to protect the town from outsiders, not to control us. And I won't let my Vin help you keep the slaves on the plantation from revolting."

Overwhelmed with emotion, she disappeared down the hall, sobbing. Cai put an apologetic hand on his mother's shoulder, then spoke to Rob.

"Dad, I'm sorry."

"It's not me that deserves that apology, Cai. Your brother's temper makes it hard to see that he's right, but he is. If we turn a militia he trained to defend the town toward controlling the town, it'll be a whole lot worse than what we've got now."

Cai sighed and nodded.

"His friend Chavez would open up on townspeople in a heartbeat," he admitted. "And, frankly, so might Shane."

"He's not entirely with us right now and that's dangerous if we aim him in the wrong direction. We'll figure something out. You said you needed to talk to me, Marnie?"

"I've got four more bodies in cold storage. Is there any way we can just dig a trench up at Beulah? That's what they did during the Spanish flu and we've got people dying of complications from the flu. They no longer have the reserves to fight it."

"That's ten this week, right?" Marnie nodded to Cai's question. She hated that she couldn't save people, but she didn't have the meds to fight starvation and cold complicated by a virus.

"Who?" Rob asked.

"Five were commuters staying at the church. There was already flu there and then the mob took their food. It was the last straw. Dr. Verheil probably had a stroke because she couldn't get Coumadin. And four others. One was an apparent suicide, who'd been on antidepressants before all this happened. I'm surprised we haven't had more of those. I've asked Jason to be on the lookout for psych meds, but the roads are virtually impassable, so ...." Her father and his crew had formed a tenuous supply line, but even their lack of trading ethics couldn't fight blizzards.

"Carl keeps reminding me that there's a deadline looming. The man is a little obsessive." Rob chuckled and then sobered. "There are houses that the chimneys have gone cold on. I don't know what to do about that."

"You think people froze?"

"Or starved. Some people have too much integrity to attack their neighbors to get food that doesn't belong to them."

"This flu's killing a lot of people." Marnie shook her head about Cai's diagnosis.

"That's not how it works. Yeah, we say people die of the flu, coronavirus, even colds, but it's almost always something else that killed them. Comorbidity made them susceptible. In our case, starvation, malnutrition, and houses we can't adequately heat. It's rare for healthy people to die of relatively minor illnesses. Remember Covid19? Ninety-six percent hardly got sick at all, three percent did, and of that one percent who died, ninety percent of them had comorbidities. We're dying of lack of calories and warmth. The flu is just the last straw."

Rob rubbed his eyes with the heels of his hands. Cai touched his shoulder. Father and son looked a lot alike now that Cai's beard darkened his jaw.

"I'll see about getting some guys together. Dead bodies spread disease." He nodded to himself, hugged Marnie, and headed out the door. Marnie rubbed her aching lower back and considered all the work she had ahead of her today.

"You need a break," Jill said to her husband. Marnie had noticed her stepping into the role Jacob had filled – a reminder when she saw Rob walking off a narrow path into a swamp.

"Yeah. I think I'm going to swing over to Lem's, ask him if he wants to go fishing."

Neither woman would argue with some real protein. MREs and farm-fresh eggs grew old fast. It was a two-birds-one-stone scenario. Rob hugged Jill and then, more hesitantly gave Marnie a sideways hug.

"We're going to get through this," he said.

"Of course, we are," Jill agreed. Marnie smiled what she hoped was a brave smile. Rob followed his sons out the door.

"Are you just saying that to keep everybody's spirits up?" Marnie asked Jill.

"Hope can work miracles, Marnie."

"Not as much as penicillin does."

"Hope works even when you haven't got penicillin."

"Is that where Cai gets it from?"

"What?"

"The mental illness that is optimism."

Jill laughed a full-throated chuckle and headed back to whatever she'd been doing before they were so rudely interrupted by security concerns.

Plans for the Day

Jazz Tully stared at the multiple sets of cross country skis on the wall of the Delaney garage attic. She hadn't expected it to be so cold up here on the second floor. Odd how the garage's main floor could be so warm with just the horses to heat it. A squeak caught her attention and Belle the cat came out of a corner carrying a vole that was nearly as big as she was. The fluffy white feline cast a suspicious look at Jazz's way and disappeared down the stairs with her prey still wriggling in her mouth.

The garage had once been a small barn and fulfilled its original purpose once more. A blast of cold air swirled up the stairs as the man-door opened and closed behind Shane who muttered something rudely Anglo-Saxon about Belle. He topped the stairs where he stared at Jazz like a grumpy owl. She doubted he'd slept more than a couple of hours any night in the last month.

"Hey," he grunted. His winsome face was pinched and losing its summer tan.

"Hey," she responded. She didn't wonder at how she looked. She'd been wearing these clothes for far too long and she smelled of horse dung and sweat from chopping wood this morning. Why worry about how you looked when you hadn't showered in weeks? "Where you headed to?" Her curiosity piqued because this section of the Delaney property had all sorts of things – tools, sleds, sporting equipment. He pulled a set of skis down from the wall and tested the odd-looking bindings, like snowshoe bindings attached to door hinges.

"Those your skis?" They looked about the right length, but they had to be older than Shane.

"Grandpa's. I'm going after those deer Andrew Bennett saw, so I need a pair of back-country skis."

"I'm borrowing your mom's today to do patrol."

"Watch your back out there. Locals are starting to go after people for their food."

"People are hungry."

"We're all hungry. That's not an excuse." He reached down a Flexible Flyer. "I hear Mace Kettridge won't be pushing people around anymore."

Jazz waited a beat to feel something, but she hadn't loved Mace.

"Bullies end up coming to a bad end sooner or later. You got your radio in case you have any problems?"

"I don't need you to mother me, Jazz. I can take care of myself."

His tone cut like a knife and she blinked at him. He reached down another pair of skis.

"Those are the closest to your size. They were Keri's in junior high, so they haven't been waxed in a decade."

He selected a pot of wax and thrust it at her. No apology, just a modification of tone. She'd take it.

"Thanks. How do you know where the deer will be?"

"For all I know Andrew is hallucinating from corn overdose, but I've got to do something because the storage food is dwindling."

"Alicia's contribution helps, right?"

"It nudged the needle but not enough. We'll starve but maybe we won't have malnutrition. If I could have brought back the rest of it ...." His gaze followed something behind her and the hairs on the back of her neck stood up. If she turned around, would she see it too? She didn't want to. His gaze flickered back to her face. "But there've been no breaks in the weather, so --." He shifted like someone stepped too close to his right arm, only Jazz hadn't moved. He moved toward the stairs. "I gotta go."

She followed him down the stairs, carrying Keri's skis and a pair of boots she hoped would fit her. "Like I said, be careful out there." Rocket the roan mare nickered. "You should ride Rocket to the checkpoint. She probably can't handle the snow up on the interstate, but she'll keep you warm there and back."

He scruffed the mare's nose and then left. While she hastily waxed the skis, she considered her options. Ride Rocket, Shane's mustang with a penchant for throwing riders she didn't like? Yeah, why not? The mare's huge liquid eyes seemed gentle enough. She had other choices. Cai's sorrel gelding Ronin rolled an eye at her. Either Alicia or Marnie had taken Jill's roan mare Strawberry. Rob had taken his horse out earlier. Cai might need Ronin and Shane said to take the mustang, who stared at her with both eyes as if wondering what she waited for. Jazz saddled her, tied the skis to the saddle, and set off for the southern post.

Agricultural Engineering

Danny Hughes shook the snow off his cap as he came in at the breezeway. Once out of his coat, he looked half-frozen, his swarthy face ashy with cold.

"Come stand by the fire, warm up," Sharon McLaughlin advised. He slowly stripped down to indoor clothing, flannel shed to hang over the railing beside the wood stove, towels protecting the wood floor. Typically, the kitchen was the only warm room in the farmhouse these days. They'd closed the northern shutters in the breezeway to keep her herb garden alive, but the temperature barely hovered above freezing at the edge of the woodstove's heat bubble. The slate counters needed oiling and were still not completely clean from the pig they'd butchered last week. Without running water, it was hard to keep things as tidy as she liked, and she found herself more tired as the days went along. She thought maybe the cancer was in her lungs.

"How did it go?"

"As good as it ever does." Danny shivered holding his hands out to the heat. "They don't make me bury them. It's just holes."

"I'm sorry." There was nothing Sharon would or could do about it except sympathize. The bombs that destroyed Chicago orphaned 17-year-old Danny. In attempting to flee to safety, he killed a man and was now beholding to Emmaus for a year's labor. Sharon took him into her home and heart, trying to teach him how to grow into a man while also mastering farming – well, not the actual crop part of that as the ground was too frozen to grow much right now. He did all the heavy lifting here and also worked wherever the town needed him – helping neighbors who couldn't do the heavy work or digging graves at Beulah Cemetery.

"It's okay. I did what I did." Raised by a faithful and tough grandma, he took responsibility for his actions fairly quickly. "So, what have you been up to all day?"

"Taking care of the goats and checking our inventory. We can make it into April before we have to butcher animals."

"Good. Mace Kettridge got himself killed this morning trying to steal food from Dell Conopher."

"Oh, my! Nobody should have to go through what some folks are going through. It's a sad truth, but there'll be more deaths before winter's out."

"Yeah. Jace is bringing equipment in tomorrow to open a trench. They'll mark each grave with a temporary nameplate and hope that's enough."

"We're a farming community. How can people be starving in a farming community?"

"Seems to me what you lack is fresh vegetables – or even canned ones."

"True. I'd have grown a garden twice the size if I'd known this was coming. We'd be able to share with our neighbors instead of worrying if we'll make it to spring. Nothing we can do about it now."

"I've been thinking."

"That could be dangerous." The older woman grinned at him. "Spill it."

"I think you ought to build a big greenhouse next year so you can grow crops year-round. One of those magazines had a story about a guy in Alaska who is doing that."

"Oh, the high tunnel guy. Yeah, that's a great idea. If he can grow vegetables year-round in Nome, we could definitely do it here." She stirred the stew on the woodstove, but there was no denying the conversation. "You know I won't be here next year, right?"

His full mouth tightened.

"Maybe Dr. Callahan is wrong."

"Miracles happen, but the tumor's getting bigger. I'm not scared of that. I'm scared of what happens to you, though."

"I can decide to stay when my sentence is up. I've got that paper – my manumission as you call it."

She laughed. She'd fostered kids in the past and everyone had been a blessing of one kind of another. Danny was no different. Killing a man had been an accident. Living with it was intentional.

"Do you think you will?"

"Stay?" She nodded. "I don't know. I've got no home to go to, so …. People have treated me well. Never really thought of myself as a farmer, but –." He shrugged. "I wanted to be an engineer."

"I think agricultural engineer might be a growth industry." She spooned up a bowl of stew and handed it to him. They took the two seats by the fire. They'd all but abandoned the living room because the kitchen woodstove just didn't keep it warm enough with all the windows in that room. She'd screened off the large opening between this room and that with some old quilts. The math said the dry wood she had on hand was only enough to stock one woodstove through the cold months anyway.

Sharon pulled out a pad and pencil and did a rough plan of the farm, showing her house, the barn, the hay shed, and her existing greenhouse.

"Where would you put the greenhouse?"

"I'd build the first one right there – a high tunnel with small tunnels inside. I'm wondering though, how to site it. Why is your greenhouse catawampus to the rest of the buildings?"

"Ah, there's a great question." She explained that she'd experimented and found too much southern and western exposure overheated the greenhouse. By turning it so the hottest part of the day actually hit a corner, she didn't fry her vegetables on the vine. Danny wondered if that might change in the winter, in which case he'd need two high tunnels.

Watching his hazel eyes twinkle with delight at designing the future made her rethink her decision to leave the farm to Shane Delaney because she had once loved his uncle. Maybe she should talk to Rob Delaney about it again.

Not that his boy wouldn't be a good steward of an inheritance like that, but Danny needed a place to stay if he was going to live here and this showed he was forward-thinking enough to make good on it. Of course, the kid had never grown any food and so would need some oversight if he was going to survive. She didn't mention any of this to him because she wasn't ready to share it, wasn't sure she knew what to say. A yawn surprised her.

"Am I boring you?" His laughing tone said he knew that wasn't it.

"I'm thinking I should go take a nap." She stood. The room felt oddly slanted. "This dying thing takes some getting used to. Make sure the doors are bolted."

"Yes, ma'am. I'll even wash the dishes."

"Thank you." She hugged him and went off to her bedroom, thinking she might need to decide on the farm sooner than she thought.

Change of Perspective

Cai Delaney walked with Click Michaels to Carl Sullivan's house so he could check on Janna Thomas. Her husband had been taken during the USDA raid in October and had not returned. She'd lost her mother a few weeks later. She had four children to feed and she'd been the city clerk before the Bombs. In other words, she had no skills that were particularly useful in the apocalypse. She now took in laundry for food while her two older children shoveled walks for the same.

Trucks knocked down the worst of the snow in the street, but sidewalks were completely impassable without shoveling. Wind shuddered through the trees, sending icy chunks into their path.

"This is like Chicago weather." Click had been a reporter for a Chicago newspaper before the September Bombings had rendered his home a nuclear wasteland and his commuter plane set down at Emmaus' airfield on its last thimbleful of fuel. He currently operated the Emmaus communication system and tried to get the old radio transmitter/receiver up so they could hear faraway communities and news.

"Reminds me a lot of Lawrence."

"That's where you went to school?"

"Yeah, six years."

"How do you get a law degree in that short time?"

"Advanced Placement classes and I CLEPPED a bunch of courses. I did college in less than three years. I was beyond sick of working at Walmart and terrified of the loans I was accumulating."

"Wow. I'm beginning to admire the self-sufficiency of rural people."

"You didn't before?"

"No. I was pretty sure you folks wouldn't survive without the cities telling you what to do. You don't have to ask how that worked out for me."

"I wasn't going to. Shane estimated that about 30 million people died in the bombings. I'm sorry for the loss of your family."

Click nodded, staring at the trees with infinite sadness. Cai couldn't imagine grieving your entire family with strangers.

"I'll be grieving that for a long time." The reporter sighed. "We do something else for now. I'm trying to get Carl to loan me his radio set so I can see if it has the parts I need, but he's refusing."

"Refusing or confusing?" Click chuckled. "You just never know which it is. He's mentally ill, but he's also smarter than a raccoon."

"I've never seen a raccoon."

"Trust me, they're smart – and completely annoying. And that's Carl. He's tricky. When he's on his meds, he uses his mental illness as cover, so people don't know how smart he is."

"So, he can convince me to clean his kitchen?"

"That's un-Carl-like, actually. He usually doesn't let people into his house. Consider yourself blessed."

"Never been so glad to suffer from sinusitis in my life."

"It's a benefit in your case, today anyway." They'd reached their destination. Cai walked Click up Carl's driveway. The portly man dumped a bucket of greywater onto the snowbank by his backdoor as they approached. The pile of trash by the door would need to be cleaned up before thaw or it would attract flies, but Cai chose not to fight that battle today. Maybe Ren would come home and render the conflict unnecessary. *He* didn't ask Carl's permission. He just ordered the crews to take care of it.

"Afternoon, Carl. How goes your day?"

"I got work to do."

Okeydokey, Smokey. Cai nodded to Click.

"I've got work to do too. You really reading at Callahan's tonight?"

"Sure. She's really your mother-in-law?"

"She really is."

"That burky woman's still following your brother." Cai glanced at Carl. It didn't sound like a question. "You ever see her?" The hairs on the back of Cai's neck stood up as it felt like someone had dumped a snowball into his coat.

"I haven't. What does she want?"

Carl sighed and shook his head.

"You don't believe me and it's going to get your brother killed. She wants his death and she's found others to join her."

"Others?"

"All of 'em ain't dead. Most of 'em are. And then there are the lights."

"The lights?"

"Jacob's one."

"My grandfather died around Thanksgiving."

"I *know* that. Went up there and said my peace private. He's that side of the veil now, but your brother needs him to get through, so he's shining through the cracks."

"Uh-huh." Cai didn't know what else to say. Carl's uncanny knack for seeing a reality just below the surface unnerved him regularly. He looked at Click who also looked to be at a loss for words. "I should check on Janna and get about my next task. See you at the house, Click."

"We will."

Cai turned aside, praying that whatever Carl saw was a delusion, and not a peek into the reality of the spiritual world of principalities and demons.

Capitalist Plotting

Wichita, Kansas

Ren Sullivan stared out the window over the motor pool. The mechanics reported eight trucks operational. A ninth truck would soon be working, to carry fuel. One of the eight would be fitted with a plow to make the roads passable for the fleet. Crispin reported that a fleet of SullCorp grocery trucks arrived from the coast with groceries this morning. Ren ordered some of the groceries diverted to his fleet. Phil Luiken came in the office door, coughing into the crook of his elbow.

"You should be resting."

Phil blew his nose.

"I'll be fine. I can't lie in that bed any longer. And you weren't any better when you started feeling better."

"I'm leaving as soon as I can manage it. You need to be well enough to take over."

"I will be. Crispin's got the security part of things well in hand. Which is why I'm here. The flu is devastating this town."

"High death rate?"

"It's not that they're dying. But you know how it is. You can't work for a week … 10 days. That's putting everything behind. There's something else happening too. It's some sort of secondary illness. Seems neurological."

"Flu sometimes develops into other problems. So long as it's not affecting our crews,

"Crispin's got one guy down with it. Doctors are diagnosing an aneurysm, but it sure seems similar to what my neighbor's kid has – paralysis, not making sense, head pain."

"Is it contagious?"

"They aren't sure, but they think it's a secondary infection, so it shouldn't be."

"Then I'm not halting my trip to Emmaus. I've been away from home for too long. If my son's home, I'll come back. Otherwise, I'll get the radio tower working and we'll get started on reestablishing communications."

Phil coughed into his elbow again.

"What else?"

"The fleet that made it through this morning reports that NATO has declared war on Miristan and North Korea for the terrorist attacks."

"Oh, good. Just what we need. A war to end wars while people here starve."

"I'm kind of glad to see someone will hold them accountable."

"It won't bring back the 40-50 million people who have died and we don't even know if Miristan had nuclear capabilities. North Korea, maybe, but the Madaris regime – I just doubt it."

"If we let them get away with it, we'll get hit again."

"Why? We're in third-world status. Without the US of *Amerika* to keep the world riled up, nobody is going to bother attacking us."

"You think it's just over? We'll never rise again?"

"I think we'll rise – or the constituent parts will. Those who have resources will survive. Hopefully, though, we'll have wiped the arrogance off our face. Whoever bombed the cities got rid of just about every politician on the national level, most of the federal administrative state, most of the infrastructure in several blue states, and the US military. They left Wall Street, which probably went the way of the dodo when the Pulse hit and it seems they left a fair amount of industrial capacity, but they clearly wanted a fairly clean political slate. And a clean slate isn't a bad place to start cleaning up a mess 250 years in the making. And it so should have humbled those who thought they ruled the world."

"Well, don't worry. I won't start any wars without consulting with you first."

"I would hope not. Wilson appears to be sticking with our agreement – oil for food, capitalism at work, a rudimentary exchange system. How's that part going?"

"The food is headed to the grocery stores as we speak. This is the third shipment. The hardest because of winter weather. We'll have more trucks up and running and they'll follow your train out. Speaking of trains – BNSF thinks they've got a locomotive that will be ready by the end of the week. They'll use that to start clearing tracks."

"Good." Richard Crispin entered. Medium height and built like a Greek statue, Crispin worked for Knights Industry and his force was under contract to SullCorp at least until spring. "Rich, what's up?"

"We received a coded message for your eyes only, sir." He held out a notebook computer. Phil stood and followed him out of the room.

Ren sat down at his desk and opened the screen. He typed in two passcodes and Carson Wilson appeared on the screen.

"Our distribution system is slowly building. We won't be able to get it fully functioning until winter breaks, but we're making a good start. Let me know if there's more we can cooperate on."

Ren hated recording himself. What he needed to say could be said in an email, he always supposed, but he responded in kind, creating a short vid to send by data burst, explaining the progress they were making on distribution in the Midwest. With Wichita as a hub, things didn't look so daunting.

Another icon blinked ominously on the screen. For Your Eyes Only. Francene Maracal appeared on the screen. Ren appreciated her handsome features and her classic French twist hairstyle. There were a lot of leftists who hated "the bimbo" as they called her, but Ren's only meeting with her had been an intelligent and sometimes challenging conversation over a Washington DC Press Association dinner a couple of years ago. They'd agreed on a few topics, disagreed on several, and parted on friendly terms.

"This is Francene Maracal, former Speaker of the House, possibly the sole remaining member of the US Congress. I've no designs on being a national leader. I am content to remain here in Alaska. In the terrorist attacks in September, many people died and many more went missing. Among the missing is my daughter Eden. Her last known whereabouts were Wichita Kansas, but she could be anywhere. If she's still alive and you have the means to bring her to safety, respond to this podcast. Alaska wasn't bombed and we've survived the Pulse. We've shattered the Jones Act and we're already selling oil on the open market. We are well on the way to becoming the independent nation many of us desired to be. I don't control Alaska's resources, but I can offer a DC3 of food to anyone who reunites me with my daughter. Thank you and I look forward to hearing from you."

Ren sat back in his chair and stared out the window. That changed his plans a bit. He called Crispin and asked if there was anyone who could help him with what came next. A young man named Michael joined him in the office.

"It came from Wasilla. The initiator didn't try to hide their location. They sent it out to a dozen live bases here in the Lower 48."

Michael showed his tracking results on the screen.

"You're from Alaska?"

"No, but my girlfriend is."

"You're dating Eden?"

"I am." The boy blushed slightly.

"You're Travis Meyer, aren't you?" The boy's eyes twittered. He'd probably thought dyeing his hair light would hide him. "I just want to get Eden to her mother, but it seems to me that you're not safe here either."

"This isn't a hereditary kingdom. I'm just a guy now – not the president's son."

"I wouldn't trust that in these circumstances. You might be viewed as a symbol. That's why you're going under an assumed name, right?"

"Yes, sir. My Secret Service detail didn't know what to do with me after the Bombs, so I suggested they bring me to Eden. We got here when you were trying to secure the town."

"Where are they now?"

"One was shot on the way here. Another died of the flu. I wanted to fit in, to hide in plain sight, so Randy, the third guy on my detail, is working for the Knights now and I'm a computer tech."

"Does Crispin know?"

"Probably."

"And you'd be all right with going to Alaska?"

"I love Eden. Of course, I'd be all right with it."

"Then let's set up a podcast." The kid smiled. Ren figured that wasn't the right term, but he didn't care. "Can you bounce it around, so folks won't know where it was sent from?"

"I can. How will Mrs. Maracal know who it's coming from then?"

"I've got that worked out. You just worry about the tech end. You need to give her a secure way to get back with me."

"I brought a notebook that is just yours. I don't know why you didn't have one before."

"I'm a Luddite. Kind of enjoying the loss of technology. But I embrace it when it's necessary. So, we don't want video on this, and I need my voice to be distorted."

Eden joined them and gave Ren some information that only she and Francene would know.

"Francene, you and I had a lovely dinner at the Hilton last year and I gave you a name for heaven on earth. All's safe. Even with multiple passcodes, I don't trust this technology. I'm going home soon. Taking some of my most valuable with me. Get back with me on the town radio station. I trust you to figure that out. I'll know to trust the overture only then, but you'll need to provide something heavenly too. Meanwhile, you can do burst transmissions to this locator."

Eden hugged Ren in excitement.

"I really didn't think you could pull it off."

"Well, it's going to be a bit of work. We need to get to Emmaus and there's 300 miles of bad winter roads between us and there. It's going to take the trucks a while to breakthrough." Eden and Travis exchanged significant glances. "What are you two keeping from me?"

"Nothing really, but – you know you have a Tucker Snowcat in your warehouse, right?"

Buddies

Jericho Ghost Town

In the corner of the two ridges that sheltered the old ghost town of Jericho Springs, the wind hardly touched them, though an occasional gust swept down from the ridge to remind them hard winter loomed on the horizon. After confirming the lake ice was too thin to support their weight, Rob and Lemuel McAddams set out chairs on the deck of the old Delaney cabin that had become a fishing hut. They tossed rocks onto the thin layer of ice until it broke enough so they could toss in their lines. Rob could see signs that others had already done the same in the last few days. This land technically belonged to his family, but hungry people cared less and less about property rights and truthfully Jacob never asserted his right to refuse people a pleasant swim or morning of fishing and Rob wasn't inclined to either. He hoped he wouldn't regret that.

"How you doing?" Lem stood a little over average height and was built like a Tonka truck. His black beard sported more than a bit of grey, but like a lot of those from distant Wyandot stock, his hair didn't have that much silver in it.

"Better." Something tugged on Rob's line, but the hook didn't set. He reeled back the slightest bit. "That was --." He shook his head. "The closest I've come since Cai was born.

I meant to pour out a libation on the ground. I've done that at dozens of wakes and never came so close to taking a sip."

"We're living in troubling times, my friend. I know I couldn't make the decisions you have to make and not feel like taking the edge off it."

Rob stared into the dark slushy water, wishing he could find answers in the depths.

"You're worrying me, buddy." Lem's tone remained companionable and calm – the perfect accountability partner.

"Sorry, just thinking about this morning."

"People shooting one another over resources. Whodda thunk that, right?"

"Yeah. Shane did – weeks ago."

Lem adjusted his reel a bit before speaking.

"That's a dark young man. How's he doing?"

"Not well." Rob felt something grab his hook. He popped the pole up slightly to set the hook and let some line out to let it run. "We all moved down to the living room a few days ago because it got too cold to safely sleep upstairs. All but him. After the first night of tossing and turning, he went back upstairs where we now worry he'll freeze to death." Rob reeled in his fish. It flopped across the ice spewing blood and mucus. Fish were actually pretty disgusting, if you thought about it. Tasty, but gross.

"Do you have any idea what's going on with him?"

"I told you what I thought I saw that night up at Beulah. I think he's still seeing it." Rob thumped the small trout in the head and stripped off a glove to run a stringer through its gills. Three months ago, he would have tossed it back as too small.

"He sounds almost manic." Lem let a little line out.

"Yeah. I wondered for a while, but Alicia knows him really well and I guess one of her brothers is bipolar. She says she's never seen Shane like this until very recently. Marnie thinks it's PTSD. There's folks who say that's how EJ experienced it." Rob dropped the trout into the burlap bag.

"But you didn't?"

"I had some dreams that might have been similar, but I thought they were alcohol-induced. Brad Snow says it's not possible to share a hallucination, so …." Brad Snow, the pastor of the Baptist church was the closest thing they had to a professional counselor locally. There'd been a couple over in Beulah before the Bombs, but even that was a hard place to get to on these roads. Rob cast and overshot the hole, his hook sliding across the ice. He reeled back in.

"Have you described what you saw to Shane?" Lem's reel whirled. He let it run, setting the hook only after he'd paid out several feet, then letting it run some more.

"He's barely speaking to me. It's like he's ashamed, but so angry that he can't say he's sorry." To avoid tangling lines with Lem, he waited to cast again.

"Angry about what?"

"I don't know. That I didn't drink the bourbon – or that I came that close to drinking it. I don't know."

"Is he still drinking?"

"Not that I know of. I know Jason Breen decided to stop supplying him, which surprised the hell out of me. It puts me in an awkward position because I don't know how to help him. He won't talk to me. He's not drinking. He's clammed up tighter than Fort Knox, but he's not engaging in behavior that I can stage an intervention on. It's like one of those seashells you can't get into without irreversibly damaging the critter inside."

Lem reeled in his fish – a slightly larger version of Rob's. A cold wind washed over them, rolling over the ridge as Lem put his fish away. Rob watched the scudding clouds in the ice blue sky for a moment before he cast again, this time landing the hook in the ice opening. Lem poured them each a cup of coffee from the pot they'd put on the barbecue between them. It tasted heavily of soy, but it was warm.

"Patience isn't something guys like you and I have in abundance," Lem remarked. He cast his own line. "With fish, yeah, but not with the people we think we're supposed to help. But I think you know Shane's going to buck like a bronco until he's good and ready to come to you. You just got to be ready when he does come and – well, I hope I don't need to tell you this – at some point, you just gotta listen."

Rob grimaced.

"My great failing with that kid – talking too much and not waiting for him to reach a point where he can't not talk. He's a tough nut to crack and I forget that he has to volunteer."

"Shane doesn't much initiate conversation. I remember sitting in a deer blind with that kid for hours and him not saying a word. It's like Cai got all the words."

Rob chuckled. His oldest son did like to talk. Right then both of their reels started spinning and they spent the next few minutes landing their fish.

"This enough for you?" Lem asked.

"Yeah. It's weird. I'm finding even turning to Cai and talking about what's going on in my head is helping."

"That's good. Just, if you start to feel that crazy bitch again – you need to come see me, right?"

"I know. I'm no use to the people of this town if I start drinking again. I got it. Which is why Cai comes in handy. He never let himself get actually hooked, but he did his time in a few rooms in Lawrence to make sure he would never again do the stupidity that led to the Callahan girl's death. So, he does know what to say, what to listen for."

"You think maybe Shane would be more comfortable talking with him?"

"I thought Shane might gut him this morning, so no. Shane's only really still talking to Jazz Tully and even then – yeah." Rob wiped at sudden tears. "My boy's in trouble and I just don't know what to do about it."

"Isn't that when you pray?"

Rob nodded. Lem poured the "coffee" into the thermos he brought before dumping the coals onto the lake ice. Rob locked the cabin and then they both picked up their bags of fish and headed home – Lem on his snowmobile and Rob on Macky the chestnut gelding.

Chasing Dinner

Shane skied along the north wire of Jericho Township, his strokes long and strong, breath fogging out behind him, ignoring how his muscles ached. You needed so many calories to sustain healthy muscle and he wasn't getting enough. There was nothing to be done about it – unless he got a deer, which is why he towed the runner sled behind him. He still held hope, though thinner every day.

They'd stopped energizing the wire to his right weeks ago. It took too much gasoline to charge the batteries now that the cold depleted the charges so much faster. Besides, there was nothing moving out there on the prairie. No one. The cold snap after Thanksgiving had stopped all foot traffic. He didn't want to think about the bodies they'd have to clean up come spring. The soldiers Cai negotiated with patrolled out beyond the township when weather permitted and they'd found the gruesome remains of people caught out in the cold, trying to shelter on the treeless prairie. They'd also seen some truck tracks that might still be people headed south. There was no foot traffic. If anyone wanting to enter the town would approach at the intersections rather than wade through untracked snow, so there was no reason to energize the fences now. According to the former soldiers, Emmaus bristled with enough armament to be intimidating. If you had a vehicle, it might be easier to go to the next town where perhaps they wouldn't be so zealous in defending their borders. He'd fulfilled his contract and protected the town.

Which brought him around to the morning topic of using the border patrol as an interior peacekeeping force. He could admit the real danger now lurked inside the wire. Joe needed a defense force for interior concerns. Shane skidded to a stop as *she* materialized right in front of him, her flowing hajib purple against the blue-white of the surrounding field. The snow to his left gave way to a mob of people with faces he recognized. He felt an AR15 in his hand instead of Jazz's SKS across his shoulders.

"You know you want to." Mike's voice whispering in his ear chilled him to the bone, forcing a shudder down his spine. *"It's the solution to the hunger and you know it."*

He needed to keep his guns trained outside the community because of this. Early this morning as they'd huddled over the warming fire, cannibalism came up among the guards. Some of them feared it. Some of them thought it was a potential solution. Shane told them to shut up. His guards on the wire shouldn't be entertaining any such notions. He still had corn from his corporate fields. They might die of boredom living on it, but they wouldn't starve. It was the rest of the town they needed to worry about.

"Not everybody can make it."

"You're not real. Mike would never say something like that." His voice echoed across the snowy field. He stood alone, screaming at willow-wisps. He'd made it four years longer than his uncle EJ because he recognized madness when he engaged in it. He was in trouble if he didn't keep reality in view.

He resumed skiing. About two minutes of skiing brought him to a section of trampled snow. He shed his skis to examine the tracks. Definitely deer, jumping the barbed wire, looking for harvest debris. He wasn't a good enough tracker to guess at the size of the herd. He guessed the deeper tracks represented at least one buck, though he no longer cared if he took a doe so long as she wasn't pregnant. Curious about some other tracks, he used a fence post to jump the wire and examine them. Wolves or dogs, it was hard to tell. Canine for sure. His crews saw increasing numbers of stray dogs outside the wire. He assumed people set out with the family pet and then realized the choices were eating Fido or setting him free so he might survive on his own. Loving choice? Hard to know and what happened when that beloved pet started hunting humans out of desperation? Would they hunt their former owners? Glister had enough food to last a couple of years, although it might start looking good to the family before winter ended. He imagined Glister defending his bowl from Cai and he chuckled.

Regardless, the canine tracks followed the deer up to the fence where they encountered barbed wire. He plucked some grey fur from a barb. They'd tried to enter and failed. Wolves were smart. They wouldn't risk injury if there was another way to get in. The pack turned aside west toward Mara Wells. The deer tracks were relatively fresh – within the last 24 hours. The canine prints were newer, barely filled in with drifted snow. A part of him said he should ski the wire, make sure the wolves didn't find a downed section, but the thought of the meat made him hesitate. Security was all well and good, but survival wasn't always about being secure.

Shane jumped the wire again, donned his skis and headed south, following the game trail. They skirted the militia compound's western fence which still sizzled when he tossed snow on it. He noted human tracks going to and from the secondary decommissioned missile silo. Dan hadn't developed it, using it instead for storage of extra food, construction materials and weapons. Shane knew about the contents there and didn't tell his superiors. He wondered if Dan McAuliff was grateful.

"You put him in prison for five years. Not fucking likely." Mike stood beside the trail, still dressed as Shane had seen him last in Santa Fe. Tall, his shirt sleeves rolled up, his jeans not even wet with snow. Heck, his head was shaved, which wasn't how Shane saw him last, but how he knew him best. Mike never knew about McAuliff's Militia and Shane's involvement. The only way specter-Mike could know is if he was a projection of Shane's insanity. Refusing to indulge grief, Shane climbed the north side of Mission Ridge.

After the long slog to the ridge line, Shane paused to catch his breath at the fence that surrounded Ren Sullivan's estate. Jace Welton mothballed the house weeks ago. Allison boarded the horses out to townspeople who promised not to eat them. News or rumor that passed as news said Ren was in Wichita, no one knew where his son and daughter-in-law were, and his granddaughter lived with the Vance family now – playing nurse to their brain-injured son.

Shane followed the deer tracks along the fence, noticing that some trees had been cut outside the fence. People planned to use wood for really cold weather, maybe during power outages. Few people expected to need wood for the entire winter and now they harvested anything that would burn. Green wood wouldn't burn well, but it might warm the house above freezing. Shane couldn't begrudge them trying to survive and he wasn't responsible for what happened inside the wire anyway.

The wind singed his cheeks as he crested the ridge and dropped toward Jusilla's Creek. He'd never known a time when anything, but spring runoff filled Jusilla's, but that had changed when the Pulse fried the solenoid to the town's well. An artesian, it had burst its valves and now flowed eastward. Shane paused at its traditional bank, eyes sweeping the snow-covered ice. It didn't look like the deer broke through on their crossing. He probed ahead and risked a crossing – probing, skating, probing. The ice groaned once at his weight but held and he turned eastward to follow the deer.

Back before electricity generated by powerplants and then wind turbines, the town had dammed Jusilla's at a natural fall of a few feet, creating a larger fall he'd have to climb to look into, building enough head for a small hydro plant. The dam, built of stone with concrete mortar, still held water, topped with ice now. The ice overflow swooped down the front of the dam like the dramatic grill of an Art Deco radiator, delicate flutes of white and pale blue. Come spring, they'd need to work on whether they could rediscover the art of hydroelectric power. For now, they lingered in the 1880s and would unless Michael Tully figured out how to make the wind turbine at Schoenfeld's work. The MacArthur Dairy produced a small turbine that Stan Osimowitz over in Mara Wells said worked fine. Producing wind turbines by hand took a lot of time. Rob offered to buy one for the house. Their crabapple jelly and ale proved valuable, even after James Vance took his cut. Unfortunately, a series of blizzards closed the road to Mara. The turbine might as well be on the far side of the moon.

A vision of Vin Barrett plowing out the road rose in Shane's mind. In the mental film Vin then went into Mara and found everyone starved to death except Abe MacArthur and Michael Tully who were gnawing on bones. Shane shuddered, skidding to a stop in the wood. He struggled against hallucinations every day now. Activity no longer kept them at bay. He needed to force himself back to reality. Any reality would do – like the deer tracks in the pure white snow. Shane blew out a great fog of breath and bent to examine them. They headed toward Alex's east field. He unzipped his coat so as not to overheat and continued to chase the trail.

Border Patrol

Rocket gave Jazz an exciting ride to the overpass entrance. She'd never ridden a horse quite like her – bold, fast, and smarter than average. Back when Shane still talked to people, he'd told her how he and Stu Mackler had *gentled* the mustang. Apparently, horses stayed wild-smart if they thought domestication was their own idea. Rocket spent two years as a feral horse before Shane adopted her and he'd taught her to be his friend, not just an animal to ride. She took instruction, but Jazz merely rode her. She didn't consider herself as the one in charge of this run. She counted herself lucky that Rocket seemed to know where Jazz wanted to go, and they went there a lot faster than Jazz preferred to go.

It impressed her coworkers when she rode up on the roan mare.

"Shane let you ride her?" Murphy caught the halter as she swung out of the saddle and dropped to the ground. Her left foot slid a little as she touched down. She stabilized herself on the saddle. Rocket swung her head back to where she hung on and tried to bite her through her coat.

"Hey, cut it out!" Jos Osimowitz tapped Rocket on the nose. Jazz pulled away. Rocket blew and tossed her mane, almost seeming to smirk.

"You think you're funny." Jazz rubbed her nose. "No biting." Rocket nickered. Jazz turned to Murphy and Jos. Murphy was a former National Guardsman, not as deadly as Shane, but still a shoot-first-ask-questions-never kind of guy. Jos was the 15-year-old owner of the local grocery, who didn't have much to sell currently, so volunteered for two security shifts a day to keep his grief over his grandmother's recent death at bay. "So, you guys will watch after her while I'm gone, right?"

"Shane might skin us alive if something happens to her." Murphy took Rocket's reins and led the mare over to where his own horse waited. "Guy's in a mood these days." He loosely looped her halter rope around a guard rail but left her reins on the saddle horn. Shane insisted Rocket should be free to run should danger arrive.

Jazz couldn't argue against that Shane's mood turned midnight-dark these days, so she chose not to comment at all. She slipped her foot into the ski bindings and slapped the catch down, then did the other foot.

"Keep an eye on that sky to the west." Jos pointed as if she didn't know which way west was. "Storms come that way, you know?"

A lot of folks who lived in the town recently learned which way the worst blizzards came from. Jazz grew up in Mara Wells, which was closer to the Rockies, and so she'd grown up watching the west for the telltale signs of blizzard development. She could argue with her former student or she could patrol the wire.

"I will." She tucked her sleeves down over the tops of her gloves and set out up the trail they'd carved into the side of the interstate.

Jazz paused as she topped the roadbed, her breath fogging the air. The sky ran into the ground, all grey-white broken occasionally by the dark brown of leafless trees and a swath of marshmallow blue to the north over Mission Ridge. The cold stung her cheeks as hunger nibbled at her belly. She'd silently joined Shane and Cai in their sacrifice of one meal a day to keep Marnie and Alicia and their babies healthy. There were days when she just couldn't do it and she'd eat a snack at midday but going hungry got easier with practice. Today, she could ignore it. She wiped snot with the back of her glove, eyes scanning the landscape below. Jacob Delaney gave her these fold-back mittens called "snot backs" as part of his potlatch goods. Might as well use them.

Except for smoke drifting up from half a thousand chimneys, the town looked deserted, no vehicles moving between the snow-covered roofs and bare trees. Most people were out of gasoline now and nobody who still had any would waste it on just going across town. Some people had horses, but increasingly people grew desperate enough to eat their horse rather than ride it. Jazz knew she could trust Murphy and Jos with Rocket and despite the mare's seemingly docile attitude, Jazz suspected she'd take a few casualties in her escape attempt.

Despite the hunger decimating their ranks, border security didn't disappear as winter descended. Shane, Murphy and Cai tried to innovate ways to guard the wire with fewer and fewer people. Today, two people guarded each gate and Jazz skied the wire between the southeast entrance and the Lufgren Crossing on-ramp. She looked at the sky, trying to judge where the sun was and how much time she had for this project. The sun hid in horizon-to-horizon cloud cover.

The interstate stretched both directions, a foot deep in virtually-untracked snow. Shane skied this route yesterday and you could kind of see his tracks, but the wind filled them in, making it almost look like no one had been here in days. She wasn't a really great cross-country skier. She did better in the tracks of others, but Shane warned she shouldn't risk Rocket's legs in snow this deep, so she had no choice but to begin the long slog westward across a field of snow.

Kansas being a relatively flat country, only Mission Ridge stood higher than the interstate and wind scoured both. Her cheeks felt chapped and her lips tingled. She scanned east. Nothing moved. She used her field glasses to get a better look that way. Jos would start the circuit that way in about a half-hour. It wasn't her responsibility, but she wanted to know what was at her back before she started out. That she thought like Shane might have disconcerted except he seemed to have developed a knack for not dying, so she thought some of his thought process good. The others terrified her.

The wind swirled snow around an abandoned truck. She shivered, reminded of ghosts. The willow-wisp was merely wind pushing snow around a fixed object, not the ghosts of the world that no longer was. She turned west and began her patrol.

Fishes & Loaves

Jill Delaney loved her family and for many years she'd baked bread once a week, using her sourdough starter to create everything from Italian loaf to whole wheat to croissants. She never thought it would one day be survival for her family.

Vi's sourdough starter birthed her sourdough starter. Vi did something similar out of love for her family. When they were first married, Rob thanked Jill for buying Wonder Bread. He'd always wanted it and his mother wouldn't allow it. She'd baked their family bread. Even homemade white bread was healthier than Wonder Bread. He'd smiled and shrugged when Jill made her first loaf of bread after moving here to Emmaus. It had been Vi's idea and Jill had wanted to overcome the sense of awkwardness born of moving into the woman's house with the son Vi clearly expected to marry someone else. Rob never complained. She wondered if he still dreamed of Wonder Bread. She did sometimes buy high-quality rye bread for corned beef sandwiches. Had. She hadn't seen a store-bought loaf of bread in months and thought she might never again.

She folded one half of the dough over on the other half and kneaded them together. Good exercise for the arms –

not that she needed that now with the wood chopping and water hauling. The dough still felt a little moist. She bent to scoop another partial cup of wheat flour out of the bin. Fortunate for the Delaneys, they owned a feed store and her father-in-law Jacob transported all of the people food to the house before the USDA raid in October. She'd designated 150 pounds of wheat flour for their personal use. The rest could go to trade. At current use, she reckoned she'd run out of flour in June. They might all have critical nutritional deficiencies by then, but they probably wouldn't die so long as she could bake bread.

The back door opened, and Rob came in, stomping snow off his boots. He lifted a sack onto the counter across from where she worked.

"Fish for dinner?"

"Fish for dinner. House feels quiet. Where is everyone?"

"Marnie's at the medical center – of course." He said "of course" with her. They both smiled. "I'm not sure where Cai's got off to. Maybe helping Marnie, which is where Alicia is. Jazz is on patrol."

Rob took a deep breath, smiling.

"Hmmm, bread. The one thing I truly enjoy about the apocalypse is having you bake bread every other day."

"At the rate we're going I'll be making bread every day soon enough." Did he still want Wonder Bread?

"That's fine by me." Rob seemed genuinely okay with her bread. My, what a few decades could do! "So, I need to go brush down Macky. Any idea where Shane got off to?"

"No, and that worries me. Has he talked to you at all?"

"Not his thing, and *that* worries *me*. So, Macky needs to be taken care of. You look like you're in your element. This house being silent – we haven't been alone here since the rain."

They both chuckled nervously, like high school students remembering a time when they snuck into the barn to lie together. He didn't even remember the name of the girl he'd done that with. She'd gone off to college while he'd been gone to the Nam and then he'd met Jill and hadn't cared. That's what he said, anyway. Jill managed to remain a virgin until DaNang and only remembered the first name of the young airman she'd tumbled with in a supply closet during an air raid. Funny how adrenaline could manifest itself as lust. She'd been so embarrassed the next day and glad that he'd never come to the hospital after that air raid. She felt no regrets with Rob, never had even when they seemed on the verge of divorce during his drinking days.

"That was a fun few days in a nuclear bunker." She held her hands so they wouldn't flour his coat and laid a big kiss on his mouth. He kissed her in return, almost promising they'd make use of the quiet – then turned toward the back door.

Jill returned to the bread, pulling off a small portion and stretching it windowpane thin. She rinsed her hands in the bowl of grey water she'd left on the sink counter and grabbed two pans to grease for the loaves.

Billy Goat

Alex grew vegetables in his east field, but it once was an enormous wheat field. Shane glided across the uneven snow, aware of the disked ridges that threatened to grab a ski tip occasionally. His gaze scanned the ground for the deer tracks. Sweat trickled down his shoulder blades as he forged forward. Two plumes of smoke rose from the other side of the fringe of trees between the field and Alex's house. He knew the plume further from the road was the house. He wondered what Alex might be burning. Had he mentioned heating the sauna? Shane was uncertain. If it weren't for the deer, he might stop to find out, but the prospect of meat overwhelmed the thought of getting truly clean for the first time in weeks.

He reached the fence at Old Highway 24. The fence wasn't barbed wire. Alex's father hadn't liked it and so the old homestead didn't have any. The straight wire was strung four strands high, though, so he kicked off his skis and climbed a post. He'd bent to re-strap the skis when he heard the truck coming. Nehemiah Lufgren was dark like his father Micah, echoing his grandmother's Italian blood. He signed *How you?"* over the wheel as he drove. *"Do?"*

"*Fine. Deer hunting,*" Shane signed back.

"*Good luck.*" Nehemiah passed him and Shane donned his gloves again before crossing the road and skiing along the fence to the wide opening that led into Alex's second wood lot. The deer tracks were muddled here. He knelt to look closely at a paw print. Wolf or dog – he couldn't tell. He got up and surged forward. He begrudged no being a full belly, but he wasn't losing out to the canines. Then he heard the barking. He rounded a bush and found Mocha, Alex's chocolate Lab, squared off against a billy-goat with its head lowered. Shane kicked off his skis and stripped off his backpack to pull out a coil of rope. He tied a loop in one end and tossed it over the goat's head. Mocha growled and nipped at the goat's heels. Shane dragged the goat out of the bush and then released it to Mocha's less-than-tender care. Mocha and Glister were litter mates, but Mocha definitely had a more work-oriented life.

The view through the trees showed him Mocha and the goat headed up the driveway toward the yellow house on its slight hill. The second plume of smoke was definitely the sauna. Its heat beckoned, but hunger gnawed more than filthy skin. He strapped on his skis again and continued following the deer. A flutter of cloth to his right materialized into a woman in a dark hajib.

"*You can't ignore her forever,*" Mike whispered.

"You're not real." The deer tracks were real. He needed to concentrate on what was real because reality was what existed and everything else out here was death.

Prayer

Macky's broad brown back absorbed Rob's attention as he slowly worked his fingers through the horse's mane, working out the knots, pulling the hair straight. The big bay gelding nickered in pleasure. Not for the first time, Shane's face flickered into Rob's mind's eye.

"God, you know I love that boy, but I don't know how to reach him and since that night up at the cemetery – is he angry with himself or disappointed in me? For being weak or for being strong? I just don't know. How do I even begin talking to him?"

"Listen, don't talk," Jacob said, leaning back on a stall at the ranch some summer day. It could have been any of a hundred times. Rob always talked before he listened and that never worked with Shane. How many times did Rob need to fail to finally try what might work?

Rob checked each of Macky's shoes. The off-front seemed a little loose. He'd have to see if Clem could come trim all the horses' hooves and reset their shoes. He picked up the curry brush.

"Worried about Marnie. She's carrying my grandchild and she's working too hard. There's just so much a woman can take and she's getting to about where Jill was when she lost the baby."

"Time's supposed to heal," Jacob said, sitting back in a chair as they fished at the lake. *"The past is foundation to the present, it's not proof of it."*

Rob wished he'd taped Jacob's wisdom every time the man opened his mouth. He guessed a lot of it could be found in the binder. The binder – that would take years to read. Wind moaned around the roof. Maybe a storm rolling in.

Cai reported he'd be going to Alex' for a sweat. He seemed to be getting better, sleeping most nights now. His shoulder still hurt him some and he wasn't explaining how he'd hurt it. There was a lot he wouldn't say about when he'd been in Wichita and Hutchinson. That both boys sought solace in silence felt ominous and yet ....

"How do I reach them, God? Or don't I? Is it for someone else? With Pa gone, I feel this weight."

A light flashed against the wall. Rob turned to look out the window that faced the house. Jill shined a flashlight at him, then gestured him to come to the house. He nodded, held up the 10 sign and then the minute sign. She flashed him a thumbs' up sign – which was really the 10. He laughed and signed *"OK."*

He doled out oats to the horses that were here and gave Macky's ears a good scruff. Glister rose from where he'd been waiting in the corner and followed him out into the blustery afternoon.

Family & Community

Alex Lufgren stacked wood outside the door of the little shed on the far side of the yard from the house. He'd fired and stocked the little woodstove in the sauna a few hours ago. It wouldn't be much longer, and it would be ready for his guests – those who showed up anyway. He'd been looking for Shane when he'd encountered Cai. Although he tried to keep the two apart for peace sake, he could invite Cai or Shane, who probably wouldn't have come anyway. They'd been best friends since kindergarten and they still connected on a deep level when they were together, but Shane had changed, and he seemed almost to avoid Alex much of the time. It made Alex deeply sad.

Keri came out of the house carrying a bucket of water. She pulled the door open and set the bucket inside the sauna.

"Thank you," he said, kissing her.

"I'm all in favor of people bathing occasionally. Enjoy it and the male bonding."

"You're being snarky."

"A little, but it's really fine. I'm making a quilt for Shane's birthday."

"In January?" She nodded. "How come?"

"It's the first time he's been home for his birthday in nine years and I'm hoping he'll – I don't know." She blinked tears from her eyes.

"He'll be okay." Alex knew he lied. Shane spun further and further away every day. Alex didn't know how to help him. No one seemed to have the answers for what ailed Shane.

Poppy and Pete came out of the house carrying their skis. Pete laughed at something Poppy signed and the chuckle carried in the clear air.

"Where you-two go?" Alex had stopped talking to Pete in anything but sign language. He would need to be fluent, not just for Poppy's sake but because his children were liable to be deaf.

"Patrol." Poppy's answer meant to put him off.

"Which way?" They were technically adults, married three weeks now, and he shouldn't be treating them like children. Still, the weather concerned him, and someone had to remind them to act like adults.

"West," Poppy signed. *"Under overpass, interstate. Come back Old 24."*

"Eyes west. Storm? Head back. Yes?"

Poppy frowned at him. Pete waited for her to answer, but she bent to don her skis.

"We'll watch," Pete assured him. "She's just annoyed by you acting like a dad."

"I am a dad. I've been *her* dad since I was 18." Alex signed and talked at the same time.

"I know." Pete signed too, using more and more ASL construction. He'd get the hang of it eventually. "My folks tried to explain it. And I don't want to die out there, so we'll watch."

Keri smiled at Alex, then her gaze shifted toward the goat running up the driveway chased by Mocha in all her harrowing fury.

"Can you --?" Alex asked Keri.

"Yeah, no problem." Keri headed after the dog and goat as Pete followed Poppy down the driveway. Alex's heart tugged to go with them, but he had people coming so he turned back to stacking wood.

Meeting the Crew

Seattle, Washington

Rain dripped steadily off the roof outside the big picture windows facing Pine Street. Geo scanned the nine men and one woman arrayed before him. Reyes and Langberg must have served. They both stood at attention, though neither saluted, nor should they, considering that none of them were still in the military. Walden, the woman, looked up from the radio she fiddled with, but then looked right back until Carlindo said for them to gather around. Marek, Myerson, and Zapata didn't even bother to stand up, though Marek and Zapata both carried themselves like predators – ready to pounce a half-heartbeat after they realize the need to. He suspected Special Forces training for them. The other four straightened and formed into a loose line that didn't inspire Geo's confidence.

"Geo Tully, this is Squad T28. Fellas – and Ms. Walden, of course – Geo's trying to decide if he wants to be your leader."

Everyone but Zapata, Marek and Walden now came to an assemblance of attention. Zapata smiled. Oh, is *that* how it was?

"You with the Teams?" Marek asked. A black man who stood at least 6'2, his dark eyes held a glint that reminded Geo of lightning caught in a bottle.

"I was. You?"

"Retired two years ago after I blew out an eardrum. Seals say I can't do underwater anymore, but I can get the job done if I don't have to go deep."

Geo nodded, filing away that he needed to check Marek's balance.

"Cassidy Walden. I'm the communications tech."

"I see that. You ever serve?"

"No. I washed out of the Air Force Academy."

"She's an excellent UAV pilot," Carlindo countered.

Zapata served as an Army Ranger in Iraq until he took some shrapnel to his head. He moved with deadly grace that belied whatever limitation forced him out of the forces.

The others had either washed out in bootcamp or never joined up, except Tanner, who was older than most of the squad by about a decade. He'd served as a Marine sniper until his retirement and volunteered to the Knights the day after the Pulse.

"I can't hump a 100-pound pack through the desert for fifty miles, but you put me on overwatch and I'll get the job done for you."

Geo rubbed a hand down his jawline, contemplating. The one man that thoroughly worried him was named Sherwin. He'd washed out in bootcamp and actually done time in prison for assault. He couldn't have been more than twenty-five. What the Knights thought he was worth failed to impress Geo.

"Do we get to hear your story?" Walden asked.

"Nothing to tell. I was a SEAL until the Knights took over here in Seattle and now … well, I'm trying to decide if I trust this offer." Carlindo grinned and Tanner snorted. "So, that radio…what's the reach?"

She grinned at him.

"There's a tower in your grid area. I don't think they know we've got a capture on it."

"Then let's see what we can hear." Carlindo lifted an eyebrow at Geo. "It's one step at a time. Let's see what we've got before we blow it up."

Carlindo nodded.

"I'll let Liam know. You want someone to swing by your truck, let your dog out to pee?"

"No. Sherwin, it's a brown-and-white Chevy, 70s era. There's a black Lab. His name is Duke. His leash is under the shell. Take him for a walk. Police his poop if needed. Try not to get bit and don't hurt him. Bring him back here."

The kid frowned but held out his hand for keys.

"It's not locked. I figure you have the skills to bring it here."

Sherwin frowned and did as told. Geo wondered if he could follow orders.

Get the Deer or Disappear

Emmaus, Kansas

A long line of specters braced his path and pointed him onward after the deer. Sera and Marie Callahan flanked *her* on either side of the game trail. Mike whispered in his ear. Kitty Vance danced at the end of a rope. The deer kept on going, past the airfield and the trucking company and they then took a turn to the south, climbing up the side of the interstate. At least there were no wolf tracks. Shane paused to drink some water, stripped off his outer coat, and strapped it to his backpack. Getting overheated held dangers – hypothermia and frostbite. Heat exhaustion in subfreezing temperatures could kill a man as surely as falling through a creek. No one had created a track up the side of the interstate here, so he kicked off his skis, slung them over his shoulder, and scrambled up the slope, stomping footholds as he climbed, glad he was running the sled empty.

"You killed us all," Mike hissed.

"You aren't real."

Mike laughed and materialized right in front of him.

"You. Are. Not. Real." Shane changed his climbing angle enough to avoid the specter. He knew it all came from lack of sleep and PTSD, but he couldn't push through Mike's "ghost". It just creeped him out.

'I'm real enough and you know it. I'm dead because you left me in Santa Fe."

Shane topped the slope and swung his legs over the guardrail. While he strapped on the skis, the man and woman he euthanized because they were suffering from radiation sickness stood on the center of the westbound lane. He rubbed a hand across his eyes, then followed the deer tracks south – dropping off the far side of the interstate, snowplowing with his left leg so he could carve the side of the highway like a downhill slope even though his skis had no edges. His thigh muscles burned.

He stopped at the toe of the slope and stared around. The vast cornfield across the road from him looked unfamiliar, but after gliding along the deer tracks for a while, he crossed a county road that was serviced by an off-ramp. He'd been here before, helping Alex clear the fields to the right. The grey-white world made his eyes burn while his nose ran from the cold. He tried to remember the way forward. The ground here was very flat. If he got turned around, he could die out here. That didn't scare him anymore. He knew that would end the hallucinations. Only the pain it would cause his parents, siblings, and Alex kept him from eating his gun just about any day. The longer he went without sleep and with reduced calories the worse the hallucinations got, and the more sense suicide made.

The county road reached a crossroads – the farm road between Alex's two fields. He glanced toward the interstate, calculating the distance. He shouldn't be this side of the highway. Nobody was looking for him here. What did he care?

"Get the deer or disappear," Mike whispered. A Miristan village populated the field to his left, men in dark clothing creeping along the roofs with AK47s strung across their backs. Shane started along the road. He'd go back if he didn't find them soon. Or he could just keep going toward the Rockies until he couldn't go any further. He wondered if Jim Bridger ran from all the men he'd killed.

The small herd of deer stood in the right-hand field, luckily upwind of him. He stopped, taking some deep breaths to calm his heart rate. Five does and a buck with a deep chest and an impressive rack of antlers, dark grey against the light grey of the snow behind him. A smaller yearling stood near one of the females. All four of the does looked pregnant, one of them with twins. That left him little choice. Either take the buck or the yearling. The yearling looked too small for his family. He looked through the scope.

"It's past hunting season." Jacob leaned against a fence post, wearing that old sheepskin coat Vi hated so much. Grief lanced through Shane.

"We'll soon be starving."

"Laws are meant to be broken and extraordinary times allow extraordinary measures."

"You would say that."

"This is how you remember me. Don't forget."

113

His grandfather's specter shredded in a gust of wind that made Shane think he should be wearing his outer coat. The stirring air must have shifted his scent. The buck's ear twitched.

"Now or never," Jacob warned. Shane tucked the rifle into his shoulder, drew in a breath, centered the crosshairs on the buck's near shoulder, paused, then squeezed the trigger.

Instinct

The white prairie stretched to the amorphous horizon where it faded into the grey-and-blue-chalk sky. Here and there, a stand of trees between fields or a bit of undisked prairie grass stood up through the white with a flash of dark wood or amber grain. The snow held off yet, but the wind out of the west rendered Jazz's cheeks and lips numb. She blinked ice crystals off her eyelashes, pausing to identify a set of tracks in the snow by the southern guardrail. Maybe deer. She'd never hunted deer in the snow, so she wasn't sure of the tracks. Several, she thought. She recognized the tracks running parallel to the deer – a skier. Looking back at her tracks, she guessed this intersecting trail to be a male or larger woman hauling an empty runner sled. Empty because it hardly rounded the snow and didn't follow the skier in a direct line as he followed the deer from the town, up over the interstate and then down into the broad prairie beyond. Going outside the cordon held risks, especially alone. Few people would be that bold.

Shane took a runner sled and he had the requisite skills and courage to chase deer outside the wire. He shouldn't be alone out here – or anywhere.

She pulled out her field glasses and scanned the grasslands. Here and there she saw the wink of fencing. And then she caught the faded red of an old barn. She didn't know what she looked for, but instinct called for her to take notice. She wriggled her toes in her ski boots. Her socks weren't yet damp. She adjusted the magnification so she might see humans better. The barn grew enormous and then she began to scan the surrounding landscape.

Judge of Character

Duke tried to drag Sherwin in the door, but the young Knight held the leash like he'd done this before, wrist-loop over his thumb, leash clasped in his hand, leaning back against the tug so not to fall on his face. Geo met them halfway, scrubbing Duke's ears and telling him to sit. Well-trained, Duke sat down and gave him a huge sideways grin, tongue hanging halfway to the floor. *See, I fetched a human.*

"You seem to handle dogs pretty well."

"My grandfather had bloodhounds."

Sherwin's accent wasn't exactly southern. It had a little western twang to it.

"Missouri?" Geo made sure to pronounce it the right way – *Missur-ah.*

"Taney County." Being from Kansas, Geo knew that was the heart of the Ozarks.

"Knights ever do K9 units?"

117

"Sure. That's what I was hoping to do when I joined, but then the bombs happened right after I finished my basic training."

Might as well not skirt around it.

"What's the difference between Army basic and Knights basic?"

"Well, Knights don't pretend to pay you for it. They actually do. And they don't have all the stupid rules about staying on base and not drinking and that. You gotta be able to do certain physical things, but how you choose to get in shape to do them is your business. You can use their facilities, but there's no idiotic PT at 4 am."

"Good to know. You got a problem with authority?"

"I got a problem with people screaming at me."

"I ain't a screamer. I'm not your training officer. My job is to form you men – folks, into a team before we hit a target that we don't yet know enough about. So you're good with dogs? What else?"

"I ain't afraid to get bloody."

"Hence the assault charge?"

"Man came at me with a bottle. I just didn't stand still to get killed."

"I'll keep that in mind. Did you bring my truck?"

"I did. Wondering where you stole it from."

"That I needed to is the bigger story. Might tell it sometime. For now, go join Zapata and Tanner." They poured over the map. "See if we can figure out what might be going on under the tarps."

Sherwin nodded and headed to the table where the other two bent over the satellite photos. Geo dropped to his knee and rubbed Duke's ears.

"You're going to have to tell me what you think, boy. Let's meet the squad."

Trigger

Southwest of Emmaus

*H*ow you going to dress that deer?" Jacob asked as Shane spread the tarp between the carcass and the sled, draping it over the sled.

"G-Pa's method, I think." This seemed like the most normal conversation he'd had lately. Something about Jacob's specter kept Mike and the others at bay. The remainder of the herd fled south after he shot their leader. He knew from experience they would be fine. The does didn't need the buck. He was more of a problem than a protector until it was time to get pregnant and they'd find a buck come the rut. His ego made him the leader, not his skill.

From the bag of gear he'd been carrying, Shane drew out a bag with his dressing gear – an ulu Vi bought when she and Jacob spent a summer in Alaska, a boning knife and stack of burlap game bags. He rolled the buck on its back for the first cut in the gutless method favored by his Wyandot great-grandfather. Shane never hunted with him, but Rob and Jacob both swore by his methods.

Starting at the genitals, Shane ran the broad ulu with its bone handle through the skin of the belly up to the base of the neck. He then circumscribed the skin at one knee joint, before running a lateral cut up to the belly slice. When all four legs were sliced, he severed the hide from the carcass.

Sweat poured down his back, soaking his undergarments. He paused, straightening to look west, seeing the darkening clouds moving his way. He bent to continue skinning. The deer's blood seemed so bright against the blue-white of the snow ....

His ribs and shoulder burned as Reynolds' blood-soaked his shirt and pants, making everything slippery and sticky. Shane grunted with pain as he heaved him up into the truck. He didn't have time to assess his injuries, bruises compared to bullet holes. He needed to concentrate on Reynolds, ignore that every breath felt like broken ribs.

"Man, you still with me?" The blood still poured from a hole in the Knight's side. Shane grabbed the first aid kit for compression bandages and a lot of roller gauze. In the distance, he heard a boom. A second later, a patch of ground 100 feet away exploded into a fountain of dirt. Shane glanced around, ears faintly humming from the explosion. Another mortar struck 50 feet away, slapping his ears. He slammed the passenger door of the truck and ....

She materialized at the end of the bloodstain, her AK47 at the ready. Shane whipped out his 9mm and pulled the trigger. Amid the phantom pop-pop-pop of the AK as she fired into the air, the specter shredded on the wind, but that wasn't how she'd died. There'd been blood and a scream of pain that penetrated his overwhelmed hearing before the next mortar round hit, making it clear Shane had to get out of there.

Sera appeared, wearing her silk hajib along with other women and Knights who had died. Mike began to laugh. The radiation couple begged him to kill them. Blood covered the entire field.

The 9 mm felt warm in his hand. Who did he shoot?

"Put it in your mouth, man," Reynolds whispered. "Pull the trigger."

Shane stared at the inanimate object in his hand – black steel and polycarbonate. The taste of gun oil overwhelmed his mouth. He set the gun on the sled with shaking hands.

Folded over at the waist in pain, **she** ran back into the village as mortars exploded all around him. He'd run that time – left her body by the side of the road, gotten into the truck and fled. What if he followed her? The village reached out its arms to swallow him whole.

Snowcat

Wichita, Kansas

W hat's your name?" Ren asked, holding out a hand to shake with the mechanic.

"All due respect, sir, but shaking hands is one way we spread the flu. Name's Kris Lawson."

Ren dropped his hand, stuck it in the pocket of his coat.

"Old habits die hard. Ren Sullivan. I know you know that, but folks call me 'Ren' and I'd just prefer it that way. Tell me about yourself before we talk about this relic."

Lawson scratched his scruffy beard.

"Not much to tell." His eyes looked deeply sad. Ren sat down on the front track of the giant snowmobile.

"I doubt that. That might have been true four months ago, but now everybody has a story. I didn't take charge here to ignore the individual stories. That's what makes life. Go on and tell me. Who have you lost? Or do you just not know?"

"No, I know." Lawson rubbed a spot above his eyebrows. He heaved a deep breath. "I was a National

Guardsman. You know about the liquidation of the containment zone at the Denver border?"

"Happened in a lot of places is what we're hearing. Not that it was right. I heard the National Guard fought back out Kanorado way. Good for you."

Lawson nodded.

"The Army was for it. My commander wasn't. Before it actually happened, some agent for the Central Security Agency shot me in the vest to get out of the containment zone, so I was here in Wichita getting patched up when the actual thing went down. The Army arrested me and tortured me until I agreed to join them. They wouldn't let me see my girlfriend and daughter. Then they shipped me out to confiscate food. I eventually ended up in Hutchinson. That's where I was when the Pulse hit. Took me another week to get back here." A tear tracked down his cheek. "When I got back to my place, the apartment complex was closed, and my girlfriend and daughter were nowhere to be found. When you took over, I asked your administrative folks to try and find them. They think the residents of the complex were taken to a camp at McConnell Airforce Base, but when they broke the Army cordon, there were just bodies."

Ren pulled on his gloves and touched the man on his elbow to show his sympathy. Lawson wiped his tears away, swallowing loudly.

"Give Phil their names and we'll see if there's something we can find."

"I already did that when I took the job a few weeks ago, but I appreciate that you care, sir."

"You got parents?"

"I do – did. I haven't been able to get hold of them either, but my dad's a survivor, so I'm not really worried about them."

"Could she have gone there?"

Lawson frowned.

"I already tried her mom. Place was deserted. Looked like a hell of a fight before they dragged someone out of there."

"Son, you're looking at the negatives. Could your girlfriend have gone to *your* parents?"

"Maybe, if she had some warning. She had their address and I know my folks would take her in, especially with the baby. But that's way out in Garden City, so I don't know."

"I'm headed that way if this thing can make it. You're welcome to come with. We'll be setting up regular convoys back and forth. This trip is just to see if we can do it. If it turns out they're not there, you can always come back here."

"The Tucker can make it, sir. She's just about as old as you are, but they were built tough back then." Lawson flushed as if he realized he'd just insulted Ren, but Ren laughed.

"That is pretty old for a machine, though I have a friend who flies a crop-dusting plane that's older than I am. What is this thing even doing here?"

"It was a museum piece," Travis explained. "You know about that earthmoving museum you own, right?"

"Ah, yeah. That was my father's baby in retirement. Have I been funding it all these years?"

"It made a profit." Eden had been standing quietly beside him the whole time. "Right up until the bombs. It was one of the most popular tourist attractions in Wichita."

"So why is it here?"

"We've been hauling pieces back and forth for the last month." Lawson nodded like it might have been his idea. "The newer stuff takes too much tech to fix – electronics fried by the Pulse either has to be circumvented or replaced. But this old stuff doesn't have that problem. We've got some of those museum pieces plowing streets, acting as busses – 50-year-old generators providing lights. We were going to put this thing into the rotation as a people mover but taking it out west works just as well."

Ren stood up and stared at the large orange machine. It looked like a truck put on a quad of tracks.

"This one seats six, but there's a cargo area where up to fifteen could ride for short distances. How many do you want to take, sir? I can probably configure it accordingly."

Ren rubbed the back of his glove along the edge of his chin. This could work…if they thought it out.

Concern

Southwest of Emmaus

The wind gusted across the snow and grass, swirling around the old barn. She adjusted her magnification and scanned the road that led from the barn to a county road and then to an underpass in the interstate. She could follow her orders and ski to the underpass or follow the tracks off the side of the interstate. She'd probably have a hard time finding the tracks again if she skied all that way and backtracked. Besides, why should she interfere with this guy's hunt? The deer were becoming scarce. People no longer cared about things like hunting season. Her job was to look for activity and breaches in the wire, but this guy had come from the town. There were no rules against that.

Right?

Rob Delaney chose not to be a dictator. People could come and go as they liked. As long as they weren't stealing from or killing their neighbors, they could get food however they wanted. Shane's border patrol might warn you it was dangerous out there, but they wouldn't stop you from going into the wilderness.

The interstate technically lay outside the wire and the underpass near Lufgren's Crossing was her takeout point anyway. So, she skied the south toe of the interstate instead of the high point. What difference would that make?

Through the field glasses, she saw something dark in a field off the road. She swept back to the deep red. The deer lay in the snow, unmoving. She could see a blue tarp beside the carcass, but no sign of the hunter. Anxiety clawed at her stomach as she scanned around the field. Shane's dark clothing stood out starkly against the blue-white. He had his pistol out, aiming at something she couldn't see. Her gut wrenched and without further thought, she stepped over the guardrail and skied a backtracking trail down the slope.

Forge

Emmaus, Kansas

The shed where Nevada Randolph had her forge was warmer than it had a right to be. Having shucked his coat, Andrew sweated as he looked over the attachment bracket for his plow truck. She'd forged a flange for it and welded it to the larger piece so he could get his plow truck working again. He'd hit something in the deep snow yesterday when he'd been three-quarters of the way to Mara Wells. He'd hoped to clear it before deep winter arrived, but the look of the sky suggested his technical difficulties had lousy timing. Well, at least he'd be ready for spring.

Nevada had been a metal artist, making weird statues for boutique hotels, just three months ago, but she'd adapted her skills to forge horseshoes and plow truck parts. She wore a leather apron over a tank top and her shapely arms glowed with perspiration. Her blonde hair grew out brown – what his wife Colleen called "going back to my roots." So many women in town revealed themselves to not quite be honest now that hair dye wasn't available.

Andrew smiled as he compared the repair to the broken flange. She'd managed to get it just right.

"You did a great job."

"I don't deserve all the credit. Clem Burroughs' father was a farrier. He showed me how to do more practical forge work. I just keep playing with horseshoes. I'm getting better."

"You're all we got, so I appreciate this, especially that you got it right the first time."

"I didn't, but metal can be reworked. At some point, I'm going to have to build a bigger forge though. People are asking me for stuff I'm just not equipped for."

"We can help you with that. When you're ready, let me know and I'll send a couple of my kids over to do the grunt labor. You're pregnant, right?"

"How did you ...?"

"I have eight kids. I know the signs."

The outside door opened in a swirl of cold and snow, accompanying a man dressed for the outdoors, carrying a barrel of coal.

"Oh, hey, Andrew."

"Max, how are you?"

"Good. Trying to earn my keep."

"You're staying here?"

"I couldn't get fuel for the house in town, so I had Jace Welton mothball it. Nevada was kind enough to let me rent her spare room."

"I kind of needed someone to do the heavy lifting after I realized I was pregnant."

Andrew tried not to speculate on how that had happened. He'd not seen Nevada with men before the Bombs, but maybe he was unobservant. He doubted Max was the father since … well, yeah. *What happened to Max's partner?* Andrew didn't know and he wasn't going to ask.

"A lot of families are combining to cut down on resource use. Two of my bachelor brothers are crashing in my basement and my parents are living with another brother. It's a brave new world out there. Nevada, thank you again. I'll send work your way, I'm sure."

"Thank you. We take food or fuel."

"Coal for the forge?"

"Yes. Or help to make a bigger one. I'm training Max and James Vance so when I get big as a house, we don't have to shut down."

"Smart. Like I said, whenever you're ready, my kids will be happy to build our credit with you."

He moved toward the door. Max turned to follow him, calling over his shoulder that he was headed to check on Kim who was shoveling.

The two men paused to stare up at the chalk sky.

"How long have you lived here?" Andrew asked.

"We were here last winter. Got here that fall."

"What were you doing before?"

"I'm a software engineer. I was telecommuting. Drew's an investor."

"I hope he got somewhere safe."

"I'm going to keep hope until next spring – promised myself until Memorial Day. I figure if he's alive, he needs to be here by then."

Andrew nodded.

"I'll pray for that."

"Even if he was clear of Chicago when the Bombs happened, though – you heard what happened at the Conopher place this morning?"

"No. What?"

"They're sitting on a big stockpile of food and some folks tried to get some of it."

"People are hungry."

"They are that and hoarders don't help. Hoarders with guns *really* don't help. Three men died for trying to feed their families."

Andrew rubbed his cheek with a gloved finger. Dell Conopher was a farmer and a friend. Like all the farmers, he had enough food to survive to spring. It bothered Andrew that he couldn't just help his neighbors, but his priority had to be his own family. Having extra food meant he could afford to pay Nevada in food for her blacksmithing. He wasn't a hoarder. He was prepared. Same for Dell and the Lufgrens and so many of the other farmers. Feeding your family was not wrong. Stealing from people was.

"I gotta go, but – if you and Nevada are desperate, let folks know. Her skills are too valuable to waste. We'll figure something out."

"But you wouldn't if it was just me?"

"Find something that makes you useful and I will. Sorry to put it so bluntly, but these are not ordinary times and it's the skilled and adaptable who will get through them. Someone like Nevada, who turned artist skills into artisan skills – that's worth preserving. Software engineer – might be useful if we can ever reestablish electricity again."

"And in the meantime?"

"Janna Thomas' kids are shoveling snow, Max. She's scrubbing clothes for people who have other things to do. You find a way to be useful."

Andrew swung up into his truck and fired up the engine. It needed new plugs and maybe a belt, but he didn't know where he would get those items in the current conditions. He probably should think seriously about that, after he was done grinding the cornmeal for today.

"It pisses me off that I'm good for nothing but grunt labor these days," Max admitted. Andrew nodded. He rolled down the window and closed the door. "But I do hear what you're saying. Did you know Mace Kettridge?"

"I did. Played softball with him last summer – for the last ten summers, maybe. Loved his family. Could be a bit of a bully when he felt he was being treated unfairly. I'm not surprised he came to a bad end in these circumstances because 'fair' is kind of a moving target in times like these."

Max frowned at the barn-like it had pissed him off, but then shook his head.

"Why didn't Delaney make everyone pool their resources so that everyone would get their fair share?"

Andrew chewed his lower lip, thinking of how he might answer reasonably.

"You didn't grow the crops. I did. I'm willing to trade with you if you have something I want, but you can't require me to give it to you. That's stealing. And, Rob Delaney knows that if he tried to take what's mine, I'd fight back. One or the other of us would end up dead. He'd rather you peacefully trade with me for what you need than that he and I go to war on your behalf. And--."

"That's bullshit!"

"I'm not finished. I'll drive away if you don't want to hear the rest of it, but you're failing to take the big picture into account."

"People are starving. How much big picture does it get?"

"And, if you make a calculation of the number of bushels harvested divided by the number of people-calories in town, you'd realize that we'd all be starving in February instead of just those who weren't prepared starving now. My family is not overeating. I've lost twenty pounds myself, not because we're out of food, but because we're rationing to ensure we make it to spring. There are no easy answers here. There's no *fair* solution. There's just the uncomfortable fact that we all starve together or some of us live separately. I'm sorry you're having difficulty grasping the new normal and I truly hope you make it through. I don't like the decisions I have to make. It's hard to watch my neighbors suffer. It would be harder to watch *my* kids starve. I do need to go. Hopefully, I'll see you around sometime."

Andrew backed up and started down the narrow driveway with the snow berms on both sides, waving at Kim Randolph as the teenage girl stepped aside to allow him to pass. She saluted him with her shovel and was already back to work when he glanced in the rearview mirror.

Sarna

Southwest of Emmaus

*T*he village called Sarna lay quiet in the midday heat until their dozen trucks pulled up at the bottom of the pedestrian track leading to its gates. Now you could see people running, small boys scampering from house to house to warn someone of what was coming their way.

A blast of icy air roused Shane as he walked toward the village into the barn.

The headman's hut glowed faintly red instead of the usual white or grey. He'd lost his gun somewhere and his bullet-proof vest constricted his breathing. He stripped it off.

"You're exposed, man," Mike warned.

"That's how you end up dead," Reynolds added.

Corn cobs littered the floor here, filling the back half of the barn. A staircase of rough lumber led to the haymow. He heard Sera's laugh, which drew him forward. The barn disappeared and he stood on a road of hewn stone through a dark forest of encroaching trees. Jacob stood against one of those trees, peeling an apple with the knife he always carried.

"You're lost."

Shane looked over his shoulder, but nothing looked familiar except Jacob.

"I know." No use arguing with reality. Realists didn't do that. A thumping filled his ears, loud and fast.

"Do you know where you're going?"

He didn't. He didn't know where he was. Forward looked as good as back – as daunting too. The thumping distracted him and he rubbed his eyes in reaction.

"Heartbeats stop."

"What do you mean, Grandpa?"

"You're in the dark wood now." Mike's specter stood on the opposite side of the road.

He looked for the light and saw only palpable darkness, hammering at him with relentless cold.

"You won't find it with the eyes you have now." Jacob still peeled the apple, but he'd often talked to Shane amid ordinary activities.

"I'm not blind."

"Aren't you?" Vi asked. Her hair hung loose this time, past her knees, gliding over the leather jacket. "God's given you so much and you can't see Him at all."

"I don't believe what you believe, Grandma."

"You don't believe in living?" Jacob asked.

"I'm doing the best I can. I can't believe in fairy tales. Where is this place?"

"The road to Rome was paved with good intentions," Jacob told him. "Take the narrow upward path. Fight the vines."

Sera laughed. Her hair flowed loosely down her back as she reached out to him from where she stood before a door. He knew if she went through it he'd never see her again.

"Don't go." He held out a hand to her. She wrapped her fingers around his wrist and pulled him through the door. He tumbled into blackness and pain exploded in his head.

Bonding

Lufgren Farm

The dipperful of water running down his back, carrying away sweat and grime, felt glorious. Alex dipped another to pour over his head. These days a whole bath was hard to come by. That much water was a luxury and it took a lot to keep it warm. Even at their house where there was running water, it was hard to bathe every day, but for the men of the town, Alex' sauna gave them a few hours of warmth as well as getting all the grime out of their skin.

His brother-in-law Cai Delaney lay on the top bench, staring into the shadows as if they held answers. Clem Burroughs came in from outside where he'd gone to cool off. When he sat down, Frank Giffin stirred from a light doze. Cai's brother-in-law Josh washed his hair and now leaned over another bucket with a cup of water, rinsing it. He sprayed droplets when he shook off.

"I used to try and imagine what it was like to live like this," Clem said. Andrew Bennett opened a languid eye to watch him while he spoke. "It's all well and good to sauna as a time of fellowship and manhood, but this needing to do it for bathing adds a different dimension to it."

"I've never done this before," Danny Hughes admitted.

"What do you think?" Alex asked.

"Relaxing."

"That's an understatement." Andrew bent to wet his washcloth with cold water and run it across his neck. "I feel like a noodle." He shifted. "How are you doing?" A lantern near the door dimly lit the sauna's interior. You guessed at facial expressions.

"Worried about Sharon. I think she's getting weaker."

"While that is unfortunate, I want to know how *you* are doing."

"You mean because …?"

"Yeah."

"I still dream about it, but not as often. I'm usually too tired when I go to bed to think much about it."

"And, you, Josh?"

"I'm good, Andrew. I knew when I went to Hays that someone might have to die. It wasn't me. I'm good." Frank stared at him. "You got something to say?"

"Everybody's got a different way of coping with it, I guess. I still see the man I beat to death. He deserved it, but I didn't want to kill him."

Alex thought about how Keri froze when it came confession time. She had stopped stealing away in the middle of the night to hide in his parents' room, but he sometimes caught her staring off into space. She admitted she sometimes dreamed of it. Alex wished he could take that memory from her, but in a world where the normal rules no longer applied, he knew he might have a tale of his own to tell at any time.

"Not wanting to kill someone doesn't make it any easier when you have to do it." Cai swung his long legs off the bench, ran his towel over his neck. "It's not healing to say 'it was him or me'. There's nothing for it but to live with it."

Keri and Cai had taken some long walks a few weeks ago after he'd come back from Hays and she'd said talking with Cai had helped her get her head straight, but she had said Cai had a death on his conscience.

"Man," Josh murmured. "Never saw that coming."

"It's not all fun and games out beyond the town borders."

"Nor inside of them either." Clem wielded the dipper now. "Those folks I had to kill at the Elevators --." He sighed heavily and sank onto the bench. "Vets don't do the Hippocratic Oath, but I felt like I violated every principle I held dear. And, they couldn't have been saved. They were dying. It was a mercy. But it still." The oldest man in the group seemed older still.

Andrew didn't confess any deaths on his conscience, so Alex still wasn't alone. A wind caught the roof of the little shed and shook it, causing the wood to groan against wood.

"Sounds like a blizzard's on its way."

"Sounds like it's already here. Can horses find their way home in weather like that?" Danny stared at the roof rafters as if afraid the wind might take the whole building.

"You can stay over if the storm is really bad. We've got extra beds."

"I don't like leaving Sharon alone."

"You're a good kid." Clem sounded surprised and then snorted. "I mean – you *are* a good kid. I had my doubts when I heard about you, but you actually care about her."

"She's nothing like my grandma, but somehow she reminds me of her." Danny's voice grew hoarse at the end.

"It's hard, losing folks." Andrew stared into the shadows. Was he thinking of his cousin Caleb Jacoby? He'd been in an inescapable prison when the Bombs went off. Shane said anyone in prison when the Pulse occurred would have been trapped and died. Alex nodded, thinking of his own parents now long dead. He'd known, at least in some way, the 80 people who had died at City Hall in September. He'd admired Dick Vance, Bart Rawlson, and Ross Winther. So many people died this winter. How to mourn them all without overwhelming yourself with grief.

A tear tracked down Cai's cheek, shimmering in the sweat on his face.

"The storms are early this year, according to Grandpa."

"About a month, according to the Farmer's Almanac." Alex rubbed a hand through his hair. "How'd he know?"

"He was 96 years old. He lived every kind of winter. And he maybe had an Almanac. I miss him."

"Yeah. Seems like all the wisdom in the world leaked away."

"And Shane lost his mind."

"He'll find his way back." Alex hoped he was right. Shane occasionally showed flickers of their old friendship, but Alex would take him even dark and damaged. Brother from another mother for life.

A wind shuddered the roof of the little shed.

"We should get cleaned up and head toward the barn." Clem frowned into the shadows above the rafters. "It's getting worse. Abby will worry about me."

He started washing off. They would take turns until they were all done. Alex stretched his neck and leaned back against the wall, feeling like he might turn to goo and flow down into the floorboards. He hovered on the edge of a doze, dreaming he danced with his beautiful wife … and then he jerked awake as the floor gave way beneath him and he fell screaming.

He stared at the men before him and wondered why his heart thundered as if he'd just run the length of a football field full tilt, but they didn't seem to have heard his scream.

Finding Trouble

Southwest of Emmaus

Cross-country skiing in Kansas normally didn't require elevation changes, so Jazz ended up rolling down the last few feet of the slope, hitting the county road hard and thinking she hadn't caught the hang of Nordic skiing. She'd skied downhill successfully at a moderate level, but the lack of edges on cross-country skis made down slopes hard, and the impact even harder.

She sat up and gathered her poles. No harm done. She'd have a bruise on her left elbow by the feel of it. Nothing to worry about. Her skis were still attached to her boots, unlike downhill skis that would have taken off downslope with a life of their own.

She stood up and tried to orient herself.

Now on the flat, she lost track of the barn, but the skier's trail followed the interstate westward, so she did too. At the underpass, he turned south, clearly following the deer tracks. Sweat trickled between her breasts and shoulder blades. She worried about how dark the sky grew to the west, but she knew she couldn't get lost between fields.

She'd run up against their fences like a pheasant in high wind, only smart enough to follow it out. The trail she chased turned westward between two fields.

The deer lay in the field. The carcass was still warm but growing stiff. It couldn't have laid here long. The runner sled held a hind quarter and the near-front quarter. Whoever had taken this deer had brought it down with a single shot, probably from the rifle that lay in the bag on the sled, next to an abandoned set of skis that she recognized from this morning. She recognized the SKS because it belonged to her.

A hand squeezed her heart and sucked the oxygen out of her lungs. The 9mm sitting on the sled said it all. She dragged her radio out of her inner pocket where she'd hoped it would stay warm enough not to kill the batteries.

"Hello, Jericho Township. This is Music Box Dancer. Anyone got their ears on? Over."

The short-range radio might pick up a few miles away, but there wasn't much within radio distance that mattered. There were mostly Lufgrens out this way and they couldn't hear, so she hoped she'd get Shane's attention.

"I'm standing by a deer kill south of the interstate near underpass two. This belong to you? Over."

The radio crackled and then fell silent.

"Maverick, this is Music Box Dancer. You out there? Over."

The radio crackled again and then an unexpected Texan accent came to her.

"Hey, Music Box Dancer, this is Loredo. Where are you? Over."

"Between two fields headed toward a barn south of the interstate. Over."

The pause that followed worried her.

"Poppy says that's Alex's barn. We store corn cobs in there. You say someone bagged a deer there? Over."

"I think Shane. I recognize his skis and rifle. But he's not here now. I can see a trail headed toward the barn, but I don't want to leave the kill abandoned. Can you come get it? Over."

"We're at the underpass now. Poppy says five minutes to your location. She might make it. It'll take me 10. Over."

"I think he's in trouble. As soon as you can get here, please. Over."

"She's headed that way already and I'll be right behind her. Out."

Prepping Dinner

Emmaus

Jill stripped the bowel line into the bucket of water and scrubbed the scales before handing the fish to Rob to fillet it. He used an ulu so to waste as little meat as possible.

"Three fish split between eight people. That's not too bad," she noted.

"If the sky hadn't been getting so grey, I would have gone for a fourth one, but it'll be fine." He paused to listen to the wind as it swirled around the house. "I wonder where everyone has gotten to."

"Cai went to Alex's to enjoy the sauna."

"I forgot about that. I could certainly use a bath."

"Good. Two more buckets and the tub will be ready."

"You're reading my mind again. Since the house is quiet, I suppose we could share it. Where's Click, by the way."

Click Michaels had moved into their basement when the weather became so cold he couldn't stay at the radio station any longer. He, Dennis Bishop, and Christiana Ceylon were the last of the refugees from the commuter airline. The rest had perished of the flu complicated by hunger. Their close living arrangements in the church basement had assured rapid transmission of the virus and people without transportation or good winter clothes couldn't earn enough food to remain healthy. Christiana earned a nice living at the clinic. Dennis had hired himself out to Nehemiah Lufgren, so he hadn't been at the church. Click – well, Rob owed him for keeping the jury-rigged communications network going. He had only been here a couple of weeks, but he was stoking the coal furnace and hauling water just like her boys. Jill didn't resent the extra mouth to feed.

"Not sure. Didn't think it was my day to watch him."

"No, of course not. He's an adult. Just wondering where everyone is. Where's Shane?"

"Another adult? We're lucky *he* left us a note. Chasing a herd of deer Andrew Bennett saw yesterday."

"Why didn't Andrew chase them himself?"

"Not sure. The Bennetts have resources. Might be leaving them for the rest of us. At the rate this town is going, only ones who'll be left come spring will be Bennetts and Lufgrens."

She didn't worry that they wouldn't survive the winter. Shane would get that deer. The hotel would release its locks and let him access his food stores. Santa Claus would land on the roof with a sleigh full of chocolate. She felt certain something would happen that would get them to spring.

She slid the last fish into the tray of snow, rinsed her hands, and turned to her tall husband. His temples were going quite gray very quickly now matching her roots that hadn't seen a bottle of dye in months. They were getting old, but at least they were living.

"Let's take that bath now." His whisper touched her cheek like a feather. By some miracle, the house was empty, and the joy of life required they take advantage of it.

Confessions

Max was a good cook and had begun to take over many of the kitchen duties now that Nevada was forging more projects for her customers. It wasn't his fault that the smell of whatever he was cooking turned her stomach. Pregnancy sucked. She'd forgotten how she'd been morning sick for six months with Kim. She'd chewed ginger and sucked on lemon drops the whole time. Those appeared to be obsolete at the moment. She sliced bread and laid it directly on the top of the coal stove to toast it. Thank God for whatever Jill Delaney's secret for making bread was. Kim promised to go learn how to do it someday when the weather was good, and Jill wasn't working at the medical center. Nevada didn't think puking would create a good learning environment.

"Where's Kim?" Nevada ran her fingers through her freshly-washed hair. At least they still had semi-hot water by virtue of warming a pot atop the stove. Max rigged up a solar shower and they could stay reasonably clean this way.

"She went to see James. She took Bosco with her." Bosco was Max's chocolate Lab who had decided he liked Kim more than Max, who didn't seem to mind.

"Good. He seems to find his way around just fine even in a blizzard."

"That's what I thought too, though I'm sure James will bring her home in the truck if the weather turns nasty."

"It's turning. The sky to the west looks bad. She can stay at the Vances if needed too. She and Allison seem to be hitting it off."

"Not a bad person to make the acquaintance of."

"She does have resources." Nevada flipped her toast. Max had cleaned the stove this morning so you could eat off it provided you didn't care about singeing your tongue. He stirred something in a cast-iron skillet. Ugh! It smelled like skunk. "What are you cooking?"

"Bacon, cabbage, and potatoes."

She saw the pile of cabbage on a plate on the counter, right next to a bowl of cut-up potatoes. There were onions mixed with the bacon in the pan. God, if it smelled that bad now, she'd need to leave the house when he added the cabbage.

"Did you used to cook for Drew?"

"We usually took turns but I'm the better cook. My mother owned a bistro."

"A San Francisco bistro?"

"In Marin County, yes."

She stripped a chunk of toast off the slice and popped it in her mouth, barely chewing it before washing it down with a good swallow of milk. Her stomach turned ominously. She did it again.

"Are we distracting you from turning green?"

"Don't mention turning green, but yes. Where did you meet Drew?"

"We were neighbors. He lived at the end of the block. I used to pass his house on my way to school."

"When you were in college or …." The third chunk of toast hit her stomach and she stopped feeling woozy.

"No, I was a freshman in high school."

The fourth bit of toast made the bacon smell good. She liked this little house she rented from the Delaneys. The kitchen was the largest room in the house, fully one half with an open utility room at one end, just the other side of the table. There were two bedrooms tucked up under the eaves and a small lean-to off the utility room where Max had made his nest.

"I'm – yeah, curious. How much difference in age is there between you?"

"About – seven, well, really close to eight years."

Nevada stared at him. Like everyone these days, he wore a hat pulled down over his ears to hide his greasy hair, but he wasn't a bad looking man. It would just be – uh – creepy to do anything with him since she'd been his husband's lover. Drew was the father of her baby and – yeah, just creepy. Max and she were closer in age than she realized – 35. Something Drew had said when they were in Chicago struck her. They were celebrating their 20th anniversary the day the Bombs went off.

She chewed on that conundrum for quite a while until they were seated at the table enjoying the meal. Colcannon tasted far better than it had smelled just a few minutes ago.

"You were 14 and he was 21, almost 22?"

"Yeah. He helped me to see myself clearly."

"Kim's father did that with me. I was 16 and he was 24."

"Oh, my! Cradle-robber much."

"Yeah. If I'd thought with my brain instead of my clit I might have realized he was just using me, but --."

"He was a child molester."

"Yes, he was. And eventually that's how he left us – not because he molested me but because he sniffed up another young girl."

"Oh! Does Kim know?"

"Not the details. She knows he went to prison, but I haven't told her why and she's not asked."

"Will you lie to soften it when she does?"

"Probably not." Nevada savored a bit of bacon and potato. Mmmm! "Drew was kind of doing the same thing with you, wasn't he?"

"Not really. He helped me to see my orientation and he was there when I came out."

"But he was seven years older than you?"

"It's different. A lot of gay men and women have their first sexual encounter with an older partner."

"So do a lot of heteros, but when we do it, the adult risks going to jail."

"You don't understand." He didn't seem upset by it. He'd probably had this conversation with others.

"No. I understand that Drew wasn't faithful to you and that he popped your cherry when you were really young. Had you ever been with a girl?"

"No! Thank god!" He made the face of a small boy who still thought girls had cooties.

"Well, thank you very much for that." They laughed. They ate in grinning silence for a bit before Nevada decided she was full and compelled to say what was on her mind.

"Don't take this wrong, but – how do you know you're gay if you've never had sex with a woman?"

"How do you know you're heterosexual if you've never had sex with a woman?"

He had a point. In the new-normal frugality-over-possible-health-and-safety zeitgeist, Nevada pushed what she couldn't eat back into the serving bowl before taking her plate to the sink. She turned around and leaned back against the counter.

"Who says I haven't?" His gaze came up to meet hers. "I was curious – and drunk. But – look, I'm just going to say this, and you can get pissed off if you like. Drew screwed you when you were barely old enough to know what sex was – maybe before you even really liked girls yet. That's child molestation. It's like having sex with Kim – which I would castrate you if you did that."

"I won't."

"Yeah – I know. But, just think about that. You were a baby having sex with an adult. Did he uncover your sexuality, or did he impose it upon you?" Nevada picked up his cleared plate from the table. "So, my night to wash. That

161

was a great dinner. You want to dip some water for me so I can get these cleaned up?"

"You're just going to drop it there?"

"I am."

The wind rattled the window at the end of the counter. Nevada shivered and hoped Kim stayed at the Vances.

Dying

*A*gony. The black red-tinged. Each breath pushed fire through his lungs. It felt as if he'd breathed in a metric ton of fiberglas.

"You're dying." His grandmother *Vi* sat on a headstone, her blue jeans rolled at the ankles, wearing a worn leather jacket. "Is this where you planned on being?"

Behind her, a tall bucket stood stark against the white of the snow. Water flowed in the top from something he couldn't see, but then flowed out of holes in the side of the bucket — seeping away into the prairie grass. How could it be summer here when it was so fucking cold?

"What is that?" he asked.

Vi cocked her head, her long braid sliding over one shoulder.

"Your life."

"I don't understand."

"You let it all leak away."

The ground beneath him shifted ominously. He stood on sloping ground, something moving in front of him. Water splashed on all sides. *Vi* sat on the turtle's head.

"Do you remember this?"

"The Wyandot legend. Yeah."

"You've fallen off the turtle's back. How are you going to get back on?"

"But I'm standing on its back, Grandma."

"Are you?" Jacob asked, appearing right in front of him. He dressed for summer now — a t-shirt and jeans. "You're killing yourself, son. All you have to do is listen, but you won't. It's like you've decided to stop living but you haven't laid down yet."

The water soaking his clothes chilled him to his soul. A boy no more than 12 set an IED in the path of the turtle. Shane tried to jump free, but the explosion slapped his ears and plunged him into the water. He tumbled, gasping, sucking in icy liquid, choking.

"You're dying," Vi whispered.

"You're dying," Jacob said.

"Wake up," Sera ordered.

"They're coming," Mike warned.

"Wake up," Vi screamed. "Wake up!"

Secondary Effects

Snow started swirling sideways in the street as Marnie met Dell in the lobby where he deposited his son Kix into a wheelchair. The boy's left arm twitched and spasmed and his knee bobbled up and down.

"Take him into Exam Room 3," she told Abigail Burroughs. "I'm in the middle of examining another patient. I'll be back in just a few."

She ducked into Exam Room 2 where Chris Ceylon was taking blood from the two Vance boys while Brian Halloran the physical therapist watched David walk down the hall. Alicia took notes.

"How's he doing?" Marnie asked.

"He's walking almost normally. His arm is still a bit clumsy, but he's able to use it if he concentrates."

"What about talking?"

David and Brian came into the room. David smiled around the room and waved with his left hand, before clumsily sitting in a chair.

"April diagnosed him as a global," Brian reported. "He doesn't understand much of what we say, but he seems to be following us when we gesture."

"Does he have any words?"

James opened his eyes, looking at the IV doubtfully.

"He says 'yeah' and 'no', but he doesn't always get it right. He's better with shaking his head, but it still depends on whether he understands us, which is not good. He seems to understand Allison a bit better."

"April says familiarity helps," Brian added. "Alicia, by the way, you're becoming quite good at occupational therapy. How close were you to your degree?"

"Not nearly close enough, but I am what we have, so …." The pretty Hispanic woman shrugged. When she'd started with David three weeks ago, he couldn't manage much with his right hand. "Part of the battle with him is getting him to understand what you want."

Marnie smiled at David and gave him a thumbs-up. He returned it. His hair grew out, not quite long enough to hide the wound scar above his left ear.

"I have another patient. Brian, could you join me? I think there's a neurological component."

He followed her into the other exam room where Abigail helped Dell get Kix up onto the exam table. Marnie started her examination with his eyes – unequal pupils, mild proptosis of the right eye, divergent gaze of the left. In addition to the twitching on the left side, he couldn't make a fist and when he did he couldn't relax his hand afterward. Dell reported he'd wet himself earlier in the day.

"Kix, do you know what day of the week it is?"

The boy focused his gaze on her. His lips parted. His eyes rolled back in his head. The shaking on his left side became faster and more pronounced and then it spread to his right side. As soon as the shaking stopped, he vomited. Brian and Marnie turned him on his side so he wouldn't asphyxiate.

"What is going on with my boy?" Dell asked anxiously.

"I don't know," Marnie admitted. "You tell me what's been going on and then maybe I can make a guess, without any of the technology we ordinarily rely on."

"He woke up running a fever and complaining of a headache this morning. We had a mob at our house, trying to steal our food. He had to shoot two men in our kitchen. Then he threw up. Leisha put him back to bed. At lunch, he refused to eat which – yeah, none of us were hungry anyway, so we weren't surprised. But then he tried to get up to go to the bathroom, but he couldn't control his left side. He stopped talking on the way here."

"He seems to understand what we're saying," Brian noted. Marnie nodded, making a notation on a chart.

"Has he been sick at all?"

"He had the flu a few weeks ago."

"Has he not recovered from that?"

"I thought he did. He was helping on the farm all this last week, not complaining at all – until – last night before bed he said something about a headache. I just figured he was tired."

"Was he hard hit by the flu?"

"No. No worse than Geneva. He was down for about four days and then he was good."

"Could it be GBS?" Marnie looked at Brian.

"No, it's not the right symptoms. I've worked with GBS patients before. It doesn't present as hemiplegia."

"Could you go see if Ami has come today? She's been studying this flu. Maybe she'll have some insight."

Dr. Amisi Ceylon joined the Emmaus Medical Center when she'd arrived a couple of months ago. Her expertise was virology and she'd taken a particular interest in the flu that was working its way through the town's population.

Since Ami hadn't come in that day, her sister Chris came in from where she'd been taking blood. By that time, they'd just about exhausted Dell's memory for childhood illnesses and Brian had done as thorough a neurological examination as he could.

"I don't think he's feeling much on that left side."

A nurse, not a doctor, Chris understood a bit about her sister Ami's work. She scanned the chart.

"I don't think it's the flu. I think we all knew that before you even asked. And, I don't know what it is. Ami mentioned another patient with symptoms that appear neurological. It sounded more cerebellum than cerebrum, but I'm no expert."

"How do you treat it?" Dell asked.

"I don't know. If it's a virus, there's not much even Ami can do. May I take blood?"

"Yes, of course."

"Not just from him. From you as well." Dell lifted his eyebrows, then nodded. "Have you had the flu?"

"A mild case. It put me on my butt for two days, but then I had to get up because Kix got sick and someone had to take care of the farm."

"Others in your family."

"Just Geneva and she seems fine."

"Ami's going to want to swing by and get blood samples from your whole family."

"Why?"

"This is a new flu strain and the more she knows, the better chance she has of figuring it out. Viruses are tricky things and sometimes they tell on themselves, but only if you know what to look for."

"Meanwhile, we'll make Kix as comfortable as possible and start tracking symptoms." Marnie continued notations in the chart. "Since he's had a seizure, we need to keep him here 24 hours."

"I'll go get Leisha. She'll want to stay with him if that's okay."

"Of course. We're short-staffed, so that works well for us."

Dell leaned his tall frame over his prone son, putting a large callused hand on the boy's forehead.

"I'll be back with your mom. You don't give these folks any trouble, you understand?"

Kix's lips parted. Dell waited.

"Hurth," Kix whispered. "Pain." He gestured to his head with his right hand.

"Is there anything you can do for that?"

"I'm not sure. Until I've observed him for a while, no, but we'll see."

"I'll be back, kid. You hang in there." Kix made a face. It took Marnie a moment to realize it was a one-sided smile.

As soon as Dell left, she asked Kix to make a fist for her, but he stared at her blankly, then stared helplessly at his hand when she moved it into his view. She checked his reflexes. The left side had grown completely flaccid and his left eye no longer responded to light. She had just turned off her light when his eye twitched spasmodically for about two seconds and then his arm twitched and then his leg. Then they went limp again. His eyelids grew heavy after that.

"What's our supply of benzos look like?" Chris rattled off how many doses they had left. It wasn't enough. They'd risk starting a regime and not being able to complete it, which might cause more brain damage than it prevented.

"I've heard rumors there's a supply of cannabis oil in town."

Marnie sighed. Chris no doubt had heard rumors from a half-dozen townspeople because Jason Breen, Marnie's father, had a reputation. It meant dealing with her father for a drug that wasn't lab tested, but truthfully, what else could she do? She supposed she could ask Cai to take a message out to the Liberty Trucking Company so she could start an experiment in patent medicine without delay. This felt like medicine must have felt – well, in the 1880s. As her dear and ill-tempered brother-in-law was fond of reminding folks … when the Pulse hit, it sent them back 140 years and there was no use trying to deny it.

She unclipped her radio.

"Malacai, you got ears on? This is Medicine Woman. Over."

School Marm

Southwest of Emmaus

Shane used an Indian technique of quartering the deer before eviscerating it. He'd removed quarters on one side and rolled the carcass to get the other side, uncovering the blood pool. Jazz used the ulu to finish the skinning on this side and had just dragged the hindquarter onto the sled when she heard Poppy breathing as she glided up the road.

Deaf people were incapable of silence. They couldn't hear themselves and so had no concept of how noisy they were. Behind the tall blonde girl in the scarlet cap, her slender dark husband of three weeks struggled to keep her in view. Neither was legally old enough to drive, but they became too foolish to refrain from sex and unable to obtain contraception. Marriage became the only sensible alternative. Historically, the odds were in their favor, but this wasn't the past. It was the present living in the technological level of the 1880s.

Pete looked half-frozen while Poppy's cheeks glowed with ruddy good health.

"Thanks for coming," Jazz signed. "Me worried Shane. Go look there – barn. You finish here, take home?" Her fingers stung with the cold.

"We can," Poppy signed. *"Me teach Pete him butcher."* She grinned at her husband in a teasing manner.

"I know nothing," Pete agreed, signing for himself.

"Storm coming." An order played on the tip of Jazz's schoolmarm tongue, but these were adults now. She couldn't tell a married couple to go back home like they were school kids. She could give them a job that would take them in the direction of safety and hope it worked out okay. Poppy's headlamp illuminated the scene better than the non-existent sun did. Jazz remembered to turn hers on.

Poppy looked west with a knowledgeable expression.

"Hour, maybe two. Snow first, then wind and snow. No see then. Shane?"

"Shane wouldn't leave a kill out here," Jazz asserted. Food grew scarcer every day and they had all stopped worrying about hunting season. Pete interpreted for her since she forgot to sign. "That blizzard's got me worried." Jazz resumed signing for herself. *"Get this kill back to your home. No waste meat. No see me, sunset, send search party. I'll find him try try."*

They nodded. Jazz checked the mag on Shane's 9mm before locking the safety and tucking it into her inside pocket. Poppy signed she should be careful and then Jazz turned away to follow Shane's trail.

Immune Response

Jericho Ghost Town

Ami stepped out of the shower, toweling off before pulling the wrap off her hair. Dressed in sweats, she left the garage to enter the kitchen. Javi stirred a pot on the stove.

"Since when do you cook?"

"Emily asked me to take over while she checks on Dylan. Since Madalyn – well, she has her hands full."

"Yeah." Emily's mother hadn't recovered from the flu and she'd passed peacefully in her sleep last week. Javi, Grant, and Jim spent two days digging a grave in the frozen ground in the corner of the back yard. Now Jim hardly left his room and the entire family mourned. "You seem to have that under control, so I'm going to go check on my patient."

"Dr. Kletti is here," Javi reported.

"Good. We can compare notes."

Kletti appeared to have just started his examination. A short dark man with a head of curls, he'd been a neurologist before going to prison for treason. Some of his examination of the Rigby's 19-year-old son didn't require any explanation. Both Babinskis were positive. Reflexes on his right were slightly spastic, which Kletti said was an improvement over the weakness of his earlier exam.

Dylan lay in a hospital bed Javi liberated from the abandoned hospital in Beulah. The crazy man came home one night with the thing on the roof of his Trooper. It did make it easier to care for the kid. He suffered from severe vertigo but could sit up partially if the bed's head was slowly raised. Vertigo seemed to lessen in the last few days, although Emily still stood guard with a bucket while Kletti manipulated Dylan's head to check for neck rigidity and other signs of cranial pressure. They'd struggled to find the right combination of medications to give him some relief from the dizziness and nausea.

"I think you're on the mend." Kletti put his instruments away in a backpack. "Did you get a walker and a wheelchair?"

"Brian, the physical therapist, said he'd bring them as soon as you cleared him," Ami responded.

"Good. You want to take this into the hall?"

Emily gave Ami a smile that said she trusted her to tell the truth after Dr. Kletti left.

"How is he, really?" she asked. They sat down in the little sitting area by the big windows at the end of the hall.

"Improved. There's no telling with viral encephalitis whether it will continue to improve, but he's no longer running a fever and he managed the exam this time without puking. Right side's pretty weak. He's still having difficulty finding words, but it's better. I'll swing by in a few days. If he's not puking, he can start sitting up in the wheelchair. How are you coming with your project?"

"I haven't made a lot of headway. The genetic and hormonal component of this is baffling. How they got a flu virus to come back with this encephalitis is – I don't know. So far, I haven't figured out a way to counteract the virus or to inoculate against it. Of course, these things are usually accomplished by teams of people working in giant labs with electron microscopes. I don't have any of that. I can only just introduce different substances and sort of guess at whether it knocks the virus load back or not. And I need more people who have the flu to keep doing those experiments. Dylan doesn't qualify because he hasn't got the flu any longer."

"It reminds me of multiple sclerosis, actually. Not that it helps, since treatment for that would be impossible currently."

"You think it's triggered multiple sclerosis?"

"No, I doubt it's MS, which is an autoimmune of neurology. The body doesn't know when to turn off attacking a disease it's already killed and turns its attention to attacking the brain instead. There are just some similarities – the ebb and flow of symptoms, for instance. It's not my area of expertise, so I could be wrong, but there is an auto-immune encephalitis."

"Hmm, maybe I need to listen to Samara's instructions again. Thank you for your second opinion and help with the neurology."

"Of course. I've missed being a doctor. I've no patience with research, however. Good luck."

Ami took the chart from him and looked over their combined notes. What if this flu deliberately triggered an auto-immune response in some patients? Dylan hadn't been able to hold down food consistently since he'd gotten sick nearly two months ago. She stared at his hematocrit. A few minutes later, she entered Dylan's room with a bag of blood.

"I think you're a little anemic, Dylan, so we're going to give you a transfusion."

"With whose blood?" Emily frowned. They'd known each other for almost two months and she still didn't fully trust Ami –or maybe that was just Ami's reading on it. Since the rise of HIV, people were suspicious of blood and she didn't have an effective way to test for it.

"Shane Delaney's." Emily's frown started to relax. "Universal donors have their use and his blood did nothing to knock back the virus load, so I might as well use it."

She hooked up the IV and slid the needle into Dylan's arm, taping it down.

"You should feel a bit stronger when that's done."

"T-thank – t-thank you." Dylan's speech improved and deteriorated from day to day. Today, he seemed to be struggling. The new hypothesis intrigued and gave her ideas for how to treat it, but there were so many things that she didn't have access to. It sucked to be Patient Zero in the apocalypse.

Ami patted him on the arm and said she'd be back in an hour to check on him. Javi still stirred the pot, talking with Grant Rigby. Ami paused at the landing to listen for a moment.

"When you guarded the borders last, how was he?"

"Tense. I think he's slipped a cog somewhere."

Grant sliced bread while they talked, but he paused now.

"He wasn't doing well when he left San Diego. He meant to rest here, but – " They both chuckled. "I need to talk to him. Any thoughts for how I get him here?"

"Not that don't involve bloodshed. He came that one time to give Ami the disk and all that and she got him to give blood, but he's become more cagey since and --. He's in town. Why don't you go to him?"

"Too many witnesses could prove a problem if anyone comes looking."

Ami shifted her weight and the floor groaned. Javi focused on her – as well as he could these days. She was the only one in the household who wore purple, which made it a little easier for him. Grant turned to glance at her.

"How is he?"

"As I said. He seems to be on an upward path, but we don't know what course encephalitis might take. He's a bit anemic, so I'm transfusing him. We'll see if that helps him a bit."

Grant nodded. He looked tired. He set the knife down.

"I'm going to get some wood." He grabbed his coat and headed out the door. Ami and Javi stood in the kitchen whispering to one another when Emily came downstairs.

"He dozed off. I'll take over making dinner, Javi. I didn't think it would take so long."

"Glad to be of use." He bent to whisper in Ami's ear. She followed him toward the stairs. It amazed her that the Rigbys hadn't yet noticed how Javi struggled with depth perception and used his hands to guide himself as his eyesight failed. She needed to have Dr. Verheil reexamine his eyes soon. The deterioration was much more rapid than she'd expected.

He didn't bother to turn on a light when they reached their room. Closing the door cut them off from the heat, but if he wanted privacy, he usually had a good reason – keeping secrets or sex were the most frequent good reason.

"You okay?" she asked.

"Yeah." He drew her over to the bed they shared – most nights. He slept on the other bed the nights he wanted to be alone. His fingers tangled in her curls. They undressed each other and soon were cuddled, her backside pressed against his lower belly, his arms wrapped tightly around her. Sometimes he fell asleep at this point, but today, he shifted his mouth away from the top of her head and told her what he was thinking. "I can't see out my right eye at all anymore."

"There wasn't much vision left after the retinal damage." She hoped it would blunt his grief. He sighed.

"Right. Left one's worse – worsening – getting worse."

He didn't want sympathy. She waited for him to tell her what he did want.

"I don't think we can keep it from them much longer."

"Whenever you're ready. You're making yourself useful monitoring those radio channels, translating Spanish. And,

180

Dylan needs medical care, so they're not going to kick me out. It's the best we can do."

"Right." A shudder ran through him. She twisted around so she faced him. Tears ran down his cheeks. "I don't know how to live like this."

"But you will, and spring will come and there's got to still be doctors who can perform cataract removal. This is temporary."

"And if it's not?"

"Then you're tougher than it is."

He sniffled. She kissed his cheek, tasting his tears.

"I've got to go check on Dylan. You okay here?"

"Yeah. We should tell them tonight."

"Whenever you're ready."

Dylan opened his eyes when she came into the room. The transfusion was about halfway done.

"Um, Ami, can you as – ask my m-mom to – to br-bring me some – some f-food?"

"You're hungry? That's a good sign."

Dylan gave her a questioning expression.

"I – I f-feel – um, empty."

"Weak?"

"N-no. Like – uh, no, uh, not eat for days."

"Hmm." She took his blood pressure with his other arm. Low since the encephalitis presented but it now registered closer to normal. She checked his temperature and noted that his left pupil was normal sized and reacting normally while the right one still reacted slowly to light, but seemed more responsive than it had been in the last month. Could Dr. Kletti's tentative prognosis be correct? Or might it be just another cycle?

She said she'd be back in another hour and headed back along the hallway to the room she shared with Javi. Dinner was another hour. No need to make Emily feed him now. Eating during a transfusion sometimes triggered nausea and Dylan didn't need to puke. Downstairs, she heard Emily and Grant talking in low tones. A plate clattered on the counter. Just the typical sounds of a suburban home, except these were anything but typical times. She doffed her clothes and slipped into the covers with the now-sleeping Javi. He draped an arm over her hip and buried his face in her hair.

Wolf Pack

Southwest of Emmaus

Jazz turned toward the barn. Blowing snow obscured the view as she set off to the south in pursuit of Shane's trail. His boot tracks labored through the deep snow, wavering this way and that. Though it was impossible to get lost here, there were fields to both sides of the road, delineated by occasional fence posts, lacking any wire. Following the road was optional. Shane's trail proved erratic, wavering all over the road and sometimes into the ditches, but it ran in the general direction of the barn, so Jazz glided along, keeping her headlamp aimed at the footsteps and one eye on the blizzard bearing down on her.

The barn hove into sight, a roof at first, and then the faded red of the barn boards. She huffed over a slight rise and looked down on the old building. There'd once been farms all over this area, but most were gone now, absorbed by the corporations or bought by people like Alex Lufgren. This barn was a remnant from a long-ago time. She skied forward a few feet and movement by the barn captured her attention. She swept the façade with her field glasses. Her heart skipped a beat. Dogs? No, wolves! And what might they be after that was tastier than a dead deer? She pulled the gun from her back holster and then glided forward, bellowing at the top of her lungs.

Spark of Life

*I*cy water flooded his nose and mouth, clawed at his churning legs and reaching fingers. Drowning, dying, darkness. Shane kicked for the surface, seeking light and air. His indrawn breath seared his lungs. His flailing hand brushed ice. Everything solid slipped from his grip. He dragged his eyes open.

Jacob stood on the shore, staring at him as icy water dragged him down into painful cold. Shane flailed, trying to stay afloat as his fingers burned like he'd grabbed metal in the depth of winter.

"Help me, Grandpa." The ferocity of Jacob's face expressed his desire, but his hands never left his pockets.

"I can't. I'm not really here. I'm in a better place."

"You're right here, Grandpa. Help me."

"I can't. You need to grab another hand."

"Another hand?"

"You know." Jacob scowled like a man looking into a north wind while dragging a tractor behind him. A dark-haired man with swarthy skin stepped up beside him. Ed Greyeyes? No, maybe GPa Joseph. A painful shudder ran down Shane's back. He couldn't feel his legs. He settled deeper into the hardening water.

"*You gotta help me.*" *His lips were blocks of ice. He sunk lower into the ice floe. G-Pa held out a hand.*

"*You know.*" *Jacob's voice shredded on the wind, but a louder voice rumbled like thunder.*

"*Take my hand before you die.*"

Shane thrust his arm out and grabbed the hand offered before he went under the water once more.

Crisis

Jazz's shout did little. A few of the smaller wolves disappeared into the swirling snow, but the leaders scented blood and didn't consider her enough of a threat. She'd come prepared, the wolves scattering as she fired her gun over their heads. She skied up to the old tractor beside the barn, kicked out of her bindings, and shouted again in case the wolves weren't thoroughly intimidated by the gunshot. Shane lay crumpled in the snow, wearing no coat, gloves, or hat. Blood smeared the snow near his temple. When something hit the barn wall above her she looked up. The haymow door slammed against the barn again, caught by the rough winds. If he'd fallen from there – the tractor --. Shane's fingers convulsed against the snow.

"Shane." Her voice echoed off the building, rolling back at her like a wave. She knelt to get a better look. His eyes opened and he grunted in pain. The wind slammed the haymow door again and she glanced west to see a world of fuzzy dark grey. The blizzard descended.

"Shane, I'm here. Hang on. I'm going to find your coat."

She surged up to her feet and ran into the barn. His coat lay atop the corn cobs. On her way back to him, the wind hit her full in the face and she had to bend her head into the wind and cling to the barn boards to make headway. She covered Shane with his coat and dragged her radio out of her pocket.

"Loredo, this is Music Box Dancer. I found Shane and he's hurt. Are you there? Over."

She held the radio to her ear and heard only static. Shane stirred, moving, hissing in pain.

"Don't move," she shouted against the storm. "You might have broken bones."

"Dying." She could scarcely hear his voice as he reached out of the coat and grabbed her arm with icy hands. "Dying."

His lips looked blue and pinched and snowflakes accumulated on his cheeks. She dragged first one hand and then the other through the coat sleeves. Shane always tucked his gloves into his inside breast pocket, and she found them there, working them over his stiff fingers and then strapping down the Velcro closures. Shane groaned in pain.

"I'm sorry it hurts. We've got to get you in somewhere warm."

"Cold."

She had to risk the broken bones. He needed heat and there was nothing here to burn. She ran back into the barn. Corn cobs burned well if you had kindling to get them started, but she saw no kindling. Of course, Alex wouldn't store them together because of the risk of fire. She grabbed the fold-a-sled Alex used to move corn cobs from the wall to his transport vehicle and ran back out to where Shane scarcely breathed.

Lay It Down

The icy water dragged him down like quicksand. The more he flailed, the lower he sank, and the colder he grew. His hands numbed so he couldn't tell if the dark-haired man held his.

"You have to decide what's important to you," Jacob said. "Your pride or life."

"I'm a little busy right now, Grandpa."

"You're always busy," Vi pouted. "The young fools are worse than the old fools."

"You know you need to turn around." Somehow Jacob stood behind him. "You need to take the other path."

"I need to survive."

"Don't worry about that. You've swept the house clean, but if you don't fill it with Him, something worse will come in."

"I'm dying. What more do I need to do?"

"What happened to Sera?"

"I don't want to talk about it now."

"What happened to Sera?" Vi asked.

"I'm drowning."

"What happened to Sera?" Mike demanded.

191

"You know."

"I do, but you don't."

"Tell me," G-Pa ordered.

"What good will it do to tell?"

"It'll free you."

"It'll heal you," Jacob added.

"It'll save you," Vi explained.

She materialized standing on the ice, an AK47 in one hand. Beside her, an Indian woman in a prairie dress held a long knife. The radiation couple begged him to kill them. The soldiers from the medical warehouse stood with blood splattering their bullet-proof vests.

"I didn't want to do this," Quincy begged. Hadn't he left him alive?

"It doesn't matter," Cai said. "So you leave a few people alive. You are death."

"I don't want to be."

"Then tell me what happened to Sera," G-Pa said.

"She died."

"How?"

"I don't know. I wasn't there."

"You were. You felt it."

"I was in Sarna and there was a mortar attack and she died in Pedaresh."

"In a mortar attack, yes?"

Shane wept. Cold crushed him.

"She was just there. I didn't mean to do it."

"Your life was in danger."

"Not from her."

"No, not from her. She wasn't even armed."

"I didn't mean it."

Pain seared down his back and legs. He bellowed in agony.

"I know you didn't mean it, but you have got to face it."

"I can't."

"You can and if you want to survive this now, you have got to face it now. You're out of chances, Shane."

"I thought she was armed."

"She wasn't."

"Maybe she thought I could get her out of the mortar attack. I don't know."

"What did she have in her arms?'

"I can't."

"You have to. It's killing you not to."

"I can't!"

The pain grew unbearable and he floated away on a raft of agony.

Desperation

G od, I need a little bit more strength for just a little bit longer," Jazz prayed as she tugged the sled with Shane in it toward what she hoped was the deer kill. She had only one goal in mind, get there before Pete and Poppy left. The wind drove ice into her cap as sweat trickled down her breasts. Shane, over six feet, outweighed her by more than fifty pounds. Jazz, strong and determined for her size, simply lacked the strength to drag him far. She could be headed in the wrong direction. She could be wandering on the prairie in a blizzard. They'd find their bones come summer. Her feet in their stupid cross country shoes felt like blocks of ice, incased in painful numbness.

"God, please help me. Please help him. I can't do this on my own. Only You can rescue him."

Tears trickled down her cheeks, burning a trail of fire. They might die out here. Shane could be dead already. She didn't know what damage she might have done when she shifted him into the sled. Keep going. Don't stop! The words of a children's tale her mother used to tell floated to the surface. There's light over yonder.

Her feet slipped and she fell flat on her back, staring up at the sky that dumped buckets of snow on her face. She rolled over to look at Shane, lying in repose like an ice sculpture. She gained her knees. The dark stain on the snow meant they'd reached the deer kill and Poppy and Pete and their precious cargo of venison were already gone.

"I'm sorry," she whispered, lifting Shane so she could slide in behind his back. She wrapped her arms around him, her legs embracing him on both sides. They were going to die out here. They might as well freeze in this position.

She shivered and the shudder made her realize Shane no longer shivered. Death slipped in while she dragged him into the middle of a field to freeze to death by the bloodstain that had no doubt triggered him.

"I'm sorry," she whispered again. Her parents stood on the other side of the field, smiling at her as if waiting for her to arrive on a train.

Objects in View

Lufgren Farm

Pete wanted to believe that hauling the sled weighted with the deer was why he couldn't keep up with Poppy, but he knew that wasn't true. They raised them stronger on Kansas farms than in Texas suburbs. Someday he would keep up with her, but it wouldn't happen quickly. Now the exertion made his lungs burn and his head hurt.

He lost track of her in the swirling snow after they passed under the overpass. He panicked for a moment, but he knew the way. They'd been doing this patrol for several days now. He just needed to turn right and keep going. The headache made his eyes water. Or maybe it was the cold that gave him the headache and runny eyes.

He reached a crossroads and swerved to read the sign. Lufgren's Crossing. He continued down the snowed-in Old 24 until he found the road to the left and he hurried up the driveway. Alex ran out of the sauna to the house as the other men from the gathering-in tried to get their clothes on over damp skin. Poppy signed for him to help Alex, then took the sled toward the barn. Keri came running out of the house to join Poppy.

These were hard people who kept their eyes on the objects before them. He admired their determination and clear-eyed resolve while at the same time recognizing his inadequacy to fit into their world. Maybe Danny Hughes and he had that in common, but Danny was already suiting up to face the blizzard after spending all morning hand-digging graves. Pete felt wrung-out and achy after an hour in this cold.

Alex came out of the house, his boots still untied, pulling on a coat. He spoke to the group gathered in the driveway.

"Pete, I need you to take us there. Weather like this, they won't last long. We need to go."

"This weather is dangerous even in a car," Clem noted.

"Stay if you like. We have to go."

In the end, Clem climbed into the backseat of Alex's truck with Cai and Andrew. Pete ended up in the passenger seat with Danny. Josh Callahan said he'd help with the deer. The headlights bounced off the swirling snow as they headed west into the teeth of winter.

Rescue

Darkness didn't improve visibility during a blizzard, but Cai trusted Alex to know the way to his fields. The road ahead seemed impassable, but Alex dropped the truck into 4-wheel drive and continued forward.

Shane left angry this morning – angry because Cai wouldn't listen to what he had to say. What sort of idiot thought he knew better than a mercenary how to defend the town and what the defense force shouldn't be involved in?

"She's trying to kill your brother." Carl Sullivan's warning echoed in Cai's brain as Alex drove under the overpass, the gates left open when Pete and Poppy came through. The road here was three-weeks-deep in snow and Alex dropped the truck into 4-wheel low.

"Hang on. It might get a little rough." Riding in the backseat, Cai thought that an understatement. Every bump brought his head concerningly close to the roof. Andrew Bennett kept his hand on the ceiling beside his head. He was a good inch taller than Cai, so he had a reason for concern.

"Pete, are we getting close?"

"I don't know. I can't see it. I'm sorry."

"We'll find them," Cai assured.

"What's that?" Danny pointed off to the right. The wind blasted from the west, but through the driving snow and darkness, they could see a pinprick of light, a guttering flicker in a maelstrom of ice.

Alex heeled over the wheel and fishtailed into the field. Jazz held Shane against her beside the burning gut pile that was all that was left of the deer. She didn't even raise her head as Alex threw the truck into park and they all piled out.

"Jazz, Shane." Jazz raised a hand.

"He's dying," she whispered. "He's freezing."

"We need to get him into the truck." Alex signaled Andrew to go to the other side of the sled.

"Wait!" Clem held up a hand for them to stop. "What happened? Jazz, do you know?"

"I think he fell from the barn, maybe hit the tractor."

"And you moved him?"

"He was going to die." She sounded like she might cry. "There is something wrong, but not as bad as freezing to death."

"Shane, can you hear me?" Cai kneeled beside his brother and checked for a pulse. Panic increased his own and he stared at Clem as the vet stuck his fingers inside Shane's coat.

"He's got hypothermia. There's still a radial pulse." Clem gently moved Shane's legs. Shane cried out weakly at a couple of points. "We can't wait. He may have broken bones, but we have to get both of them into the warmth as soon as possible. Andrew, Alex, chair carry to the truck. Jazz, can you walk?"

"I've got her," Cai said. As soon as they'd lifted Shane, who cried out weakly but didn't try to resist, he scooped Jazz up. She didn't weigh much. As he straightened, the snow at the edge of the glow from the gut pile swirled and he swore he saw his grandparents in one of the eddies.

"Put her in the back. She can hold his head. We'll have to ride in the back." Andrew Bennett jerked his head toward the bed of the pickup. Danny didn't argue, just climbed as ordered. Pete scrambled up beside him. Shane's long and stiff body proved unwieldy, so it took all of them to get him into the backseat. After they got Shane settled, Clem told Cai to climb in and elevate Shane's feet. He climbed in the front and Andrew joined the youngsters in the bed.

Wind caught the truck and shook it on its springs as Alex adjusted the heater to blow full blast defrost to make it into the back. He rocked the truck to get out of the snow. Shane moaned. The men in the back piled out to give the truck a push and then ran after the fishtailing truck to scramble back inside. The truck jostled, dumping someone on their backside in the back, and causing Shane to snap rigid with a weak bellow.

"Try to keep him stabilized," Clem ordered. By the glow of the dash lights, Jazz looked blue.

"You okay?" Cai asked.

"I'll lllllive," she stuttered through shivering lips.

Alex broke through to the other side of the overpass and wheeled hard right on the Old 24. The wind grabbed the truck and shook it like a dog with a retrieving dummy. Shane's body stiffened, but he didn't yell this time.

Way Station

*T*he darkness faded to light and the world around him bathed in sunlight, mountains unfolding in waves in all directions, touched by fall colors, and scented with the warm spice of autumn. He felt colder than death, like an ice sculpture wrapped in snow. He'd moved beyond the pain to numbness.

Shane turned and entered the cabin. It looked like the fishing cabin in Jericho Springs, but the back wall was the door Sera had gone through, standing slightly ajar.

Jacob leaned against the counter, flipping pancakes. The aroma of frying bacon permeated the air.

"Where am I?" Shane asked.

"I guess you could call it a way station."

"To where? Between where?"

"You ain't dead yet. You could be. If you don't fight you will be."

"I'm so tired, Grandpa."

"I know. But you're just starting, Shane. You've never really been alive before. It would be a shame if you went now."

"Eric," Sera sang from the doorway.

"You didn't kill her."

"It doesn't matter."

"No, to your conscience it probably doesn't. You're all mixed up."

"Eric, I need you."

Shane stepped toward the door.

"If you go that way, there's no coming back," Jacob warned. Shane turned to him. "You must choose. You'll have other times of choosing — some of them soon — but if you go through that door now, it's over. You'll leave behind everyone you care about and there's no going back."

"What do I have to stay for?"

"You know. He's still got you and she is laying down her life for you."

A Strauss waltz embraced him and twirled him around. The cabin dissolved and they were in the Emmaus high school gym dressed for his senior prom. Alex wore a blue suit dancing with Lise Webber. Whatever happened to Lise? Shane hadn't heard. Alex's parents died a week later and Lise just disappeared in a puff of smoke. She'd never wanted to be a farmer's wife. Joe's date Joilyanne Shoenfeld had gone to college in Chicago. Since they weren't married, Shane figured she'd found someone else to look googly-eyed at. The whole school turned out, guys with girls they didn't like, girls, looking silly in taffeta. Shane took Marnie to the prom, of course, but the woman in his arms as he moved in complicated patterns that he never would have allowed his classmates to see was not Marnie, but Jazz, laughing at him, snowflakes on her eyelashes, blue lipstick on her pinched lips, wearing a snowmobile suit instead of a prom dress.

"I think we're both in trouble," she told him. "Just keep dancing."

Hard Choices

Cai pushed open the door into the kitchen. Mark Ramirez took one glance at Alex and Andrew carrying Shane and began snatching things off the big harvest table to create a hospital. Clem peeled off Shane's gloves, revealing white fingers. He pulled off the coat, making Shane groan. When he stripped off the snow pants, Shane's eyes rolled back in his head and he passed out completely and didn't stir as Clem stripped him down to his bare skin.

"His hip's dislocated, so's his shoulder. That ankle might be fractured. Ribs bruised, maybe fractured. Now he's got hypothermia and probably frostbite, but long-term life is an issue here. We've got none of the muscle relaxants we usually would use to reduce the dislocations. He might die from this, but if we don't reset them before he warms up and the swelling starts, we won't be able to do it later."

Alex and Cai stared from Clem to Shane.

"You need us to make the decision?" Cai asked.

"Yes."

"If we don't do this, he'll be crippled, right?" Alex asked.

"He might be crippled anyway. I'm a vet, not an orthopedic doc. I've got a really good record with dogs and horses. The risk of doing this when he's still cold is that the shock might kill him."

"Shane wouldn't want to live unable to walk." Alex directed his statement to Cai. Keri moved into the circle, nodding.

"Yeah. Do it. What can we do to help?"

"You're going to have to hold him down, and someone get that girl a hot beverage." Alice Ramirez scrambled to provide the beverage as Cai, Andrew and Alex restrained Shane.

Bath Interrupted

Rob gently rubbed the soapy sponge down Jill's back, caressing the freckles. It had been decades since they'd shared a bath in their own house. They'd done it in bed and breakfasts. There was something about water that wrapped you in tranquility and love.

She leaned back against him, water dripping off her fingertips.

"It's too bad we have to add more warm water. I could stay here for days."

"Yeah. Remember trying to get Keri out of the tub when she was a kid?"

"That child! They each had their challenges, but she thought she was a mermaid." Rob laughed and he could feel her chuckle through his chest. On the table beside the tub, the radio crackled. Rob and Jill both looked at it, daring it to interrupt their time together.

"... Pathfinder? ... accident ... home. Over."

Rob reached over to catch up the radio.

"This is Pathfinder. I couldn't hear what you said. Repeat, please. Over."

"Dad, … Cai. Shane … accident. We're bringing him home … cold and hurt, but Clem thinks … okay. Get the living room as hot as you can make it. We already called Marnie … meet us at the house. Over."

Jill had already climbed out of the tub to dry off. Rob stood up.

"Speaking of children with challenges," he quipped.

"The weather's nasty out there, Rob. Why didn't Shane just stay at Alex's?"

"I don't know."

When Alex threw open the door, they were dressed and Rob had stocked the living room woodstove and opened the damper. Andrew Bennett and Clem Burroughs carried Shane straight through to the living room and set the camp cot in front of the woodstove.

Clem quickly explained what happened while Jill scurried to get blankets. Jazz lay cozied into Shane's belly. Marnie came in at that point, taking a history. Radial pulse only of 38, body temperature of 83, fixed dilated pupils.

"You reset his shoulder and hip?" Marnie sighed, trying to get a blood pressure reading. "You could have stopped his heart."

"Don't start," Cai said. "Alex and I made the decision. He's still alive. What do you need from us?"

"He needs a warm glucose drip and gentle handling. Jazz, you doing okay there?"

"Yes. He's so cold and he's not shivering."

Marnie did her own exam while Jill prepared the IV.

"I need to get back," Alex announced. "This storm is much worse out my way and he got a deer, so I probably need to make sure Josh doesn't steal any."

"Thank you," Rob said. "Cai, can you go get more wood. We need to build up the fire." Cai nodded and followed Alex out. Rob leaned into Shane's slack-jawed face. "Hang in there, kid. We've got you and you're safe."

Marnie looked up from her examination, mouth set in a grim line.

"We need warm water to try and warm his hands. Feet look okay. Think this ankle's fractured?" She directed that at Clem. Rob knew exactly where to get two buckets of warm water.

Hesitation

A *giant grabbed his legs and pulled them apart, tearing his body in two. Pain raged through him like fresh lava that slowly faded to black. A thundering drum overwhelmed him as he fled from it. Mike, soldiers, women in hajibs, the Indian woman with the long knife, children, Sera, and Knights – all reached out and tried to grab him as he careened side to side, trying to run free. The wind grabbed him, tumbling in darkness and a thousand cuts from flying grass and leaves, terrified of where he landed, unable to gather a breath. He landed in a field and a million vines cossetted his limbs, holding him to the earth. He strained against them, tore at them with his hands, then whacked at them with a machete, struggling to stand.*

Ahead, the door appeared, and Sera beckoned from it. He hacked to remove the vines from his ankles, stumbling to his feet, staggering ahead.

"Wait. Don't go!"

She smiled like a lover.

"You killed me," Mike accused.

"You killed me," **she** *said.*

The accusations flowed one over another as he fled down the path, stumbling to a stop occasionally to break free of the vines, striving ever

211

forward toward the door, tripping, falling, hacking, failing …. Jacob said there was no coming back from that door.

"You owe these people something better than your death," Jacob said. "Go through the door and you don't live. Stay and you can do better."

Shane hesitated.

"I'm not that strong," he admitted.

Sera crumbled to dust in the wind that caught him and sucked him into its churning maelstrom.

Critical Condition

Shane shuddered and tried to pull his head back away from Jazz's hair. So claustrophobic that he couldn't stand low CO_2 even when barely conscious. Fortunately, for him at the moment, Marnie and Jill were preparing a pelvic girdle which required they roll him onto his back. His teeth chattered, his muscles spasmed and his eyes twitched back and forth.

"He could have internal injuries," Marnie told Jill. "But I think we've got everything we can fix. We need to assure that hip doesn't slip again. I can't believe Clem did that without x-rays. Far too bold. Are we ready for this?"

"Yes. Rob, Cai, hold him down. This is going to hurt."

"On three," Marnie instructed. They pulled the girdle together and Shane snapped straight, bellowing in pain. For the first time, his eyes opened.

"Urghhh."

"Hey, you're back with us," Marnie said. "Good. You might wish you'd stayed asleep a bit longer because the hard part of warming is still ahead."

"Jazz?" His whisper sounded like a finger brushing parchment.

"I'm right here." Jazz doffed the blanket she'd wrapped in and climbed back onto the mattress with him. Shane shivered, looking frail and defenseless. Rob unbuttoned his shirt, stripped off his pants, and climbed in behind Shane, drawing his cold son into his chest. Jazz slid lower as Shane protested against her hair in his face.

"Shh, we're just going to keep you warm until you can do it for yourself. Don't fight us. Shh."

Big shudders ran through Shane's body and then, unexpectedly, a sob wrenched from him.

"I'm sorry," he croaked.

"It's fine. You can't help it."

"Not that." Shane shuddered again.

Rob made soothing sounds until Shane calmed and then he just lay there with his hand against Shane's chest right above Jazz's head. Bump-skippy-skip. Bump-skippy-skip. Bump, bump, bump, bump-skippy-skip.

Marnie warned Shane's heart might throw arrhythmias as he warmed. Rob supposed it was better than no heartbeat at all, but the distinct possibility existed that Shane might arrest at any moment. Shudders periodically ran through the boy. His teeth might chatter for several minutes before he'd doze for a bit. Rob almost felt his body heat seeping into his son's cold body. He flexed his hand and grazed Jazz's shoulder. She felt warmer than Shane, but not by much.

"How you doing?" he asked her.

Shane shifted as if in protest.

"Shh, I'm good. Let him sleep."

God, help my son survive the night.

Rob concentrated on syncing his breathing with Jazz. Shane dozed, still periodically shivering. Rob almost wanted to shiver himself, feeling the transfer of heat from himself to Shane. The house grew quiet. His eyes grew heavy.

Rain drizzled down his neck as he made his way along Cloverdale, sticking to the shadows in case the old man came looking for him. He would just get a small bottle, something to tide him through until the nightmares stopped. He could control it. He just needed to keep good sense in mind – don't drink during the day, only have a couple of beers a night.

The convenience store lights ached behind his eyes and he paused on the sidewalk. He'd promised Pa a month and it had only a week. But he wasn't sleeping and surely Jacob could see that he needed to.

"You're killing yourself, son. I don't blame your wife for cutting bait where you're concerned. Until you want to save yourself ain't nothing she can do for you."

Vi wasn't talking to him. She'd hung up in the middle of a conversation and now she hung up whenever she heard his voice on the other line.

"Can you blame her?" Stan asked when they'd gotten together during his leave a few weeks ago. "She just buried your brother. You call her up drunk, that's gotta be scary."

Stan had just been home to see his folks and reported that Carl was in a mental hospital. Carl, EJ and now Rob. What was the world coming to?

The neon lights on the convenience store turned out and when he pushed on the door, he realized it was locked. He raised a hand to knock, to beg for just a moment, but in the glass, another neon sign shivered. He looked over his shoulder and saw the cross about two blocks over.

A mission church — wooden benches, a simple altar. He sat down in the back row, shivering in his soaked clothing. The lights were low in here and it seemed almost as if someone had forgotten to lock up the building for the night. He stared at the cross on the front of the pulpit, his mind empty of all real thought. Why in the world would he come to a church? Such a waste of time. His head hurt. He lowered his face into his hands, elbows on the back of the pew in front of him. A Bible lay open on the seat, a bookmark stuck in the spine. He stared at it.

If we confess our sins, he is faithful and just to forgive us our sins and to cleanse us from all unrighteousness." 2 John 1:9

He looked at the cross again.

"You don't know what I've done," he whispered.

Such a strong sense that he was wrong washed over him that gooseflesh stood out on his arms. An old Morgan Cryer tune he'd heard years later filtered through his mind.

"What sin, what sin? It was gone the very minute you confessed, buried in the sea of forgetfulness. The heaviest thing you'll carry is a load of guilt and shame. You were never meant to bear them, so let them go in Jesus' name."

He didn't know what he was doing. He just did it and Jesus kindled him alive. He walked a dusky path unable to see the next step before him and yet it was there, waiting, promised … as he took each step in trust.

He lifted his head from his folded arms and grasped the rough hand held out to him.

"G-Pa?"

"Hmmm, better." A deep warm voice like a pleasant wood fire washed over him. *"I've got you. Rest."*

Snuggling up to Shane still felt like cozying up to an ice sculpture, but warmth ran through Rob's arm and into his boy. He was a conduit of radiating heat floating on the edge of a dream.

"I've got both of you. Rest."

Honesty

December 23

Jericho Ghost Town

The Jericho B&B had once been home to the richest family in Jericho/Emmaus – the Sullivans – so there was plenty of room even for a large blended "family" like the Rigbys – except at breakfast, which they ate in the eat-in kitchen. Even with Dylan still in bed and Emily trying to coax him to eat some of the mush he was able to swallow, the kitchen overflowed. Grant and Jim were tackling breakfast while Ami helped Miranda with her math assignment. Her younger sister Lainey sat cross-legged on the floor examining an English assignment her mother had given her a poor grade on. The door from the living room swished open as Javi entered the room. His forward foot encountered Lainey and he grabbed the counter to keep from spilling right over on top of her.

"Whoa! Did not see you there."

"Lainey, you shouldn't sit there." Jim indicated the table as a good alternative. Miranda slid over to make room for her sister. Ami could see Javi struggling to bring the bright room into focus.

"Why don't you come to sit by me and get out of Grant and Jim's way?"

Her suggestion gave him something to hone in on without drawing attention to his being disoriented in a room he'd been in a hundred times. It also let him know that the floor was clear of stumbling hazards. He slid into the booth seat beside her, hands identifying the silverware and placemat.

"Javi, Ami, I need to speak with you in the other room, please." Grant held the door to the living room open. "Jim, if you could get breakfast on the table. We'll be right back." Javi squeezed Ami's hand. They both knew they'd waited too long.

Grant used the sitting room near the back of the house as his meeting space. Ami and Javi sat on the couch while Grant stood by the window, rubbing the back of his neck. Just as Javi opened his mouth to say something, Grant spoke.

"Your eyes are getting worse, aren't they?"

"It's cataracts," Ami admitted. "He lost vision in the right eye a few days ago and the left one is deteriorating quickly."

"And you thought a trained spy wouldn't notice?"

"I knew you'd notice." Javi sighed heavily. "It just would become more real when you did."

"Then it must have been real for you weeks ago because I've kind of known for a while. Kept waiting for you to say something."

"We didn't intend to lie to you." Ami didn't know what else to say.

"Yeah, I did." Javi shrugged. "I kept hoping it wasn't really happening. And, Ami – she's just trying to support me. It was my decision not to tell you."

Grant rubbed the bridge of his nose.

"Now that I know officially, you can start preparing for when you can't see. Is this something that surgery can fix?"

"Before, yes." Ami considered explaining the details but decided that wasn't what Grant asked. "Come spring we can figure out if there's anyone who can still do that sort of surgery and how we get to them."

"Good. He's too good at what he does to be permanently blinded." Grant walked to the door. "We'll have to explain to the girls that they can't leave stuff lying around, that it's a tripping hazard. I'll still need you on the radio channels. I suppose you worried that we'd kick you out."

"Thought occurred."

"Well, I'm not angry. This is a different situation from when I was your handler. If I don't act like that – well, Emily's trying to teach me how to be human."

With that, Grant left the room. Javi lowered his face into his hands. When Ami touched his shoulder, he sloughed off her hand.

"Sorry. I just --. Rigby's not the only one who needs to learn how to do human. You should go eat breakfast. I'm going to go somewhere and just think for a while."

A lot went unspoken between them. Ami sometimes felt they were two wild things in the woods, circling one another, testing out what sort of danger each held to the other. Javi hadn't had a lot of emotional intimacy in his life and he didn't know how to grieve for his eyesight with her.

"I'll save you a plate."

She followed Grant to the kitchen where Emily ate with the girls.

"How's Dylan?"

"He ate the whole bowl. It wiped him out, but he has an appetite. His improvement is like the best Christmas present."

Dylan had good days occasionally. Ami wasn't willing to pronounce him healing just yet. Javi didn't appear by the time she was done eating, so she announced she would be in the garage lab. Maybe something would work today.

What's Happening in Georgia?

December 23

Columbus, Ohio

Julian Raines never hated a town before. He'd wanted to get out of New York City because it was turning into a police state where you could be killed simply for existing, but he'd liked the City well enough before the bombs went off. Julian *hated* Columbus, Ohio. He couldn't lay a finger on why he wanted to get the hell out of town, but he spent a good deal of every day talking himself out of abandoning his traveling companions while they were sick and just flee westward. It seemed irrational and, yet, every instinct said it was wisdom itself to do so.

When they'd arrived in Columbus just before Thanksgiving, it seemed a haven. Food was rationed, but fairly plentiful. Their housing had heat. For the first time in a month, they'd been able to take showers and don clean clothes. Joseph Sullivan held a position of privilege because his father owned SullCorp. For the first week, it seemed like they could spend the winter here.

Julian sent a message to his family in Seattle, promising that he'd be home eventually. He didn't hear back, but the shattered and shuttered communications grid meant the message had to be routed and eventually printed out to be physically delivered to his parents, who would then have to find a way to respond. The world in December was very different from the world three months before and they were all learning novel ways of working around shattered systems.

Meanwhile, Joseph Sullivan hadn't been able to reach his father directly but had been told his status would be reported. Julian's spidey-senses, honed by his years in prison, piqued at that point. Were they being held against their will? Not exactly. Were they being delayed by misdirection? The hair on the back of his neck stood on end every time he contemplated that question.

He could live with that question, but then the flu hit around the first week of December and the mood in Columbus changed. You couldn't leave your home, you weren't allowed to drive, there were lots of rules that made leaving Columbus impossible. You'd never reach the edge of town without being arrested and, if you did, snow blanketed the area so you wouldn't get far beyond the town limits.

To get his mind off the very real feeling of incarceration, Julian accepted that winter prevented their westward movement and asked SullCorp to put him to work in their impressive computer lab. They wanted Columbus to become a hub for a new Internet. He'd served years in prison for being an extraordinary hacker and then gone on to use his skills for Bunnell & Wilson, building unhackable software. Of course, when you put a hacker in charge of building unhackable software, he will leave backdoors that allow him to hack those systems when needed. SullCorps computer engineers had struggled to overcome barriers that Julian could merely unlock. Those backdoors revealed the Internet was still there. Europe had it, Africa and Asia had it. The United States had huge holes in it, but more, there were blocks on it. He guessed the United States government had used its "kill switch" to try and shut down the Internet in the aftermath of the September Bombs. Whatever their plans for that had been, the blocks were in place when the Pulse shattered the grid. But the satellites remained circling the earth and they'd not been hit by the Pulse, so it was just a matter of removing the blocks to allow the reconnections SullCorp wanted.

Julian had hoped to be able to reach Seattle and Joseph's father in Wichita, but so far, the brightest US connections were regional. He could reach Cincinnati, Louisville, Pittsburg, and Indianapolis. The guy in Pittsburg was hiding in a basement, saying the city had gotten worse since the Sullivan group had fled there. While Julian worked on high-level unblocking, the less-talented techs were monitoring what was out there to "hear."

His private messenger bleeped, and he pulled up Andi's incoming message, asking him if he wanted to meet her for lunch. He glanced at the clock on his computer and suggested they meet in a half-hour to eat their sandwiches. Although he liked the cantina, it gave them time to talk in private if they met in the front seat of the Sullivan group's truck.

"Oh, my god!" Connie stared at her computer screen as if in shock. Julian had turned around, expecting a rat had run across her keyboard or something. A handsome black woman of East Indian descent, she usually smiled a lot, but she now looked horrified.

"Something I can help you with?" Julian had been working on a particularly snarled connection all morning and needed a break. Working on *anything else* would do.

"Um." Connie stared at him over the top of her screen. "I – well – you might *need* to see this to believe it."

He came around to her side of the monitors.

Concentration Camps Strained with Social Refuse

Over 10,000 noncompliant interlopers have been placed in long-term detention at Hunter Airfield. Mayor John Halford says the gathering of minority dissenters will continue until the resistance is taken in hand.

Then in Publius:

All those who harbor escaped slaves will be prosecuted to the greatest extent of the law.

"Where is this from?"

"Savannah Tribune."

"So the South has returned to slavery. Not surprising there, right?"

Connie frowned, scratching a finger in her natural hair right above her ear.

"Where are you from?"

"Seattle. Why?" Julian braced for a white privilege lecture, not exactly sure what he'd said wrong, but knowing he must have misspoken.

"Pacific Northwest. That explains you. You're all pretty color-blind there. And why would you know about *Publius* if you live in a color-blind state? It's a black magazine. Remember the whole Black Lives Matters movement?"

"Hard to forget." There'd been a minor riot at Coyote Ridge during one of the BLM dustups.

"Well, they took over *Publius* a couple of years ago."

Julian frowned at the screen again.

"You're saying black people are – no!"

"Yes! It sure looks like they've overthrown the government there and are enslaving white people."

"I don't buy that."

Connie looked immensely sad, like a teacher whose best student has just failed to answer a softball question correctly.

"*I* don't feel this way. Most black people in America don't feel this way. But there is a sliver of the population that does feel this way."

"Just because they put it out on the Internet doesn't mean it's reality."

Connie cocked her head, considering Julian's statement.

"I will do more research."

"That seems like a worthwhile use of your time, although I'd go get some lunch first. I know I need to eat before returning to my current task."

"Goodness, it is past noon. Are you going to the cantina?"

"No, I'm meeting a friend."

"That pretty girl you live with?"

"It's not like that, but yes, it's her."

"You go enjoy. You're probably right about this be just chumming the waters, but I'm going to dig into it now that I can reach Savannah."

"Let's hope you find out it's all fantasy."

Andi already waited in the truck with the plate of sandwiches, chips, and off-brand soda. Julian supposed Coca Cola no longer existed, headquartered as it was in Atlanta. Maybe one of their regional bottling facilities would resurrect. One could hope. He didn't wholly trust soda with Chinese lettering.

"Thank you. Sorry to be running late. Got to conversing."

"It's fine. Joseph's status rubs off on me. The Distribution manager won't dock me if I'm late." Twenty-year-old Andi spoke with a mellow Atlanta drawl. She stood a few inches shorter than his 5'10", with blue eyes and caramel brown hair. "I think he has the flu."

"The Distribution manager?"

"Joseph."

"Well, that's not surprising since Perry has it. You want to lay bets as to who of us will be next. Or does Katharine have it already?"

"Could be, though I think that's not why she's sick at all."

"What do you mean?"

"It's only if she hasn't eaten in a while. Reminds me of my sister when she was pregnant."

"Oh? Oh! Well, they are exceedingly affectionate for people as old as they are."

"Shh, don't let them hear you say that."

Julian laughed.

"Three months ago, someone might have cared about the ageism. Now, do we?"

"No idea. I apologized to Chris yesterday for a microaggression and he looked at me like I was out of my mind, then told me that it would be silly for my black boss to think I was showing white privilege. I guess he's right."

Julian thought about the hierarchies that existed in prison and thought Chris was absolutely right.

"You're from Atlanta. You ever get over toward Savannah?"

"I've visited a couple of times. Why?"

"Connie, one of the techs, came across an article in the Tribune that was celebrating the overthrow of the white hegemony by black forces."

"That can't be real. Blacks are still the minority in Georgia. Someone's having fun."

"That's what I said, but Connie's going to check it out."

"Connie is – the redhead?"

"No, Jamaican."

"Seriously? Why would she care?"

"My experience is that not every black person holds all whites responsible for something that happened in past generations."

"Shouldn't they? I mean, one of my ancestors was probably a slaveowner."

"But you never were." Julian sighed. "So – I don't know. The world is just going nuts and all we can do is cope with it. If it's true, going to Georgia is not your best option."

"Nobody's there anyway." A momentary sadness crossed her face, quickly set aside. The death of her family in a nuclear wave seemed a long time ago under current circumstances. They lacked the luxury to grieve while they tried to find safety.

"This is a really good sandwich." Julian preferred his tuna fish with lettuce and tomato, but fresh vegetables were as scarce as hens' teeth -- an expression he'd learned from Andi and still didn't wholly understand, so he embraced chopped onion, olives, and pickle relish mixed in the mayo. The chips were a bit stale and there was the Chinese soda, but years in prison had taught him not to complain about the quality of the food so long as the calories were sufficient.

"Sometime we should slip down here after everybody's in bed and – you know?"

Andi always teased him with sexual advances. He thought he might take her up on it sometime soon. He liked her well enough now.

"Maybe."

Her gaze cut to his face.

"Seriously?"

"Considering. Anyway, I should get back to the node. Do me a favor?" She lifted an eyebrow. "Ask Chris what's going on out there."

Andi nodded, collected the empty plates and soda cans, and slipped out of the truck. Julian made sure they weren't leaving crumbs before returning to work.

·

Suicidal

Emmaus, Kansas

Cai wallowed through two feet of snow from the wood shanty to the house, dragging a sled full of firewood right up on to the back porch since the snow was drifted that deep. He stomped the snow off his boots in the mudroom while Jill pulled biscuits from the oven. Marnie came into the kitchen wearing one of his coats over her expanding belly.

"Where do you think you're going?" Cai blocked the way with his size and armload of wood.

"To the medical center."

"There's no way. I could barely see the barn. I don't think even Rocket could get you through."

"Lila and Abigail can handle it." Jill pushed past Cai to flip the biscuits onto a plate. "Besides we have a critical patient here now."

"He's not critical any longer. He's broken and still shivering, but he's going to live. His heart rate's near normal. Body temperature is still up and down, but that's his other injuries."

Cai carried the wood into the living room. Shane shifted when Cai lowered the woodstove door. Jazz sat on the couch. She put a hand on Shane's shoulder.

"Just relax. It's Cai stocking the woodstove. Go back to sleep."

Shane's eye closed.

"He okay?"

"I think he's feeling kind of vulnerable. Sounds agitate him."

When Cai finished, he headed back toward the kitchen. Jazz rolled over the back of the couch to follow him.

"You doing okay?" he asked.

"I just really need to brush my teeth."

"Me too."

"No need to wait."

They each dipped their toothbrushes in salt and baking soda and stood on either side of the table Jill had designated as the bathing station, grimacing at the horrible taste of dental hygiene. A clawfoot tub Shane dragged up from the basement occupied one corner of the old well room, filled with soaking clothes.

"That was an incredibly brave thing you did last night." Cai looked in the mirror. Should he try to shave today? It was so hard without shave crème.

"Yeah – bravery and foolishness kind of look like the same thing." She laughed ruefully. Her lips and cheeks peeled, but she appeared none the worse for wear.

"Thank you for saving my brother's life."

She nodded, rinsed her toothbrush, put it away.

"The thing is – I'm not sure he wanted his life saved."

An icy fist formed in Cai's belly.

"What do you mean?"

"He went to a remote location on a very cold day and took his clothes off. It's possible he meant to hurt himself."

"Seriously?" Cai almost wanted to scoff, but Rob came to the well-room door and nodded to Jazz. "You think she's right?"

"I don't think he maybe planned it out, but yeah. He's apologized about five times since."

"My god! I've been so angry with him over his attitude that it never occurred to me that he might be that desperate."

"Alicia said he was that desperate before he left San Diego." Jill set a platter of biscuits on the kitchen table next to a crock of butter and another of crabapple conserve. "We're going to eat in here so he can sleep." They all gathered at the little table as Rob poured soy "coffee" for them.

"We'll see him through this. That boy is made of strong stuff. We'll just have to make sure he's not alone for a while."

Alicia and Click came up the stairs from the basement just then. They'd both been informed of what was going on when they arrived home last night, Click going to the medical center and bringing Alicia home before the worst of the blizzard hit.

"He's down for at least a month anyway," Marnie said. "We need to enforce bed rest on him or that hip won't heal."

"This should be fun," Jill quipped, putting a hand over Rob's.

"What does that mean?" Jazz asked.

"Oh, we were just talking about the special challenges each of our children presented as they were growing up. The words 'Shane' and 'rest' are mutually incompatible."

Marnie grimaced at the non-coffee.

"Well, for at least the next few days, he's going to need lots of rest. And we cannot leave him alone because that will tempt him to try things he's not currently capable of. Right?"

"Right?" Jill and Rob snickered together. Cai shook his head and changed the subject.

"I'm going to go sit with him. Any idea what he might need?"

"There's a jar if he needs to pee. He's been holding it, but eventually, he'll have to let go."

Cai felt his cheeks grow warm at his mother's suggestion.

"It's Christmas Eve tomorrow." Marnie often spent Christmas Eve with the Delaneys, both when she dated Shane and when she and Cai began dating. Christmas Eve was a big club night at Callahan's Bar & Grill. This would be her first Christmas Eve at the Delaneys as an official Delaney however. "Are we just going to postpone it?"

"No, we'll do something. The venison will be ready and we have cranberry sauce."

"And potatoes." Jazz sounded almost fond of the idea.

"It'll be enough," Alicia said. She smiled at the biscuit she devoured. Her belly stretched a t-shirt to its limits. Last night, the baby had turned and you could see a knee or elbow deform her abdomen.

"Grandpa used to tell how things were during the Great Depression, how gifts were simple." Cai stood. "I'm going to go sit with Shane. You guys can plot and plan."

"You know you have to keep the lights low, right?" Marnie nodded her head toward the living room. "He has a concussion. Don't overstress him."

Cai nodded. Glister had taken up a position against Shane's back while his brother shivered. Cai crept around to the front to see if Shane was awake, but his eyes were closed, the left one nearly swollen shut. He took a book over to the front window where there was enough light to read by. He managed to read a page before Shane convulsed, whimpering.

"Hey, hey, don't move around too much." Cai knelt in front of him. "Is there something I can do for you?"

Tears poured down Shane's bruised face. The salt must sting his chapped lips.

"Where am I?"

"The house. You need anything?"

"What's behind me?"

"Glister is trying to keep you warm."

"Nnnot wwwworking." Shane's teeth chattered.

"It's the pain. Your body's pretty stressed."

Shane tried to shift, wincing, muttering a swear word.

"You dislocated your shoulder and hip and maybe fractured some ribs and an ankle too. If you need to shift positions, I'll gladly do that for you."

Jill came from the kitchen, carrying another bag of warmed glucose. She swapped the IV before she and Cai gently maneuvered Shane so he was lying on his back, using pillows to keep the stress off his injured joints. Shane stopped shivering and drifted off to sleep. Cai watched while Jill put a makeshift pad between his legs. She saw Cai's questioning expression.

"Moving him to change the bed right now would just be cruel, so preventing him from wetting it is a better solution."

"Shane, helpless. I never expected to see that."

"Shane sleeping. Didn't expect to see that either, now did you?"

Cai smiled at Rob's comment as his father set an armload of wood beside the woodstove.

"I'm going back to reading my book if you guys have stuff to do."

"Where would we be doing this 'stuff'?" Rob asked. He sat down on the sofa, opening his Bible on his lap, using a headlamp to read by.

"I've got a bucket of laundry to do in the well-room," Jill announced. "Call me if he needs anything you can't handle."

Cai nodded. He sat down by the window, listening to the wind howl around the roof of the house. He twitched the curtain aside to look out and see snow piled up on the bottom quarter of the glass. He'd never seen so much snow in his life. Laurence got a lot more snow in a typical winter than Emmaus and he still hadn't seen this much snow before.

Glister settled down next to Shane's left arm and laid his head on his shoulder. Shane's breathing slowed. Cai opened his book and began reading.

Helicopter

Jericho Ghost Town

Grant Rigby watched as his wife Emily attempted to feed their 19-year-old son Dylan. He couldn't feed himself because his right arm lacked coordination due to some sort of brain illness. After weeks of pain and crippling vertigo, Dylan turned a corner and was able to sit up in a wheelchair. Opening and closing his mouth on command tired him quickly, which was why Grant stayed nearby, prepared to help Emily put Dylan to bed when his strength ran out.

"What these?" Dylan slurred when he spoke, but he was remembering words today.

"Peaches." Emily watched Dylan's eyes. She seemed to understand him better than anyone else. "Peaches." The second time she said it she emphasized the "p" and "ch" sounds.

"Pea-sus." Dylan didn't talk much these days. Ami said the physical and speech therapist – a married couple -- would visit tomorrow to assess Dylan now that he seemed more functional. "Mmm."

"Tasty, huh?"

"Em-emp-ty."

Dylan lost a lot of weight in the last few weeks. A runner, he'd never carried a lot of pounds, so his skin stretched over his bones now.

"You're hungry still?"

"Um…nnot…eat…days."

"Well, I can do something about that. Can you wait a few minutes?" Dylan smiled. Emily stood. "I'll be back with some oatmeal. You can stay, right?"

"I can." Ron Patterson arrived about an hour ago and Grant really should be downstairs working with him, but Dylan sitting up was too much to ignore. While Emily and the stimulus of the food gone, Dylan focused on his own body, pulling at his right pajama leg. The foot slithered off the wheelchair's footrest and the whole leg slowly pushed itself straight, rigid to the point of shaking.

"Do you need something?" Grant moved up to stand in front of Dylan. His son slowly angled his head so he could look at him.

"Lishen."

Dylan used his left hand to gesture toward the window. Grant pushed back the curtain and stared as a helicopter seemed to set down at Emmaus Field. With Shane injured, he doubted anyone was there and was surprised to see a helicopter anywhere since the Pulse. The only one he was aware of was the Kiowa Shane saw on his trip to Santa Fe.

Javi pushed in the door and joined Grant at the window.

"That's what I thought I heard. That sounds like the same assholes who chased Jacob Delaney and me. I'm going out there to see what's up."

"Javi – you sure about that?"

"Don't coddle me, man. It's coming, but it's not here yet and I'm going to keep being useful for as long as I can manage."

"You'll be useful even when you're blind, Javi. Just recognize you have limitations now. Take a radio with you."

Javi left and Grant turned back to Dylan who sounded distressed, hand to his head.

"Light bothering you?"

Dylan gestured clumsily to the bed. Grant just got him settled when Emily came back with a bowl of oatmeal.

"We may be forgot he's photosensitive."

"I'll still try to get this down him. I'm just so excited he has an appetite. Ron wants to talk with you."

Ron Patterson came from the McAuliff Compound a few times a week to try to maintain the servers Dylan had kept humming before he got sick. The server room was off the basement, under the garage, in a hardened bunker.

"What's up?" Grant saw no reason to stand around making nice. He was paying the man to be here.

"I found this podcast in a data capture. How the hell did Francene Maracal become Speaker of the House in her second term?" Patterson had, like most of the men in the militia compound, spent the last five years in prison and so didn't know all that had passed in the world.

"It wasn't a CSA plot if that's what you're asking. And what does that have to do with the price of tea in my living room?"

Patterson grimaced, then snorted.

"That was actually funny." He booted up something and Grant watched as Francene, former governor of the State of Alaska and currently the most likely to succeed to the presidency if the United States still existed, asked for her daughter's safe return.

"Good to know she's looking. Can you see if there's any chatter on the girl?"

"I already started. How's your boy doing?"

"Making progress. You get any radio chatter? A Kiowa just landed at Emmaus Field."

"I get ghosts sometimes – off to the west. Nothing that comes in clear. There was a power source near Cheyenne Mountain, but I haven't picked it up in a week. Javi tells me the Mexican border is completely sealed now. Those people who survived the cities and came by this town are pushing up against that wall now and they've got nowhere to go."

"How many?"

"Rough estimate – Mexico television has it at two million. And, they ain't sharing food and water. They shoot attempters on sight."

"Jesus! The conservatives were right that if it were the other way around, Mexico wouldn't let Americans in."

"Yeah. It's worse. That flu – it's sweeping those camps and it's the deadly southern version."

Grant sighed, rubbing the back of his neck with both hands.

"And, there's some sort of secondary infection cropping up. Like what your boy had."

"So, Mexico is keeping out the plague?"

"Looks like. You know we got the flu out at the compound now?"

"I'm sorry."

"Probably not you. Plenty of people coming and going, breathing and sneezing. Dan wants Nick to help your girl."

"Ami? That's no girl."

"I get that. It's just the way I talk. You think she'd be willing to work with him?"

"I think she needs a team, yeah."

"She here?"

"Nope. She's in town working a shift there."

Ron showed Grant some more notes he'd made. The radio growled to life.

"Grant, there's two people from Cheyenne Mountain here. They're asking for sanctuary. Over."

"Are they now. So? Over."

"They have food – enough to feed them through spring, I think. Over."

"That puts them a little closer to a paying guest. Anything else? Over."

"They claim to have intel on Cheyenne Mountain."

245

"Make it clear to them that if they're not legit, I will plant them in the backyard. And blindfold them on the way here. Over."

"Yes, sir. I'll even drive them around a bit, so they don't know exactly where they're going. Over."

Grant took a deep cleansing breath. Emily and Ami taught him that a few days ago when he caught them doing yoga in the family room.

"I always wondered what you'd do if I failed to produce for you."

Grant cut a glance at the tall, lanky computer genius who kept his hair pulled back in a ponytail.

"The military is usually more trouble than its worth. They think they're extremely important, but they aren't. You are extremely important. Keep it that way and you and I will have no problem."

Grant went upstairs and met Javi in the driveway to escort his blindfolded prisoners into the motorhome. It was colder inside than out. When he muscled the woman into the seat, she pulled her hands back from the Formica table with a hiss. The guy was less sensitive. Grant pulled down the blinds and sat down across from them. Javi stayed standing, leaning against the counter, a graceful panther ready to pounce.

"You can look now."

They lifted their blindfolds away, using two hands since theirs were bound at the wrists with zip ties. The woman looked around suspiciously while the man donned glasses. Grant guessed them both in their early 30s. Their hair looked ragged where it poked from their stocking caps and they'd been wearing their clothes for far too long. The man had quit smoking – his breath no longer stank, but the brackets to each side of his mouth gave him away. While neither had seen a shower in a good long while, their faces and hands were clean, and they had access to toothpaste.

"Your names."

"Captain Broussard," the woman said.

"Staff Sergeant Kevin Perez."

"My name's Grant. I suppose Chavez introduced himself."

"He did." Whatever Chavez had done hadn't made Broussard a fan of his. Chavez didn't seem worried about the loss of potential friendship.

"And he says you have intelligence on Cheyenne Mountain. Do tell."

"Cutting the shit, sir?" Broussard was career-military. Grant met her gaze and waited. "We knew about a CSA listening post east of our location before the Pulse taking out our telemetry. This is the only community with a substantial electrical signal for a hundred miles and this building is brighter than the others. I understand why you don't trust us, but we're all on the same side."

"What side is that?"

"We all work for the same government."

Grant glanced at Javi, who still held his gun on his lower belly, casual but deadly. He gave a barely perceptible shrug.

"I'm not willing to break out the scotch and cigars just yet. I'm sure Chavez explained that I'll kill you if you're scamming us, right?"

They exchanged glances between them and then Broussard continued.

"We were part of a flight team at Patterson, ferrying a diplomat to base. We'd just landed and shut down when the Pulse hit. Because of rumors of hostilities, the base was on lockdown, the shutters closed. They never opened."

"That was about seven weeks ago. Any communications?"

"No, sir. We even tried some of the old landlines and nothing."

"Cheyenne Mountain is heavily shielded against nuclear blasts." Chavez almost scoffed, but he was well-trained. Broussard didn't read his sarcasm.

"Yes, sir. The military has been less than certain about EMP warnings. That's why that Kiowa is the only airship still functioning."

"If the Mountain's gone silent, how many people on the surface?"

"Well, that's the odd part, sir." Broussard looked at Perez, who gave his report.

"There was some sort of drill going on at the time, so there was fewer than twenty personnel on the surface." Chavez pinned Grant with a look. Red flags all over the place...if they told the truth. "I was ARFF – fire suppression. My partner and one of the mechanics greeted

Captain Broussard. We turned the diplomat over to an escort team and then we started post-flight."

"The Pulse hit and basically fried everything." Broussard kept her gaze on Grant. She wanted to be believed. "We went to the base entrance, but the blast doors were closed. We held up in the maintenance shop. Early on, we thought we heard some chatter, but we haven't heard anything for six weeks. Some of our folks went to Colorado Springs and never returned. We all had the flu. Two of us died. Two walked away with all the supplies they could carry and that left Perez and I staring at a hole in the ground with real winter headed our way."

"Why did you decide to come here?"

"There's a lot of air traffic out of that airfield. I figured we'd have a better time among pilots even if we couldn't find you. And, we stripped the base of all food stores, so we hoped we could buy our way in somewhere if nothing else."

"What were the last known radio codes for Cheyenne Mountain?"

She blinked. Her broad cheekbones jived with her New Orleans accent. Perez had moved more as a child. He didn't have an accent to pin down.

"Give me a pen and paper."

Grant provided it.

"You have a choice. We can detain you until we're satisfied with your story or you can return to the helicopter and wait for us to contact you."

They exchanged glances and then Broussard nodded.

"We'll take detention if there's heat."

"Let's get those blindfolds on then."

The attic of the Sullivan Bed & Breakfast had a small side room that lacked windows but got enough heat from the room below that they wouldn't freeze to death. Javi said he could get them secured without help and Grant went down to the basement to ask Patterson to scan the radio frequencies with the codes. Javi joined them a little while later.

"Emily provided them with bedding. Anything?"

"There are no transmissions, but I ran a scan on past transmissions." Rod tapped into the keyboard and a waveform came upon one of the monitors. They listened to several minutes of transmissions with Broussard's voice, including some log entries. There were no answers from the Mountain.

"What do you think?"

"They couldn't have known we were passively monitoring?" Grant asked Patterson because he frankly wasn't sure.

"Doubtful."

He cast a profile on another screen. Elena Broussard had been an Airforce pilot mostly ferrying dignitaries and colonels. Perez was a flight line grunt.

"The two of them probably never exchanged more than orders and yes, sir, ma-am, sir, before the lights went out." Chavez grinned like he thought it was funny. He'd served in the military. Grant hadn't and would never understand all that hoorah crap. At least Javi mocked it.

"So, what do you think?"

"I think we need to know more before we trust them around my children."

"Ami will want their blood." Grant laughed at Javi's Count Dracula impression, wondering if his former asset now turning friend had been the class cut-up. Funny-odd how he'd never thought that before. "That Kiowa is a sweet bird. Could come in handy. The food they brought won't. Meals Ready to Expel, baby."

"If this continues past the summer, we'll be glad to have them."

Javi nodded, then blinked and rubbed his left temple.

"Eyes starting to bother you?"

He sighed.

"Seeing through the fog gets to me after a while."

"Go take a nap, sit in a dark room, whatever you need to rest them. That'll give Rod time to crunch some data."

Javi left the room. Patterson said nothing, just watched him go. Grant could practically hear him counting seconds.

"Shane Delaney becomes more important the more of your crew falls out, right?"

"Don't speak oblique. What are you getting at?"

"Assassin's a young man's game, right? Dylan can't stand and Chavez can't see. What are you going to do?"

"First, I'm not the head of the League of Assassins. I'm primarily an analyst who used to run assets. Dylan never was one and Javi was retiring after his latest gig anyway. And, Shane is no assassin. He's a pilot with small arms skills. I'm fine with not having to kill people. And, for your information – I was young when Dylan was born, so I'm not as old as you think I am."

Patterson grinned.

"Josh Callahan."

"The guy that went with Javi and Shane to Hays?"

"He can do that whole suppressing his conscience thing – if he even has one. Just so you know."

"I don't think you quite understand the qualifications, but I'll file it away for future reference. The storm eased a couple of hours ago. You might want to get back to the compound before another rolls in."

"I knew the storm eased. I've got a bit of time before it picks up again tonight and then there won't be another one for – well, at least a couple more days. Clear and cold is the forecast for Christmas Day."

"Where you getting that?"

"Satellite capture. I took a weather telemetry course during my time at MIT. Betcha I'm more accurate than the network weather guy used to be."

"That wouldn't be hard. Lainey could more accurately predict the weather with just a barometer."

They laughed together.

"I am going to go, though. Three days here is more than enough."

"Has it really been?"

"More than enough or three days?"

"Time doesn't fly in the middle of a Kansas winter."

Patterson nodded, then shrugged.

"Beats prison."

"I put your payment in the back of your rig."

"Thanks. I'll see you on Boxing Day, I guess."

Grant reached over and plucked a cell phone off a shelf.

"Would you be willing to take this? You could text me with it."

"I can also email you."

Grant blinked at him.

"You didn't know that?"

"I knew some government assets could, but – how?"

"I worked for Microsoft for a half-decade. Might have left a few backdoors. And, you know B&W's Apollo webserver?" Grant nodded. "Developed by a Microsoft affiliate." While he talked, Patterson wrote down his email address. "Before we went down, I had developed a domain for the community and the fees were automatically withdrawn from an account. Never even thought about it while I was inside, but I decided to see if it was still there since everything satellite-based appears to be intact. I wouldn't mind having free access to the backdoors your kid developed though."

"We don't trust each other that much yet."

"That's what I thought you'd say. Just think about this, though. You could pay me every bottle of scotch you have, or you could let me be a partner. I've gotten quite a way into Microsoft, Amazon, and B&W without federal clearance. Imagine what would happen if we connected our two networks."

Grant felt like a well-trained dog with a steak dangling two inches from his nose.

"What advantage would that be to me?"

"US military is gone, man. There's scattered chatter, but less every day. Knights are on the rise and that's B&W. You want to know what's really going on, that's where you want to snoop."

Grant rubbed an earlobe and imagined a combined network. If only he trusted Patterson and McAuliff.

"What would this partnership cost me?"

"Nothing more than you're already paying." Grant raised an eyebrow. "Technically, I work for McAuliff, but we're anarchists, so he's not going to say 'no' to my freelancing as long as you pay me for the time you take away from the community."

"Then what's in it for you?"

"You don't notice if I siphon off funds from companies that no longer exist."

"Funds? What funds? It was all ones and zeroes, wasn't it?"

"Maybe. But let's say I find something?"

"Have you *already* found something?"

"No, but – I'm knocking on the door to something, I think."

"Are you Matthew Broderick playing *War Games*?"

"No, I'm smarter than that. And, here's the real treat. It's my money to begin with."

"Do tell."

"Before we went down, I transferred some assets into a holding company that has done very well. It's behind a Department of Treasury firewall."

"Thus, why you need to combine networks?"

"Yes. I found the door. I need the key. I'm pretty sure your boy Dylan has that ability."

"My boy Dylan can barely string two words together, but he was an awesome analyst and hopefully will be again. I'll think about it. Let you know."

Patterson nodded and stood, reaching for his boots, coat, gloves, hat. It paid to be prepared these days since if you broke down, nobody would just happen to be passing by to rescue you. Grant walked him to the SUV and wished him a Merry Christmas.

Grant paused on the way to the front door, eyes on the clouds above him. He shivered, a feeling of foreboding running down his back. Maybe he was just cold, but he felt something bigger than winter lurking just beyond the fences.

Liberty Trucking

Cai felt the judgment as Lucky showed him into Jason Breen's office at Liberty Trucking Company. Lucky left the door open and Cai sat there listening to the men and women talking in the main room, which was where the coal stove was. It seemed like Jason's staff had grown and now included wives and baby-mamas and they appeared to all be living here now. That made sense ... live where you work. Combined housing meant fewer resources spread over more people. The fragrance of the cannabis plants made Cai's eyes water.

Jason came in, closed the door, which immediately reduced the heat transference.

"What's up?"

"Marnie wants me to talk to you and I figured you ought to know that Shane's been hurt."

"Hurt?"

"Yeah, wandering around out there in the blizzard, he fell and dislocated a hip and shoulder, rang his bell pretty good."

"Jesus! Those are some bad injuries given the state of medical care right now."

"Clem was there. He reset the joints while Shane was still hypothermic. There's a good chance he'll heal, but it's going to take months."

Jason scrubbed a hand down his craggy face. Like everyone else, his hair needed shampooing, although Cai still felt pretty clean since the sauna at Alex's house."

"Have you seen *my* kid around?"

"Yeah, he took a sweat at Alex Lufgren's last night and then butchered the deer Shane shot before he got hurt. I think he probably stayed at the farm last night since the weather was really bad." Jason nodded.

"I don't have anything for him to do just yet, but he keeps slithering away on me, trying to start side hustles like that trip to Hays."

"You got your cut, right?" Jason nodded, but he still looked irritated. "So Marnie wants me to see if you have any cannabis oil."

"That ain't good for babies."

"She doesn't want it for herself. She's going to test the theory that it works on seizures."

"That's anecdotal at best, but okay. We don't have a lot. It's popular. And I'm not the one producing it, so I can't just give it to you. I can trade an 8-ounce Mason for two bags of salt, a bag of corn or wheat, or something you think I might find equally valuable."

"Four bags of dog food?"

"If we're talking the 40-pound bags."

"We are. I came on horseback, so I'll be back as soon as the weather allows if you'll hang onto some for me."

"We got a few dogs here at the compound. They'll be glad to see some kibbles. How's my daughter doing?"

"Marnie is fine. She's stopped feeling morning sickness and she's outgrowing all of her scrubs."

"She's too pretty a woman to wear those anyway. How do you feel about being a father?"

"It's earlier than we planned and the circumstances suck, but all children are a gift from God."

"Hmm." Cai didn't know his father-in-law well, but he assumed he was an atheist, and the hum sort of confirmed that.

"I'd better be headed back. It looked like more snow coming."

"I'll probably be headed into town to check on Maggie. If I do, I'll swing by your place with it."

"Nope! My parents would not approve. It's a medical center request. I'll leave the dog food bags there unless I'm coming here."

"Fair enough. You want a drink? Shane and I usually toast on our deals."

"No. Settle for a handshake?"

Jason met palms with him.

"Just remember, I love my daughter. If you hurt her, they won't find the body."

His sharp blue gaze met Cai's directly.

"I earned that," Cai agreed.

"That's the closest I've ever heard you come to admitting it."

"I have – to Marnie, to Maggie, to Shane."

"Maggie thinks you're full of it."

"I'm trying not to take that personally. And I promise you – I won't hurt Marnie and I'll try to keep anyone else from hurting her."

"That's where I always knew she was safe with Shane."

"My brother the risk junkie? Jazz Tully nearly died with him last night. Just think about that." He shrugged. "Gotta go."

He headed out of the building. The low-hanging clouds obliterated the horizon in all directions. Fortunately, his horse Ronin knew the way back to town. The wind blew up his back as they minced their way toward home. By the time they reached the garage beside the house, snow blasted in hard waves. Winter without snowplows and streetlights was difficult and it was only a month old. By spring, they might all be dead, and his stomach clenched as he considered all the houses with cold chimneys. He needed to gather a crew for that and yet there were few volunteers. He could only hope the volunteers would come before the cold eased because once things started to thaw, body detail would be more difficult and dangerous.

Hiring

December 24

Jericho Ghost Town

Josh Callahan looked older than his 23 years, consistent with the half-decade in prison. His gaze challenged Grant to push his luck, kind of like Javi and Shane could when they needed to present a dangerous aura. Grant returned his gaze with equal candor.

"So what do you want from me?" he asked. Patterson arranged for them to meet by the Jericho Hotel. In this bowl behind Shane's closed building, the wind teased without tormenting.

"I might, from time to time, need a hired gun." Josh's grey eyes turned aside warily. He might have been a simple Kansas kid once, but that was a long time ago. Patterson might be right about the conscience. "I'll pay you in food, booze, cigarettes. What do you think?"

"Not corn."

"No. Food."

"Not Mountain House either."

"Nope."

"One meal a day as a retainer. Two meals to look tough. Five if there's shooting involved." Grant nodded. "And, if I have to kill someone, you deal with the burying and I get a bottle of scotch."

"I can do that. I'll give you a cell phone so I can text you. You want that retainer paid daily or weekly?"

"Your wife cooking or is this MREs?"

"Retainer is MREs. It's the easiest to apportion. I don't know you well enough to invite you around my children."

Josh's face transformed with a smile.

"Yeah, I wouldn't trust me around them either. MREs are fine. Retainer's in advance, right?"

"It is."

"You got anything you want in trade for cigs?"

"What do you have?"

"Cannabis, corn, salt, crabapple conserve, and cider. Could probably get you some milk."

"That crabapple conserve sounds good. So does the salt. One jar or bag for two packs."

"Hard bargain."

"I know the worth of what I hold"

"And you can promise Chavez won't gut me sometime when my back's turned."

"As long as you don't deserve being gutted."

Josh laughed.

"Yeah, that all sounds fair. I'll bring the trade by tomorrow."

"Nope. Text me and we'll meet somewhere."

Grant pulled a cell phone out of his pocket and handed it off.

"It's all programmed."

"And it'll work even with the towers down?"

"Better if you're outside, though."

"Good to know. You know Shane's hurt, right?"

"That's why I'm talking to you."

"And there's stuff Chavez can't do?"

Grant shrugged.

"Okeydokey. Nice talking to you. Bring my retainer with the trade, okay?"

"That was the plan."

"And I assume you'll shoot me in the head if I screw up."

"Depends, but that is a possibility. Just so you understand."

"And any idea how long this relationship will last?"

"I'm hearing Shane will be down for a couple-few months and well, we'll see how you work out."

"A man could live on one MRE a day if he had to."

"Yup, if he drinks enough water to keep things flowing."

Josh grinned again.

"I'll watch for your text then. Oh, you should know that I'm working and living at Liberty Trucking, so I might need to bug out occasionally for trading trips."

"I don't pay you if you're gone and if I discover you're double-dipping – gun to head, right?"

"Got it. I'll let you know before I go and when I get back, but -- you know, you're not offering a roof, so …." Josh shrugged, tugged on the bill of his cap, which covered a stocking cap and then turned for his vehicle – an ancient truck that was more Bondo than metal but seemed to run pretty well. After he was across the bridge, Grant went to the backdoor of the hotel and tapped a code into the keypad. It didn't work, but it also didn't zap him. That bode well for the future of the seed corn and storage food contained behind the fried security system – if only Dylan were able to help with figuring it out.

The girls were playing something loud downstairs when he shrugged out of his winter gear. Upstairs, Brian showed Emily how to stretch Dylan's paralyzed limbs.

"Can I talk to him for a minute?" Grant waited for them to get to a stopping point.

"He's probably tired, but you can try," Brian said. "I need to head home. April and I have been invited to the Vances for Christmas and she wants to take a bath. That takes hours these days."

Grant considered a moment.

"We maybe could pay you in access to hot running water."

Brian's eyebrows shot up toward his curly dark hair.

"Yeah? Not today, but yeah. That would be lovely."

He said he could find his own way out, but at a signal from Grant, Emily followed him. Dylan focused on Grant.

For a while, the right side of his face had sagged with paralysis, but now it was only asymmetrical when he smiled.

"Dylan, you were keeping track of the security codes for Shane's hotel. Where'd you store them?"

Dylan's forehead creased. His mouth twitched to the left. His tongue came out to lick the left corner. His breath came faster, and his eyes narrowed.

"It's all right. I'll ask you 'yes/no' questions."

Dylan nodded.

"Are they stored on your phone?"

Dylan's lips tightened again and then he whispered "D-d-don't know." Grant sighed. Of course, if he hadn't understood the first question, he wouldn't know.

"Do you remember Shane's hotel?"

Dylan nodded.

"Do you remember trying to guess the security codes?"

Dylan hesitated before nodding.

"Do you remember where you kept them?"

Dylan shook his head, then frowned and nodded.

"Did you store them on your phone?"

Dylan shook his head.

"Did you store them on your computer?"

Dylan frowned, then shook his head.

"Did you store them on the network?"

Dylan's right arm curled into his chest as he yawned, his tongue pulling sharply to the left. Then he nodded.

"What directory?"

Dylan looked confused and shook his head. While Grant tried to figure out the next question to ask, Dylan wriggled the fingers of his good hand over an imaginary keyboard.

"Yeah. That might work. Not now, though. You're tired. Maybe tomorrow."

Dylan nodded, his eyelids already growing heavy. Grant patted him on his good shoulder and left so the boy could sleep.

Christmas Presents

Emmaus

Jazz never wanted venison as much as she did Christmas Eve afternoon. Shorting yourself one meal a day in the dead of winter taught you to appreciate what food you had. She poured the ground corn from the mill into a bowl and carried it into the kitchen.

Someone knocked on the back door and Jill opened it.

"Carl? Hey, how are you? Come in."

The rotund man who was a neighbor of a few blocks over entered the mudroom, kicking snow off his boots.

"I got a Christmas present for you, Jill." He set a box on the counter. He pulled off the Santa hat he was wearing and brushed the snow off before he donned it again. Although Jazz had seen Carl around on many occasions, he kind of scared her because he was a schizophrenic prone to saying disturbing things. "How's your boy?"

"Hurting, but he'll heal."

"I peeked in the window before I came to the door. The only ones still in the room are friendlies. She's maybe around, but he's lit the lantern to keep her back."

267

Jill's mouth opened and closed several times.

"I could take a picture if you don't believe me." Carl fumbled in his jacket for his camera.

"No, I – I do believe you, Carl. Who are these friendlies?"

"Don't know all of them. Jacob and Miss Vi. But they're fading to memory. There's a soldier in one of those black uniforms. He's got the light now, so he'll be able to keep her back like Pastor Greyeyes did."

Jill's back straightened. Jazz didn't know if she should step in or flee. Carl scanned Jill's face a few times and then fumbled in his coat again.

"Well, I brought something that might help." Carl pulled a pint jar out of an inner pocket and held it out to Jill. She took it, her forehead creasing. "It won't bite, I promise."

"No, I'm not worried about that. What is it?"

"Cannabis oil. I traded Jason Breen a case of canned goods for it." Jazz stared openly. She'd never seen that much cannabis oil in one place.

"Why would you do that?"

"It's a pain reliever and your boy sure sounds like he could use it." Jill's face opened into an "oh, my" expression and Carl laughed. "Yeah, it was against the law before the bombs, but I don't think the Federales are going to come after us now."

"Do you know what the dosage is on this?"

"A little dab will do you. I tried it the other night." He smiled. "An eye dropper-full and I hardly heard that damn blizzard."

"So, you got it for your personal use?"

"Yeah, but I'm not going to need it. I thought it would be a good idea, but it's not for me – or anyone else. Me and it – bad combo. But your boy – he needs the help, right?"

"It might help him. Why are you giving up your food, though?"

"I've got enough to meet my needs. Don't worry. Is what I told that niece of mine too. So, I'll be headed on. You folks have a good Christmas."

Jazz remembered to pour hot water into the bowl and stir the corn mush while Jill thanked Carl out the door. Jazz watched her wipe her face and scrunch her nose as Carl left. A heavy smoker, Carl also didn't bathe regularly – even less regularly than the rest of the town these days. The mush felt soft enough, so she mixed butter and corn syrup into it. She carried the bowl into the living room. When she sat down on the edge of his mattress, Shane opened his swollen eyes, shielding them using a shaking hand with rough and reddened fingers.

"I'm here bearing calories," she announced.

"Not hungry. Can you turn out that light?"

A single lantern by the dining room lit the room.

"It's not bright in here but hold on."

She leaped up and moved the lantern behind the silk floral arrangement Jill had used to replace the fake fruit that nobody wanted to be teased with when they couldn't have the real thing. He'd closed his eyes by the time she got back to him.

"Nope, stay awake. You need food."

Shane opened one eye.

"Not hungry," he repeated through tight and chapped lips.

"You're going to eat a little bit of this whether you're hungry or not."

He opened the other eye a slit, staring at the spoonful of mush as if it might be a snake.

"I can't. Left hand. I'll stab myself in the eye."

"That's why I'm holding the spoon. Open up."

"My head hurts."

"Could be because you're hungry."

He frowned, licking peeling lips. When she brought the spoon close, he opened his mouth and took the mouthful, grimacing. She offered a sip of milk to wash it down, lifting his head for him.

"I can't," he whispered when she offered a second bite.

"You can."

He accepted the food and then another sip of milk. When she tried to get a third bite into him, he turned his face away from her.

"Yeah, this might taste better if they found another name besides 'mush'. Such a turn-off. Would you like some grits? C'mon, just one bite of grits." He looked like he might hurl, but managed another small bite, gagging a couple of times before swallowing it.

She set the bowl aside and went to her bag in the corner. They all lived out of bags since it was too cold to live upstairs. She came back, squirting a small amount of ointment on her hand and then coating Shane's left hand with it. Much more carefully, she coated his right hand, studiously not disturbing his shoulder.

"Hmm, that feels good," he whispered.

"Close your mouth. I'm going to get your lips."

"What is it?"

"The best ointment I've ever encountered for chapped skin. Close your mouth and then I'll let you rest."

"Thank you." Tears squeezed from under his long lashes. "I'm sorry."

"For what."

"Everything." He took in a shuddering breath, wincing in agony. He finally let her coat his lips and then she sat quietly beside his bed, gaze averted for the most part. When she did glance at him occasionally, tears quivered on his lashes. She put a hand on his left shoulder. He shuddered, breathing out. A single tear trailed along one cheekbone to hover above his ear.

"Just rest. It'll feel better when you're a little stronger."

He didn't argue and she counted that as a victory.

Republic of Afrika

Columbus, Ohio

Christmas Eve. Julian remembered it fondly. His father always waited until the last minute to go shopping, reasoning that stores were reducing prices rather than get stuck with gifts. Always a stressful time, running through the store in Dad's wake, trying to find something for Mom, who was the hardest to shop for.

Julian scored a brick of cheese. Perry had stopped puking but mostly slept while Joseph's fever raged. That meant Julian and the two women would share what they could gather in the kitchen. Far more stressful, but they were infinitely more grateful for what little they had. They weren't starving or freezing, and it was likely Perry and Joseph would recover.

Connie glanced around before she opened the tablet. They sat at one end of the node center, their backs to a wall. Connie didn't want to advertise what she'd found before she ran it by Julian. Or so she said. She'd set it up as a slide show of the various blog posts and newspaper headlines, but then she handed him earbuds.

"You'll need these at the end because there's a radio broadcast."

Concentration Camps Strained with Social Refuse

The proclamation in the local newspaper read:

Starting November 1, all unaffiliated white people must report to Maxwell Air Force Base for processing.) After November 7, 10 am, unaffiliated white people found outside the cordon zone will be shot.

Julian rubbed his free hand on his neck as the hairs there stood on end.

"This is the Voice with Raz Parnell. Welcome to the Struggle, my brothers and sisters.

"Some years ago, President Barack Obama promised us a fundamental transformation of the United States of America. Other white men promised us much the same thing. Since Lincoln pretended to free the slaves, we've been hanging on these lies and living for a day that was never gonna come. You know it as well as I do. They replaced slavery with Jim Crow and then they replaced Jim Crow with prisons. Black men slaughtered in the street while white kids can shoot up a mall and get a few years in prison – maybe not even that. And we kept waiting, kept hoping, kept begging for a seat at the table. The weak among us gathered around the feckless words of Martin Luther King Jr. – he had a dream of something that was never gonna happen, ya-all. Five hundred years of white

274

men owning black men, even when they pretended they didn't, and we were still living in a poor condition while white men lived nice lives on our stolen labor.

"The white race is the cancer of human history and racism has been so universal in the United States that it became so normal it was invisible. The majoritarian pigs kept electing the white supremacists who put their boots on our necks and held us to the ground so we could not rise as our traits should allow. Oh, white people pretended they were shocked and cared, but then they went back to their lives as if nothing happened because it did not happen to them.

"They were in charge and their guards were nothing more than killers, rapists, and thieves – no different than the people they incarcerated for the crimes of inconveniencing white folk. They breathed a heavy sigh that the lynchings had stopped while turning a blind eye to the lynchings occurring every day on the streets of Western society.

"Every time a black man, woman or child was pinned to the ground by the knee of a police officer, chased down a street and shot just for being there, judged purely because they were black – it was a modern-day lynching. Every time a white woman crossed the street to avoid a black man, woman, or child, avoided sitting beside a black person on the bus, or ignored the abuse of these people, it was a modern-day lynching. And since it was not happening to them, they thought it wasn't happening at all.

"We were told that electing a black president would balance the scales and we believed it, only to find that the black president was a white man in blackface and the scales

275

of justice were even more weighted against us because now the white man thought he was absolved of 500 years of abuse because he'd voted a pretend-black man to be his leader.

"'What have we done wrong that you hate us so?' They'd cry as they crushed us beneath their boots. Maybe my grandfather did something and that's why I live in this nice house now, but I didn't do it so why should I be held accountable? Here, have a public housing project and an Obamaphone. All settled now. And on and on, making excuses, not taking responsibility, lording it over us. No more, we cried over and over and they did not listen.

"And then the bombs went off. Oh, bless the Lord Almighty Shango for raining his fire and lightning on the white centers of power, bringing us the hope of justice after 500 years of darkness. Thank Babalú-Ayé for bringing the sickness that weakened them and emboldened our strong right arm. The world was tired, racist, and volatile as hell, ripe for a hostile takeover by a benevolent regime. Their society was already divided. The conquering was easy."

"And now we must take up our own salvation, brothers and sisters. What was done to us must be done to them, so that they might correct their spirits. The recompense as already begun – white folks removed from the houses that should have been ours – assigned to work for our folks – provided rations like the cattle they are.

"I know there are some who question this action, but we've given them centuries to change their minds and we stayed in the condition they left us in. And now we're correcting them like the privileged brats they've always been. In time, you'll see the wisdom of this and many of them will as well. The natural superiority of the black man and woman will bring about a time of peace and prosperity and even our slaves will eat well.

"For this midwinter season, we must look toward the light and accept the gift Shango has put in our hands. In the spring, comes the planting."

The transmission ended and Julian pulled out the earbuds.

"Damn." He didn't know what else to say.

"Looks like something happened in Savannah – a mutation of the flu maybe."

"No." Julian saw no reason to keep it a secret. "According to what I'm hearing, it's more deadly in the South and they might also be getting secondary effects we have here. Why that would result in the overthrow of the majority population is a mystery, but we're not there, so --."

"What if it spreads?"

"The flu?"

"No. This anger? This reverse slavery?"

Julian laughed, unnerved by the thought. He sought to comfort her.

"You won't have anything to worry about."

"Not true. My husband's white. My children are mixed. One looks like me, the other looks like her father."

"Oh. My bad. My prejudices are showing."

"No need to apologize for what I didn't tell you until now. I also worry about you and everyone who doesn't look like me. Nobody deserves that. Can I work on how far this has spread?"

"As long as you're making connections in the net, I don't care what you work on. And this might be worthy of some scrutiny. I'm going to take this to Green. I think it's best we don't tell anyone else for now, but he should know."

Connie nodded.

"I surely wish I could get home to my husband and children."

"I know. This quarantine sucks. Have you spoken with them?"

"Every night, but it's not the same as being there."

"It's not, but hopefully it'll be over soon."

"And if it isn't?"

"You sure ask a lot of hard questions." They laughed together. "Sooner or later, my group has to bust loose and head west."

Connie nodded. Julian sighed, closed the tablet and left the node to go talk to Fred Green, the manager of the Sullcorp hub. This was not how he'd envisioned spending Christmas Eve.

Mysterious Spread

Emmaus

Marnie and Ami met in what passed for the staff lounge at the medical center – the small room behind the reception desk where Jace Welton installed a coal burner that Shane had been faithfully stocking until his injury. Ami set down the hod, closed the door, and adjusted the air intake.

"You look like you've been doing that forever."

"We used something similar to heat our home when I was a child. You'd think it doesn't get cold in Egypt, but we do get something like fall that we call winter."

Marnie smiled to show she appreciated the sharing as she hung up her scarf and coat and exchanged her boots for tennis shoes.

"How have things been here?"

"I've only had the one patient thanks to the storm."

"Kix Conopher?"

"Yes. When I got here, he'd just had a grand mal, and he was quite confused for a few hours, but then he perked up and we talked a bit. He couldn't feel anything on his left side, but his head wasn't hurting as much."

"Well, that sounds better. Do you think it is?"

"I don't rightly know. I suppose I should just tell you and ask you to keep it confidential. One of the men at the B&B has similar symptoms. He'd had the flu and then he got sick again – headache, neck pain, seizures, some paralysis. Dr. Kletti from out at the McAuliff compound was a neurologist and he thinks it might be encephalitis."

"Could it be GBS? Brian doesn't think so, but the link to the flu has me curious."

"In Dylan's case, it's not GBS. It's sort of a rare disorder, so I don't think you'd find two people with it in a small town like this."

"Hmm. I wish I could tell his parents something. Perhaps he's on the mend."

"Perhaps. With only one case so far, it's hard to say anything about it. We don't even know that they're related."

Ami caught Marnie up on the charts she'd completed and reported that Chris had passed the Conopher family blood samples onto her.

"I'm headed back to work in my lab. Kix is asleep, so hopefully, it'll be a calm shift for you. I'll make sure the stove is completely stocked before I leave and I'll haul some water to the stove."

"Thank you. I'm going to go check on Kix now while you finish up. I'll be praying that you figure this out soon."

Ami smiled in that way people had when they didn't know how to react to prayer. Marnie didn't bother to argue.

As much to save generator fuel as because of photosensitivity, the lights in Kix's room were off. With the door propped open for heat, enough light came in from the hall that Marnie could see to navigate and she'd adopted the habit of a headlamp. While she scanned down Kix's chart, the boy in the bed flailed his right leg out of the covers. Marnie directed her lamp to the ceiling and approached him.

"How are you feeling?"

He made a soft strangling noise and her stomach turned over queasily. Probably another seizure. She turned on a nearby light so she could see what was going on. Kix's left arm lay limp at his side, while his right fist twisted against his chest. While his left eye wouldn't open, he stared at her with his right and she could see terror there. He wasn't seizing. She moved to the bottom of the bed and lifted the blankets. Positive Babinski in both feet. The left leg was flaccid and the right one toed in and down.

She called Ami to join her.

"It's somewhat similar to Dylan's. I agree it's worth charting and considering if they are similar."

"Can you get Dr. Kletti to consult?"

Ami frowned, her swarthy face turned away.

"I don't know. You know they're fugitives, right?"

"I couldn't care less. Have you met my father?"

Ami smiled. Apparently, she had made Jason's acquaintance.

"I'll ask. And, I was wondering – is Dr. Verheil about? I've a question to ask her."

"I'm sorry. I suppose you've not been here in a few days. Dr. Verheil died in the early part of this week – I think it was a stroke."

Ami looked devastated, but only for a moment. It was so brief an expression that Marnie thought she might have imagined it. Out in the lobby, they heard the bell at the door jangle open. One of Jacob's last acts was to hang wind chimes so that when the door was opened about halfway, they rang out. Both doctors moved toward the sound.

"Help us," Marilee Johanson cried as her husband labored under the weight of their teenaged son Calvin. He set the boy down on one of the sofas.

"What are the symptoms?" Marnie asked.

"He woke up this morning complaining of a headache and now he can't move his legs."

Marnie glanced at Ami whose only tell was to swallow tightly.

"I'll stay. We'll do the work-up together."

Team Building

Seattle, Washington

The Knights weren't Navy SEALS so it was good that Geo had never commanded a Team. He constantly had to remind himself that this crew was a different profession – different, not less-than. Myerson, Zapata, Marek, and Walden gathered with him over the strategy table.

"There's a school right about here. A nice big public building where you could hide a pretty large group of people fairly successfully. We're receiving coded messages from that general vicinity that. The code isn't aligning with your earlier matrix, but why would it be in code if they weren't trying to hide something?" Walden stepped back.

"Can I make a suggestion?" Marek asked. Geo hesitated a half moment before nodding. *Different, not less-than.* "Someone should go in and see if they can get close enough to check things out."

Geo rubbed his jaw. He needed a shave, but he and Duke didn't go home last night. The crew lived here at the old Fredericks & Nelson Department Store, so he'd stayed to do some team-building exercises, trying to respect that most of these people had signed a voluntary contract just like he had. He wasn't a military commander, so he couldn't act like a slave-master.

"Anyone want to volunteer for that?"

They all looked anywhere but at him, although Reyes and Langberg both blushed because only a few weeks before, they would have stepped forward and marched into the fires of hell if their commander asked them to. Now they wanted to know more before they even considered it.

"There's an apartment complex right about here." Walden indicated the location on the map. "I'd be willing to go with you to check it out."

"Knights commanders lead from the front?"

"Something like that," Zapata said, smiling. His eyes had that crazy glint that dared Geo to argue.

"If we pretended to be a couple – may be looking for food – maybe we could get close enough, radio back our findings." Walden shrugged. "I'm assuming you have the skills to get me out if needed."

Geo stared at the map, trying to decide what he thought of this plan.

"We go in filthy, make it look like we're desperate. Who's going to run the base station while you're mobile."

Reyes held up his hand, explaining he'd trained for a radio tech, though he'd always been a backup grunt.

"Now, let's work on how we get there."

"Canoe." Marek pointed at a spot on the west shore of Lake Washington. "We pick it up there and drop you both here." He pointed at Mercer Island. "You paddle across. I assume you know how to do that?"

"I've paddled dinghies."

"Good thing I grew up in Puget Sound." Walden grinned. "I'll take the stern."

"We'll need concealable weapons."

Meyerson's smile flashed white.

"Have you seen our armory yet? Carlindo scored big time. Come on, I'll show you."

He signaled one of the four barely-trained Knights to follow him. As he walked by Duke, the black Lab growled low and got up to follow them as Peger fell in with Geo and Walden.

"Supply officer?" Geo asked.

"Until they train me in arms, might as well be useful. I worked for a gun store until the Pulse."

"Where?"

"Here in Seattle. Ballard Tactical Goods."

Geo tried not to flinch. He and Wes Marcus had followed up after looters when they'd run from the Knights' sweep at the Ballard Mall. Peger narrowed his eyes then grinned.

"I didn't own it, man, and a lot of bad stuff went down those first few days – especially with you military types. How were you going to know they weren't looking to kill you?"

"They killed a few military," Meyerson reminded. He paused to unlock the weapons room and swing the heavy door open. Geo stared around at the fully-stocked shelves – tactical gear, rifles, pistols, grenade launchers – even parachutes. Meyerson stepped back to allow Geo an unfettered look around at the inventory.

"How much small-arms training do you have, Walden?"

"Just boot camp."

"Why'd you wash out?"

"You ever been to Lackland?"

"Twice."

"Hot as hell. I couldn't handle it. I was fine in the morning and evening, but I couldn't function in the heat of the day. I wanted to be a UAV pilot, but the physical part was just too much in the midday heat."

"You don't have to apologize to me. About two-thirds fail BUD training for a whole bunch of reasons. I don't need you to be a SEAL or even an Airman. I need you not to shoot me when you're defending yourself from the bad guys. Can you do that?"

"I can. I did fine in that."

They spent about a half-hour gearing up. Watching her load the Sig Sauer 9mm and three extra clips told him she had a good background in arms training. He briefly lamented that they couldn't make full use of the tactical closet, but it didn't fit the image they were trying to present. He gave her a few extra clips to fill.

The Knights had a uniform, but of course, they would go in dressed in civvies. They used each other's first name – Geo and Cassidy – as they got ready. They didn't have a long acquaintance so he figured there wasn't much risk they'd use the wrong name, but he considered their options if it happened. He decided to go with a half-truth.

"I'm military – a SEAL who's been hiding since the takedown. You knew me through my brother Jim Tully. No way'll trace back to us since he's never been here, but if someone knows me, they aren't going to know about Jim. You met him in training. We met before everything went down – a bar. Where'd you grow up here in Seattle?"

"Port Angeles, but I went to college at Seattle U. There's a bar not far from there – the Elbow Room."

"Tiny place?"

"Corner bar. Hang out for college students, but Jim wanted to see me and dragged you along. What does Jim look like?"

"Me only about 30 pounds less muscle. And his eyes are hazel."

"Yours are … blue. Good to know. Are we a couple?"

"I don't think I'd be good at faking that. We're friends. We've been on the move since the takedown. Heard there might be some of my types gathering over on the eastern bank. We'll exchange some personal information as we go. We need to sound like people who have been hanging out for weeks together. Just remember, they train SEALS to keep our lips tight, so if they throw something at you that you can't answer about me, I'm not that chatty. I also don't care that much about your past. That way when we don't know something about the other, we're not sending up red flags."

"How'd we hook up after the takedown?"

"We ran into each other in that camp that was developing by Pike's Market. We were staying there, but food's tight, works day to day, and getting hassled by the Knights was getting riskier for me."

"We aren't bothering that camp." Geo stared at Zapata. "I'm just saying. We're encouraging those people with work and trying to get them to move on, but we're not harassing them."

"He don't know that," Sherwin said after a moment. "*We* know that. But when you expect the cops to hassle you, the cops will seem to be hassling you."

"What he said," Geo responded. "And I doubt the people east of the lake will know any better either. The more I think about it, the less we need to hide these weapons – at least the ones I'm carrying. It gives us cred."

Walden nodded. Geo thought they could pull this off.

Code Talking

Wichita, Kansas

Ren shrugged snow off his jacket as he entered the tiny room Travis used for an office. The boy sat bundled up in a coat and a sleeping bag because heat was at a premium even with fuel coming from the Gulf Coast. Ren offered to give him an office up on his floor, but the boy pointed out that he was trying to fly under the radar, and assigning one of Crispin's Knights to him was attention-grabbing enough.

"What you got for me, kid?"

"I didn't want to forward it in case there's something hidden in it. Look at this."

ICY - I'm looking forward to seeing your shack. I hear Eskimo kisses are popular in Shang-ra-la during wolf's moon. Listen for it."

"What the hell does that mean?"

"The only time I met Francene, we talked about our homes and I told her the locals call mine 'The Shack' because it's the nicest house in town. She also told me that her husband calls her 'icy" because the day they met, a roof dumped on her head. He teased her and it stuck." Ren

289

looked to where Eden sat huddled next to the heater. "Those are things neither of us tells anyone we don't like, so not a lot of other people would recognize it. Eden, maybe you can tell us what the rest of it means."

"Eskimo kisses is me – an inside joke with my dad who nicknames everyone. I don't know what Shang-ra-la is, but Wolf's Moon is January."

"Shang-ra-la is a kind of garden of Eden from an old book and movie, so my guess is she threw that in to assure I knew she meant you. Travis, is there any way to reply to her that doesn't risk detection?"

"Sure. Keeping them guessing is the best way. Some sort of code."

"You know Morse?"

"Who?"

Ren laughed and opened his mouth to explain about Morse code when Eden spoke up before him.

"Alutiiq, maybe."

"You speak it?"

"Well, not to have a conversation in it, but enough to say a few words so she knows I'm with you."

"There can't be a lot of people who know even a few words in that language," Travis admitted.

"Well, regular readers of the Kodiak Mirror – and my dad, who is the one who taught me."

Ren nodded. Travis suggested she make the message something personal.

"No, that'll be too easy to figure out if someone intercepts it." Eden frowned. "Numbers. The last four digits of my Social."

"Why?"

"Because it was always my bike combination growing up and she and Dad will both understand it, but nobody else will. Can you distort my voice like you did his?"

Travis nodded, busy typing into his computer.

"I've got it all set up. You just press the button and say the words."

Eden sat down in his seat and stared at the screen. Ren and Travis exchanged glances, holding silence. Eden spewed out some sounds that hardly seemed like language. "*Allringuq, talliman, mallruungin, pingayun.*" Eden then hit the Stop button. She stood and Travis took her place, playing back the audio, which made her sound more like Ren than herself. She nodded.

"It should work."

"I'll bounce it all over the country before it gets to her, so it can't be traced back to us."

Eden turned to Ren.

"When do we leave?"

"Now that we know she can find us … tonight."

"Travis?"

"I was ready to leave here the day I got here. Go get packed. All I need to do is put my toothbrush in my bag." He stood up from his seat and laid a kiss full on her full lips.

291

"You sure you want to go to Alaska." Her skepticism seemed well-founded. Ren had been to her hometown in the winter a couple of times. It was like Kansas with mountains and wind.

"I told you. I'll go anywhere you want to go, so long as you're safe being there."

"Alaskans are well-armed, son," Ren assured Travis. The kid snorted. "We leave as soon as the drivers are ready to go and it's going to take us about four days to get there so anything you two want to do that you can't in the back of a Snow-Cat better get it done in the next few hours."

"Ooo, we should take a shower," he heard Travis say to Eden as he closed the door. "Might be the last time we have hot water for a while."

Kids surely don't think adults are that dumb, do they?

Swapping Stories

Christmas Morning

Emmaus, Kansas

Rob rolled over and stared at the ceiling. The moon sent a silvery sheen across the plaster. The storm had passed finally. The house felt cold ... colder. Something awakened him. It had to be Christmas morning. Vi's birthday had been Christmas Day, so the Delaneys celebrated on the eve. He didn't have a tradition of waking up early to slide presents under the tree. Maybe just the absence of howling wind woke him.

Belle the cat's purr rumbled from the couch behind his pillow. How a cat who weighed five pounds could sound like a hundred-pound jungle cat was a mystery Rob had yet to solve. Glister's tags tinkled as he shifted positions on the other couch, now pushed up against the window wall to allow room for mattresses in front of the woodstove. Jill snored lightly beside him, turned away, face snuggled in her pillow. Cai and Marnie slept to the right as far from the woodstove as she could get, but tonight Cai slept alone because Marnie had gone to the medical center. Jazz slept to the left, between him and Shane, her back toward him, facing Shane.

Now he recognized the sound that had awakened him – sobs of grief. Careful not to uncover his wife, Rob rolled out of bed and stepped around Jazz's mattress, settling on the left side of Shane's mattress. Without a word, he slid an arm behind the boy's back and rolled him up against his chest. Shane hissed with pain and then sniffled, sobbing in low slow shudders.

"Bad dreams?"

Shane answered with a convulsive swallow.

"That's why I drank. To stop the dreams."

"I'm sorry," Shane croaked.

"You didn't do anything wrong, kid. I am responsible for my sobriety. You know, that's really what I learned the night I was saved – that I couldn't expect anyone but my Higher Power to rescue me. When I quit running from Him, admitted what I'd done, the pain became bearable, so I could see a future."

"I can't. You don't know what I've done."

"Because you won't tell me." Shane shifted uncomfortably, grunting in pain. "Shh, you don't have to. You just need to listen. Can you do that?"

"Mmm."

Rob let three years of Vietnam experiences filter through his mind. What could he tell Shane that would address his need? He'd prayed about that since holding his shivering son all night.

"My first tour in we were ordered to pacify a village. Of course, pacify was a euphemism. There was nothing peaceful about what we did to that village. Being homeless and rendered starving is not peaceful." Rob sighed. He'd chosen the incident that most shamed him. He almost wished he'd chosen another one. There are no trophies for just showing up in God's army.

"I acted as interpreter a lot. Vietnamese is a tonal language, so being musical is an advantage. The LT called me over so he could interrogate this woman. She kept insisting they weren't a VC village, but they were all VC. Or not. They were whatever their tormentors at the moment were. It was how they survived. But when you're 18 years old, you don't know that. You think they're lying just to you and wouldn't the LT know – the LT who is 22 and is only a lieutenant because he went to college before getting called up in the military. So, he gets rough with her and this kid – he's maybe 12 and he comes running over shouting for us to stop. He puts his body between us and her and when the LT raises a hand against him, he shoves back, knocks the man down. He's defending his mother and there are all these other people shouting, and I hear a gun shooting somewhere. I try to push the kid back, but he's strong – wiry, been working the fields -- and he pushes me and the next thing I know, I've driven my knife into his chest." Rob wiped a tear away. "I've never gotten that one out of my head."

Shane heaved another long, slow sob.

"I kept re-upping. Didn't think I fit back in the world anymore. I still had a little hope. Your mom and I met in

Danang, got married in Tokyo on leave, and I thought love would rescue me." Rob scoffed at his own stupidity. Shane winced, but he still listened. "I got back to the States and I couldn't make it stop. The memories were everywhere. I'd been drinking in the Nam, but I just fell off the cliff in Seattle. Your mother wouldn't put up with it, not after I showed her some of my soldier moves. I could have hurt her. Maybe I did hurt her. The stress may be caused the miscarriage." He'd had to learn to stop hating himself for that one too.

"That didn't stop me drinking. I drank more. She kicked me out and I moved into the barracks. More drinking with nightly keggers. I fell apart quick, ended up on report. Somewhere in there was a phone call home – I pissed off Vi. EJ had just died and she was in no mood to watch another spiral down. And, then your grandfather showed up. He got the CO to put me on leave – probably saved my career. He got me to this hotel, and he sat on me for a week. It wasn't easy. I hadn't been sober – no alcohol on board – in maybe six months to a year. I was dependent on it by then. And, sober I felt it – all the crap I did. One night I got away from him. I looked in the window of this liquor store and I could see this neon sign – a cross on top of the church down the street. While I hesitated, the liquor store closed. Of course, there were others, but it was raining, so I just went to the church and sat in the back pew. And I prayed. I just put all the thoughts – all the memories – on the altar and I confessed. The pain eased and I knew I didn't need booze to salve it. Which didn't mean I didn't still want it, just that it could no longer lie to me."

Shane hiccupped.

"Whenever you're ready, son. I absolutely will listen to you."

Shane swallowed tightly, struggled to breathe through a stuffed nose.

"I k-killed her."

"Killed who, Shane?"

"I d-didn't know her n-name. She wore a dark hajib. We were in a firefight. I'd already taken a few rounds to the vest and my buddy was bleeding to death beside me. She just showed up in my peripheral vision and –." Shane sobbed, pain wracking through his body.

"It'll be easier if you tell it all, Shane. I know it hurts, but really, it gets better after you lay that burden down."

"It hurts so much."

Rob waited, listening to a log fall in the woodstove, the soft pop and crackle of the warming fire. Just when he thought Shane had flinched, the boy shifted slightly, hissing in pain.

"Sh-she – she h-had a-a b-baby."

The import of Shane's confession cut through Rob. After leaving home following Marie Callahan's abortion and subsequent suicide, he'd killed a child. The automatic response came to Rob's mind – "It'll be okay, kid. You were in a war and these things happen." He bit his tongue. Shane didn't want or need platitudes. The same could be said for killing that kid so long ago. Rob knew platitudes wouldn't soothe this pain.

"Shit," he whispered because he sensed Shane needed a response to continue.

"I left them there on the side of the road and saved my own sorry ass."

No, it wasn't time to talk yet.

"And when I got back to Pedaresh, I was going to tell Sera. I swear I was. I was going to quit the Knights and tell the CSA to fuck off, but – but – there'd been a bombing. The building was-was gone and now they both follow me everywhere I go, accusing me of – of what I did. And, I can't – I can't live with that."

Shane's tears wet through Rob's t-shirt as he wept, sobs shuddering through his body amid paroxysms of pain and grief. Rob just held him. He guessed Sera had been a girlfriend. Guessing instead of asking, the need to say something dissolved into the night. Rob prayed for God to provide him answers, but they never came. Eventually, Shane quieted. His strength ebbed and he slept, and Rob surprised himself by waking up to the dawn with Cai stocking the woodstove. Shane looked peaceful as Rob dragged his numb right arm out from under him. Except for a quick glance when Rob sat up, Cai seemed focused on the fire. Jazz, however, met Rob's gaze and gave a small, sad smile before she nodded her head like they agreed on something.

Brain Pain

Pete groaned as Poppy left the bed. Pain lanced behind his eyes, stabbing his neck. He couldn't focus on her hands to see what she said. Clumsily, he signed "headache". Some signs were so appropriate – his spear fingers jabbing and turning in his skull. She left and took the attacking light with her, although leaving the hallway door propped open for the heat. Slowly the room grew light. His eyes still watered and teared as he contemplated the need to urinate. He sat up, fighting a sudden urge to throw up. He shivered uncontrollably as he swung his legs off the mattress. He stood to head for the door, surprised when his right leg buckled. He grabbed the chair by the window and stood gasping as pins and needles rippled like fire up and down his leg.

Taking another step poured agony the length of his leg and he had to grab the dresser for support. He clung to the chair rail in the hallway when Alex cleared the stairs.

"You okay?"

"Feel like crap." He gagged convulsively.

Alex grabbed his arm and helped him into the bathroom that was only a few impossible steps away. After he puked three times, Alex helped him sit up on the toilet. He'd not peed sitting down since his trainer days, but his leg still wouldn't hold him. After he was done, Alex helped him back to bed.

"What's wrong with your leg?"

"I don't know." Pete wept for the pain in his head.

"You hurt your back trying to lift too much?"

"I don't think so. I don't know."

His head hurt so bad he could barely remember yesterday. Alex put a hand to his forehead.

"You feel cold. Hmm. You need another blanket?"

Pete said "yes", but it didn't help. Keri brought up an electric heating pad and that helped a little, though when he shifted it to his right side, it felt like the heating pad shocked him. He dozed, his headache overwhelming all other senses but his hearing.

"I think we should have Marnie or that other doctor come out to look at him." He couldn't make out the reply from whomever Keri spoke to, but it was a sure bet it wasn't his wife since she never spoke aloud.

He needed to puke again, but this time when he sat up to toss back the covers, his right leg didn't move at all, effectively pinning him to the bed. He spewed the wood floor beside the bed and then fell face-first into his own slime.

It's Over

Columbus, Ohio

Sleeping arrangements in the tiny apartment above the maintenance warehouse were always tight but having two sick people made it even more complicated. Joseph and Perry slept in the same room in the vain hope of keeping the other three from getting the flu. Ordinarily, Andi slept on the couch so Katharine and Joseph could share a marital bed. Julian shared the other bed with Perry. With Katharine displaced from her bed, Julian was forced to sleep on the couch because he surely wasn't sharing a bed with Katharine, who surely wasn't sleeping on a couch.

Andi handed him a cup of coffee as he straightened from tying his shoes.

"If there were heat, I'd sleep in the truck." She rubbed a hand through her hair, which she'd taken scissors to yesterday. It looked good for a self-trim.

"She snore?"

"She's hot and she steals the covers. Maybe we could just pretend to be lovers so we could take the bed." She cast him a hopeful look.

"I could suggest a rotation. Becoming lovers isn't necessary."

"Friends with benefits?"

Julian laughed nervously. Sex would be fun, but it always came with attachments and he wasn't sure he wanted to bind himself to anyone. He could still bug out from these people if he had to, but could he do that after he'd bedded Andi. Probably not.

"I gotta go. Lunch in the truck?"

"Sounds good. Oh, by the way, Chris says something is going on with this flu."

"Yeah?"

"Some sort of secondary infection. Someone said it was like Guillain Barre Paralysis."

"What's that?"

She rolled her eyes upward, clearly trying to remember details.

"You get a virus and then the fat layer on your nerves – which is what carries the messages to your muscles – disintegrates and leaves you paralyzed. It gets better, but you can die of respiratory failure before that happens."

"Wow! And they're getting a lot of that?"

She nodded, then shrugged. Julian hoped Perry and Joseph wouldn't experience that.

"Good to know about it. There's been some chatter out there about a resurgence of polio."

"Polio?! How does that happen?"

Julian shrugged. He had a meeting with Fred Green he needed to get to. He grabbed a slice of bread and headed across the compound to the administrative building. The building was typical Midwestern low-slung concrete and glass. Fred was a middle-height black man with a face shaped by laughter and an enjoyment of carbs. He wasn't fat, but his clothes were loose, suggesting he'd lost a few pounds for the Apocalypse.

Julian waited while Fred scanned through everything Connie had uncovered, then scanned back through it, then sat quietly staring at the snow falling outside the window. Julian wondered where he hailed from. He thought Memphis or Savannah. His accent just didn't seem deep enough to be from Alabama or Mississippi.

"God, it's over." Fred's Southern-honied baritone felt like the last note of a requiem.

Julian didn't nod. Prison taught him that the US had been an ideal never realized, unattainable for most felons certainly.

"Those are majority-black cities headed by black mayors. Their stated goal is to found the Republic of New Afrika by taking control of the territory in and around their cities."

"It'll spread. The RNA's been a dream of black radicals since the 1960s. Mobile's more than half. A lot of New Orleans relocated there after the levees failed. Columbus Georgia's just about half. It's a long way away under current conditions, but I should let the City Council know about it. The milder winters in the south mean they're more maneuverable. We don't want to see them at the town limits come spring."

Julian didn't know what Fred wanted from him. He thought preparing sounded like a good idea, but it wasn't for him to say. He was just trying to wrap his mind around black people who were concerned about a black uprising. Either way, he'd be headed west before the situation got here. His concern was for Andi, who felt a natural affinity for the South.

"We need to get the Internet back to a robust state."

"We're working on it, sir. Although we haven't connected yet, B&W is also working on it. I keep seeing tracks in the cloud, so I think we're getting there."

"Good. I need to be able to get consistent communication with Wichita."

"I understand. Now, can you tell me something?" Fred nodded. "What's going on outside this compound, in the city?"

Fred tugged on his nose a moment, perhaps considering his answer.

"Flu."

"Lots of people dying?"

"No, not that I've heard, but they're trying to keep it from spreading."

"I'm down with that. What about people who want to leave?"

"I wouldn't try it. They're taking their quarantine seriously and we've had about twenty people sick here."

"I mean, leave the city."

Fred stared at him, then chuckled.

"Seattle. You guys don't have winter, right? The highways to the west are feet deep in snow and nothing is knocking them down, so you wouldn't get far from the city, and then you'd have to come back and they'd put you in prison for breaking quarantine. I hear the jails are pretty bad these days."

"Good to know. How are supplies?"

"I think we can make it to spring if we're careful. And I've heard chatter that Ren Sullivan is moving some goods. I wouldn't be surprised if a convoy showed up any day."

"I'd like to see that. I need to get back to the node. I'll let you know if we learn anything more."

"Of course, and I'll share as I can."

"Thank you. Merry Christmas, by the way."

"Wow, is it?"

"Yes."

"It was my favorite holiday. Can't believe I didn't know it."

"Now you do."

"Tell the node to take the day off. Jeez! I need to tell people to go relax. There'll be alcohol around sundown, here in the big conference room."

Julian grinned and excused himself so Fred could make arrangements.

Christmas Morning

Emmaus

For the first time in a while, Nevada woke up without morning sickness as daylight slipped through the curtains. She lay there in sheets that hadn't been washed in far too long, listening as Kim sang a cappella in the kitchen. It smelled like she'd baked something – maybe the pies she'd made at the Vances the other day. Bosco barked at the back door and Nevada supposed that was Max's tread across the floor to let him in. The storm passed sometime in the night. Nevada pulled on her clothes before rolling out of the warm covers into the chilly room. She peeked out the window at the wind-blasted yard, the snow piled against the fences and forge-shed. She rubbed the small bump under her sweatshirt. Three months. She was a fool.

Kim turned from the stove as Nevada came down the stairs. She flipped two slices of French bread onto a plate.

"There's butter and crabapple jelly," she announced.

"What are you doing for James that he's being this generous?" Max asked.

Kim's cheeks grew a little pink, but she laughed.

"Nothing like that. He's – like True Love Waits. He said it was my Christmas present. Dinner is the two pies his mother taught me how to make. Turkey pot."

"Sounds delicious." Nevada slid into her chair as Max joined her at the table. Kim flipped two more slices onto a plate and dredged replacements.

"How is David these days?" Nevada spread her napkin on her lap. They each had one designated to them, so they didn't have to wash them daily—washing being an all-day ordeal now.

"Allison says he's doing a lot better, but I can't really tell. He's walking, but he doesn't talk."

"Poor kid." Max's compassion always surprised Nevada who had heard from Drew that Max had a temper. She'd seen no real evidence of that. He could get passionate about some things – children going hungry, for example – but he always treated her and Kim with patience. If he weren't gay …. "Imagine being trapped in your head like that. At least he's not completely paralyzed."

They all three nodded, a little sad. Kim flipped the last two slices onto the plate, donned oven mitts, and conveyed a rasher of bacon and the French toast to the table where she sat down. Max retrieved a pot of something they were calling coffee from the back of the stove.

They talked about pleasant subjects – Christmases past – while they ate, then put the dishes to soak and went into the living room. Thank goodness for artificial trees. Theirs didn't have lights, but every ornament the Randolphs owned weighed it down. They exchanged one present each. Max gave Nevada a blue vase from his house. She'd admired it once when visiting Drew to discuss a business venture and Max remembered. So odd. That was before she started sleeping with Drew. Max gave Kim a pair of really warm gloves.

"Drew bought them for me a few years ago, but they are too small."

They were way small because they fit Kim fairly well. Kim gifted both of them with a painting – Nevada's was of her working in the forge and Max's was of the prairie before the snow fell. They both were photo-realistic. Nevada gave Max a small metal sculpture of a curious cat that she'd done for a client who was probably dead now and gave Kim a forged bracelet of twisted wire.

"This might be the best Christmas I've ever celebrated," Max reported as he washed up the dinner dishes while Nevada wiped down the counters and table. Kim had headed upstairs after a walk in the snow with James.

"Really? How so?"

"Drew didn't celebrate Christmas. He thought it was too commercial. So it's been years since I've celebrated it. This has been great." He drained the sink and dried his hands. "I've been thinking about what you said the other night."

"Oh?" She waited for more, but he just hung up the dish towel and nodded at her.

"I'm not done thinking." He turned for his room. "Good night."

Operation Launch

Seattle, Washington

Meyerson, Zapata, Sherwin, and Duke accompanied Geo and Cassidy to the Cedar Point shoreline where they had the most direct access across Lake Washington to the state park on the eastern shore. Kenmore College was a couple of miles inland from the park. They could do the whole trip in a day if they went the most direct route. That made the tiny pocket park perfect for launching a canoe in the December fog.

Geo dropped to a knee in the mud to scruff Duke's ears. Three months and the black Lab had become his family.

"You be a good boy while I'm gone." He looked at Sherwin. The guy had a way of not-quite smiling when something pleased him, but he didn't want to show it. Duke liked him more than anyone else on the team. Despite Geo's misgivings, he knew dogs were usually good judges of character. They smelled or sensed something subtle human beings missed. "Watch out for him."

"Like he belonged to me. Which he doesn't. If I fell and broke a leg, he'd leave me in the woods. But you – he'd follow you through a desert and we both know how Labs feel about places with no water. He's a great dog, Sergeant. You can trust me with him."

It would take time to get used to the designation.

"I secured a gun up in the gunnel," Meyerson explained. "Just in case, you know. You'll have to reach up under and behind the float."

"Good to know."

Duke waded into the water, trying to stay close to Geo. When Meyerson stepped between him and Geo, he growled.

"Sorry, boy, but you can't come with. I know, Labs and water, but I doubt you'd like the risk of gunfire."

Sherwin leaned back on the leash and Duke reluctantly moved along the shore with him. He didn't seem to like Meyerson. Some dogs didn't like black people. Geo always thought it had to do with their eyes being so dark. That didn't explain why Duke seemed to like Marek. Geo would have to work that out later. Meyerson showed him the GPS coordinates and then the compass so there'd be no question of getting lost. Geo marked his map.

"We ready?" Cassidy donned a life vest. Geo tried to decide if that was a good idea or not. It could make them look staged. But it was a Seattle Parks life vest as was the canoe, so it seemed legitimate. She wore filthy jeans and a ripped t-shirt covered with a jacket that had seen better days. She'd covered her hair with a stocking cap. Geo wore similar clothes.

He clamored into the bow of the canoe and gawked as Cassidy pushed off from the shore and stepped into the canoe without getting her feet wet. With a few strokes, they were away. Duke barked a couple of times, but Cassidy kept stroking.

"That dog loves you."

"He's a good friend." Hearing himself say that surprised Geo. He liked dogs, but he'd never had one of his own. He'd joined the Navy at 18 and dog-ownership didn't work with life in the Teams. He sneezed. The damp air rendered breathing into a cold wet experience. "Wow, this is pea soup."

"This is nothing. Merry Christmas, by the way."

"Is it? How do you tell here?" Geo pulled on gloves.

"I'm sure there's some weather-related phenomenon that would tell me, but I looked at a calendar this morning. I guess that the holiday's been canceled."

"Yeah, probably." Geo picked up his paddle. "How do I help you?"

"Stroke on the right side and keep your paddle perpendicular to the canoe. You'll get maximum power that way without messing with my steering."

"Okay. Let me know if I'm doing it right."

"A little more right angle. How long have you lived in Seattle?"

"I don't live here. I'm stationed out of Whidby. Was. You said you were raised here."

"Yeah. Granfolks moved here during World War 2."

"I had a great-uncle who moved here then too."

"Lots of people did. My folks were from North Dakota."

"Kansas."

"They might practically have been neighbors."

They laughed. Paddling a canoe was harder on the shoulders than rowing a dinghy. That was more forearms and back. Cassidy was doing most of the work. He'd never really served with a woman before. Buds training tended to weed out even tough men. Despite what the movies portrayed women hadn't broken through yet. But Cassidy was making him look bad at canoeing. Usually, she did some sort of paddle magic that overcame whatever stupid thing he did to swerve them off course. Every now and then she'd ask him for a course correction, which usually required paddling on the left. As the morning wore on, the fog lightened so they could see the way ahead. The far shore became visible before midday. By that time, he and Cassidy knew a lot about each other's families, and she'd told him made-up stories about the friends they supposedly knew in common. Geo almost felt like he met these people. She had a gift for description so that he felt like he knew the places she referenced.

When they approached the beach, Cassidy paralleled the shore until they reached a place where the trees reached almost to the water. They carried the canoe up into the trees and covered it with debris. He told her to memorize the location.

"If we get separated, this is our rendezvous. Whichever one of us gets here first, assuming we don't have a pack of wolves on our tail, waits half an hour and then pushes off for Seattle. Got it?"

"Yes. And if the wolves are on our heels?"

"Shove off without me. If I don't make the rondy, whatever information you have is more important than I am. Got it?"

"Being a SEAL, you'd probably survive and swim the lake."

He laughed. She wasn't far off the mark. Cassidy hid each paddle separately – just in case. She might have washed out of Basic, but she had a Special Forces kind of mind.

"You only need one paddle for a canoe."

He knew that, but he could see where she might think he didn't.

"That way." Geo pointed uphill sighting off the compass, and they started their hike inland.

Heat

A Dream in Emmaus, Kansas

*T*hey landed in the late afternoon in early January, the town appearing like a diamond bracelet spread across black velvet. *According to the internet, Fairbanks, Alaska, was more than four times larger than the town he'd grown up in, with bedroom communities that brought the greater population to 100,000. Still a small town if you compared it to San Diego ... or even Anchorage, where they'd spent two hours on the ground between flights. Anchorage was like 400,000. The snow outside the windows there had been deep and you could see it because the sun deigned to show its face. Not in Fairbanks. The days were only about four hours long now, with a long dusk, but they'd missed it, catching the last of the northern sun kissing Mount Denali as they flew past it.*

Shane's CSA training taught him to take the aisle seat where you had more flexibility in responding to situations, but he still preferred to see the ground unfolding beneath him. If he couldn't fly the craft, he at least wanted to enjoy the view. He'd seen plenty of mountains in his life – gone skiing in Colorado and New Mexico, rock-climbing in the Grand Tetons and navigating smuggler routes through the Andes, but the Alaska Range seriously impressed him. Denali hove up into the sky like a fist, standing above some of the tallest mountains in North America, a symbol of a bellicose state two-fifths the size of the entire United States. Denali stood at their port wingtip for 15 minutes of the hour flight as if to emphasize just how big the state was, that it needed a mountain that big.

And, then they landed in Fairbanks for a six-hour layover. They ate dinner in The Local, which wasn't a huge restaurant but was the only choice, and then his traveling companions crashed out on the floor in the gate area. Shane had slept on the plane from Seattle, so now he was wide awake in the last place on earth you'd want to be unable to sleep.

The Fairbanks International Airport sounded far too pretentious for a glorified Greyhound bus station and he quickly became bored with the gift shop and watching Mike sleep. After drinking a beer in the bar, he stowed his carryon with Mike and breached security to wander the lower level. Yeah, FIA displayed some unique art. He spent a lot of time taking pics of the Flying Jenny, Ben Eielson's plane that had been the first to fly into what had been the largest town in Alaska in 1924. The blue-and-yellow Curtiss JN-4D looked kind of like a box with wings, but it would have been cutting edge back then, a mere 20 years after the plane had been invented. Shane stared at the stuffed polar bear for quite some time, trying to imagine seeing one in the wild and just as glad that a taxidermist had seen it first. The standing Kodiak brown bear made something move in his bowels. Its claws were as long as his fingers and razor-sharp. You could see all of the airport in a half-hour if you spent an extra-long time in the bathroom. Eventually, he couldn't take it anymore and he walked out of the automatic doors in front of the Alaska Airlines departure desk.

What a weird experience! You didn't go outside from there. The first set of doors closed behind him. You could turn right, or you could turn left for another set of doors. He turned left, exited the doors, and *inhaled razor blades. The hair in his nose froze solid and felt like it broke off and ran over his lips and down his chin. His tonsils felt scorched by an ice wraith. He coughed as his eyes burned and his fingers informed him that he should be wearing gloves.*

A man and woman came out of the fog. He carried a large green duffle over one shoulder, and she pulled a small carryon on wheels.

"See, I was right, you're going to miss the lines." All Shane could see of her was a red coat, black gloves, and brown Ugg boots. The man wore dark pants and a heavy tan coat with a dark stocking cap.

"It's refreshing, isn't it?" Surprised that a total stranger would just greet him, Shane breathed in through his mouth to reply and coughed instead.

"Breathe through your nose," the woman said.

They disappeared into the terminal and Shane decided to go back inside. He sat down on the bench inside the door, back to the triple-pane windows, and watched as the couple stomped the snow off their boots and removed their headgear. Her hair tumbled dark-red down her back. He paused at a reflective surface to straighten his light-brown hair. He peeled off his coat, tucking gloves and hat in the copious pockets.

"You'll remember to bring these when you pick me up?"

"I'll leave them in the car the whole time, so yeah."

She teased and he mugged disapproval, reminding Shane of his parents. Would he ever see them again? He'd bought the Jericho Hotel thinking he would but shipping out to a warzone meant the possibility that he might not.

His fingers no longer tingled, so he went back upstairs, let security screen him again, and bought a coffee at Starbucks. He sat down in a line of chairs staring out the dark windows facing the tarmac. Nothing moved out there in the foggy black. He imagined white walkers prowling the runway just out of his sight, grabbing planes out of the sky and generally spreading a lot of blood.

"Waiting at this airport is the worst." It was the man from downstairs, who sat about four seats to Shane's right. They were the only two people in the boarding area. "Where you headed?"

"Over the pole."

"Cool. You get a few days in Iceland?"

"That's what they tell me. Pictures look interesting."

"And then?"

He was about Shane's dad's age – 50-ish – and had one of those ready smiles that make for easy conversation.

"Middle East."

Now his blue-green eyes scanned Shane, probably taking in the jeans and not-high-and-tight. Shane hated military cuts and he would not be shaving his head like Mike did. He'd probably go real short for the heat of summer and curly for winter. Miristan supposedly had winter.

"Contractor?"

"Yes. I'm a pilot by trade – got my degree in aeronautical engineering." Shane figured it would freak the guy out to know that he was going to go to war as a civilian contractor authorized by a bunch of government agencies to kill Miristani rebels.

"Brad."

"Shane. So, I take it you're from here."

Brad grinned.

"Kinda. Not a lot of people are really from here. When my wife was growing up, she didn't know a lot of kids born here. The adults who stayed here weren't born here. And if you were born here, you mostly left as soon as you could. But now – I guess it's more common. Our kids were born here. Our daughter is in the Lower 48, but our son lives here. I'm originally from back East."

"Your wife's from here?"

"Her family goes back to the 30s in the Panhandle and then they moved to Fairbanks in the 50s, before she was born."

"And, she stayed?"

"Yeah, University of Alaska-Fairbanks is a good college, and – you know, once you're used to this." He pointed to the window where that ominous fog swirled. "It's survivable."

"Which is worse – the cold or the dark."

"Depends on who you ask. The dark gets to me – so I go out to visit my father in Texas sometimes. The cold is harder on her."

"My mom wouldn't let my father leave for long in the winter and they live in the Midwest."

"Yeah. I think she'd prefer it if I were here for the cold, but you know – it's also dark. And, she knows how to handle it. Long as she keeps the woodstove going, the house will stay warm."

"You heat with wood?"

"And, diesel fuel. Mostly with wood."

"Man, your bedrooms must be freezing!" Shane remembered the bite of the air outside the door and knew woodstoves heat one room very well and the rest of the house was a tad chilly. Here, it had to be downright frozen.

"Nope!" Brad took a sip of his own coffee and Shane remembered to sip his own. Starbucks always tasted like someone burned the beans, but it was all that was available, so he told himself to embrace the bitter. "How do your folks heat their house — you said in the Midwest?"

"Mid-Plains."

"My wife's mother is from North Dakota."

"Further south, but we get winter — winds out of the Rockies. Probably 20 below on really cold days, with a 30 below wind chill. And my folks heat with diesel fuel — although some of our neighbors have natural gas — and they use wood heat as a backup."

"Boiler or forced air?"

Brad was just making conversation, Shane supposed. He didn't have anything else to do for the next four hours. Mike hated planes, so he'd sleep like a log here.

"Boiler."

Brad drew something out of his carryon, a small stack of papers stapled together.

"I invented this. You interested in looking? It might be up your alley with the engineering and all."

"Sure." What else would he do with the hours? It beat reading a book on his phone.

Brad's company name blazed across the cover — Waste Energy Resources Company. The WERC-U was their sole product — a vat that sat on top of a woodstove. Couplings in the side of the pot connected to a heat exchanger plumbed into the home's forced hydronic heating system. Pumps distributed the heat around the house using the existing baseboard.

"Wow, this is a great idea. This is the kind of stuff people in the Midwest have tried to figure out for years — how do you get the heat *from your woodstove room to your bedrooms. Propped doors and fans just never quite do the trick."*

"Why do you think I invented it? Our yellow Lab was complaining it was freezing in the master bedroom one day and I went downstairs to fill my humidity pot. I'm an electrician by trade, so I used the temperature probe on my fluke meter to check how hot the water was. One-eighty. I looked over at the boiler which is maybe eight feet away and I thought 'That's one-eighty also. If I could just get the heat from that pot – wait. There's baseboard running right behind the woodstove.' It didn't happen that fast. There were pieces to put together, but once I had the idea, it was like a lightbulb went on."

The door of the woodstove clanked loudly, and Shane jerked awake, glaring at Cai who stocked the stove. The light of the fire hurt his head, so he squeezed his eyes shut. He could hear a strumming guitar and what sounded like Jazz singing *Silver Bells*. He no longer quaked with cold and felt over-warmed and slightly sweaty. His fingertips felt raw as he wiped them across his forehead, encountering the dried blood matting his hair.

"Is there water?" His voice sounded weak, raspy as a cat's tongue, and his throat felt like sandpaper. Cai continued what he was doing, though he glanced toward Shane.

"I need some water."

"I'll get it in just a minute."

Thirty seconds of waiting felt like an hour of torture, but eventually, Cai closed the woodstove and came to hold a water bottle to Shane's lips.

"It's so hot here."

"You have hypothermia. We're just trying to keep you warm. You want me to fold down some of these blankets?"

Shane nodded. Cai helped him roll onto his left side, facing the woodstove, his back to the family festivities he was too sick to care about. It took a little while for the pain to dissipate enough for him to grow drowsy and while he lay there staring at the woodstove, he thought about how you could run pipes from a pot to the baseboard and get heat throughout the entire house. He wiped the sweat from his brow. Maybe not run the heat to his room. He drifted away, buoyed on dreams of heat exchangers, and running hot water.

Sharing News

Hutchinson, Kansas

Ren pushed back his hood as he got back into the Snow-Cat. Lawson climbed into the other door. Travis sat up on the back seat, looking like a teenager woken up on a Saturday morning. Eden didn't wake up.

"Where are we?"

"We're at Hutchinson. There are soup and warm showers."

"I thought we were just going to push through," Travis said.

"That was the hope, but Lawson wants some time to baby the machine and we've all been in this tin can for nearly twenty-four hours. I need some alone time in a bathroom. Let's go."

Eden sat up and shrugged off the blanket she and Travis shared.

"Is there coffee?" She settled her concealed rig into the small of her back. Travis grimaced from behind her. He hadn't been raised in Alaska. His Secret Service agent Randy taught him how to shoot on their journey and gave him a gun to protect himself, but he couldn't make him like it. Randy stayed in Wichita.

"I'm not sure, but the soup's hot."

Outside, the Hutchinson Fairgrounds lay knee-deep in snow, but a set of bright lights directed them into one of the buildings where a man named Jared greeted them with something resembling coffee.

"Thank you for hosting us," Ren said.

"Least we can do since you're resupplying us." Helen de Wald wore her coat indoors because this building was heated by a barrel stove that just didn't spread the heat around. She brought bowls of soup to them. Jared provided them with a plate of pilot bread to sop it up. "Until your first trucks got through a few days ago, we were talking about closing down. People aren't able to trade when they don't have food to eat."

"My crew tells me you're trading high-quality goods. There's lots of people in Wichita who will appreciate it."

"Well, now that we have food to trade, we're helping the local area."

"What are the roads like around here?"

"We haven't been further than Ellsworth since the Pulse." Although Helen said she was FEMA, Jacobson commanded the Knights and she deferred to him to a large degree. "These storms keep coming every few days and some of the towns have gotten quite combative with interlopers. The road to Ellsworth has no hostile communities, but with this latest storm – you might want to stay until the storm breaks."

Ren glanced at Lawson, who seemed to know Jacobson. He used a tablet to talk with the Knights drivers operating the plow that worked to clear the road for the trucks. The Snow-Cat could go forward without that help, but the point was to get the trucks through.

"They'll let us know. If they can clear the road as well as they believe, we should be able to set out in about four hours."

"Couldn't we go out ahead of the convoy?" Eden asked.

"No, that isn't a good idea." Ren knew when to ignore his instincts to forge ahead. "There's safety in numbers. Go ahead and use the shower, maybe catch a nap. It'll be about noon when we set out again."

"Okay." She and Travis left with a Knight by the name of Kriczek. Ren, Lawson, Jacobson, and Helen looked at each other from around the barrel stove.

"Any idea how much snow is expected in the next twelve hours?" Lawson asked.

"There's no weather service anymore," Jacobson explained. "We can only cope with what comes, and I'm told by people from around here that there's never been a winter that was so snowy."

"I haven't seen so many winter storms in my lifetime either." Ren sighed. "There was a winter back in the 1880s like this."

"*The Long Winter*?" Helen asked.

"Wilder?" She nodded. "Read those to my granddaughter. Great stories. Based on real events. Where were you from?"

"Kansas City."

"I'm sorry for your losses."

"Nobody there but an abusive ex-husband. My parents died a few years ago. My brother lives in Italy. I did have good friends, though. I've mourned them already."

Ren looked at Jacobson.

"Chicago's gone."

"Not close with your folks?"

"You don't join the Knights because you want to be a pastry chef. My folks weren't in Chicago. They were visiting Boston and Boston's still with us. They're good people. I'm not. They might be better off without me."

"Seems like you're doing a good thing here."

"I'm getting paid. Let me show you to the showers. Then, Lawson, if you don't mind, maybe you can tell me a bit about what's going on in Wichita."

"If you don't mind hanging out with me while I change oil, sure."

"I've got no pressing duties at the moment."

"I can find my own way to the showers," Ren assured.

"I'll show you," Helen said.

He nodded and followed her out the door to follow a trail through the snow. Eden had small feet and she knew how to walk on ice and snow – with a wide stance. Travis slipped and slid beside her. He wondered which of them held onto the other.

"You're not what I expected," Helen admitted.

"What did you expect?"

"The great Warren Sullivan – king-like. Imperious. A libertarian firebrand, ordering mere humans around like Genghis Khan."

"And I'm not living up to expectations?"

An icy blast of wind took Ren's breath away. Helen pulled up a facemask over her mouth and nose.

"My God, that's cold."

"Definitely. Probably minus 20 and then there's chill factor. You're more like ordinary people."

She led the way up onto a wooden porch and pushed a door open. They could hear Travis and Eden giggling.

"I'll shower there to stay out of their way. Thank you for showing me."

"Jacobson won't let his men fraternize with FEMA workers." Helen stared at him, communicating volumes.

Ren felt himself blushing.

"You're not married, are you?"

"A widower. I still love my wife."

"I'm not looking for a lifelong commitment – just a shower together."

"Not my thing, young lady, but I appreciate the offer."

Helen sighed and unzipped her coat.

"I'll just go over that way and grab a shower of my own."

Ren realized that meant she'd be able to see him as he showered. He'd been married at least a decade when he'd been her age. He'd had the opportunity to cheat on Lottie while she was alive, and he'd never done it. Would this be cheating now? Yeah, he kind of felt like it would. He was flattered, but —no, he wasn't a sex-in-the-shower-with-a-random-acquaintance kind of guy.

The wind shrieked around the shower trailer and shook the building ever so slightly. A four-hour respite from this storm might not be enough.

Grief

December 26

Emmaus

Shane opened his eyes when Jill swapped the IV bags. He rubbed his forehead with a chapped hand, eyes narrowed.

"How you doing?" she asked.

"Okay. Weird dreams. You're dosing me with cannabis oil, aren't you?" Jill's flinch gave her away. "Where'd you get it?"

"A friend. I think Jason Breen is his source. He brought it yesterday. How'd you know?"

"Sativa always gives me weird dreams. So, that bag – what's in there?"

"Glucose and a little something-something."

"No more, Mom."

"Your pain would be so much worse."

Shane sighed. With a wrench of will, he blurted out a new confession.

"Mom, cannabis is my whiskey. It's not a good idea."

"You never told me that before."

"It was a long time ago. Marnie wanted to quit smoking cigarettes, so I gave up pot as a solidarity thing. We nearly broke up. We weren't nice to one another for a while. When I went back to school that fall, I didn't start again, but I'm tempted sometimes and I'm scared of that."

"I'll reduce the dose, but you need it for now. Okay?"

The pain spiraling through his body warned him that he needed pain relief and the options were limited.

"Fine, for now."

"You need anything else?"

"Yeah." He sighed again. He hated that he couldn't do anything for himself. "Could you – um – bathe me. I just feel disgusting."

"Of course. I'll go warm some water."

Shane rubbed his forehead and tried to relax back on his pillows. Everything hurt, most especially his back from lying flat all day. He wanted to roll onto his side but knew he couldn't. He couldn't move either leg without nearly passing out from pain and his right arm lacked any strength. Mike materialized on the couch, wearing black fatigue pants and a white t-shirt, eyes narrowed as he laughed at some joke. Shane felt the lancing thorn of guilt pierce his heart. Jazz settled on the floor beside him.

"What are you seeing?" she asked.

He wiped tears. From the swelling around his left eye, he guessed he had a heck of a shiner.

"He had the flu and he insisted I leave him in Santa Fe. And, now, even if the weather breaks, I can't go get him. Even if he's alive, I can't."

She grabbed her pillow and positioned it over his bruised ribs so he could sob without quite so much pain. Not bruised. Cracked. He could feel the cartilage crackling as he heaved a deep breath. Bracing it helped.

"I wasn't trying to kill myself." She didn't argue. "I left the gun behind."

"I wondered about that. So, you remember what happened?"

"Not really." Skiing and deer. Then cold. It made no sense that Jacob had been there. And something about a turtle. What was real and what was a hallucination? "I remember you. Thank you for coming to get me."

"No problem – this time."

"I'll try to accommodate that." He paid for his chuckle with more pain. Jacob appeared behind her, his leathery face smiling. "Um, can you do me a favor?"

"Sure."

He wiped tears and snot on the back of his hand.

"Could you go up to my room. There's a Bible on my dresser and there's envelopes inside. Can you bring them here?"

"Of course." She left the pillow and stood. "You're okay on your own?"

"Mom's just in the next room and I am definitely not going anywhere."

She disappeared up the stairs. Mike leaned against the newel post.

"Hey, buddy. You know you didn't have a choice, right?"

"Doesn't feel like it."

"That's the grief talking," Jacob said. Mike's ghost nodded in agreement.

"How do I make it stop?"

"You don't. Jesus does. You set it down every day until it's second nature."

"I don't know how."

"You'll figure it out." The old man faded as a beam of sunlight came in between the drapes.

Jill set two bowls of steaming water on the hearth beneath the woodstove.

"You okay?"

"Just really emotional right now."

"That's the injuries. It'll get better."

He nodded. He wanted to believe her. She just slid an arm behind his back and he tensed.

"Just relax, and I'll do it all, starting with washing your hair, which requires I get rid of the pillows. Trust me. I've done this hundreds of times with people far more injured than you. And, you're right. When it's done, after you've had a little nap, it'll feel so much better."

She turned out to be so right. It hurt to move, and it hurt to be moved, but he felt almost human by the time she'd finished, and it was only mildly embarrassing to have Jazz help turn him when he wasn't wearing any pants. When they were done, they left him on his left side and Jazz set his Bible just to the left of his mattress where he could easily reach it when he had the energy to do so. He didn't right then. For the first time in a long time, he wasn't afraid to close his eyes. He dreamed and some of his nightmares still lingered, but he saw light at the end of that dark tunnel now.

Dealing

Ami lifted the top layer of gauze on Kix Conopher's belly and smiled slightly. The bleeding from the PEG tube had slowed and would stop soon judging by the rate of coagulation. She'd successfully catheterized his rectum and bladder. Although he could no longer move much beyond a few muscles in his right thigh, his breathing sounded good.

"You hold on," she told him, placing a gloved hand on his forehead. His eyes didn't open this time, but his right eye rolled upward under the closed lid and the right corner of his mouth twitched.

She heard weeping in the exam room across the hall.

"I'm so sorry," Marnie said. "The paralysis just kept ascending and without mechanical respiration, there was nothing I could do when he stopped breathing."

Wanda offered to drive them back to their house. Marnie promised the body would be transported to wherever they chose. Ami sat down in the lounge and tried to think of what she would say when Marnie finally turned her way. Death stalked all in the third world and Ami had often been accused by her fellow doctors of being heartless on the subject. Death and life played back and forth, and you could spend all your time grieving if you didn't understand that. What some called heartless was truly pragmatism.

Marnie lowered herself onto the sofa and dropped her head onto the back. They sat silently for several minutes.

"How Kix?"

"Still living. He's pretty much lost all bodily functions except breathing."

"Your boy Dylan?"

"His breathing was never affected."

"That makes no sense. Calvin was classic signs of polio or possibly transverse myelitis. Kix appears almost like double hemiplegia."

"Dylan's presented almost like a cerebellar stroke, but now it's hemiplegia and aphasia."

"Is this the start of another epidemic or are these three totally different illnesses?"

"Yes, absolutely."

Marnie raised her head to stare at Ami.

"You have no idea?"

"I don't. It's too early in the process to be sure. Did you get blood from Calvin and his parents?"

"I did."

Ami stood, feeling like she was 50 years older than she was.

"I'm going back to the B&B and run panels on all three victims and their families."

"What should I tell the Conophers when they return?"

"If the seizures are stable, they should take him home. Jason said he can supply cannabis oil to anyone who asks. Show them how to feed and drain him. We're not equipped for coma patients." Ami sighed. Marnie nodded.

The situation flowed and answers hid, but Ami spoke the language of viruses. Sooner or later this one would tell on itself, if only she stared at it long enough.

Sharing a Novel Idea

Rob loaded quarter logs into the woodstove. They'd need to clean the ashtray in the next few days, which would mean moving Shane. Maybe he could just scoop coals from one side to the other. When he closed the door and locked the handles, he saw Shane wasn't asleep.

"How are you feeling?"

"Awake some. Not so in and out." Shane shifted his shoulders, grimacing.

"How's your head?"

"Clearer, I think."

"That's not what I mean."

Shane sighed.

"This is giving me plenty of time to think. It's still not ever going to feel good, is it?"

"No. You learn to live with it. You don't ever learn to be comfortable with it."

Shane nodded.

"I noticed you've had some different reading material. Is that helping?"

Shane stared at the ceiling. Rob figured he'd overstepped and moved to retreat.

"They – okay, I *think* I was dreaming, but – Jacob and Vi were there. And – yeah, I just want to answer some things for myself right now."

"I'm not going to push. I did notice, however, that you're using unopened letters from your grandparents as bookmarks."

"I keep meaning to read them, but then I get tired."

"I think the trick there is probably to read the notes first."

"Yeah. That doesn't feel right for some reason."

"You warm enough?"

"Plenty. It's still freezing upstairs, isn't it?"

"Polar. If I could just figure out how to get the heat from this room and the kitchen or even the basement to upstairs…." Rob sighed and shrugged.

"Guy showed me something – up in an airport in Alaska. A pot on top of the stove."

"That does make the kitchen more humid."

"He plumbed it into a heat exchanger and the other side into the baseboard."

Rob stared at him. It sounded like a fever dream, but then he stared at the space between the woodstove and the baseboard behind him. He'd drained the baseboard this fall when it became clear they couldn't keep the system going, but with a couple of pumps – wow, heated bedrooms again.

Shane's eyelids slid toward closed, but he pulled them open again.

"What do you think?"

"I think we should look into that when we aren't worried about starving to death. It's a novel idea, though."

Shane nodded.

"Need to sleep now."

"Yeah, enjoy. We'll talk later."

Shane's swollen lips curved in a slight smile and Rob left him to his dreams.

Infiltration

Kenmore, Washington

The sun visibly lowered in the sky as they scanned Kenmore College with binoculars. The college started life as a seminary but had become some sort of New Age Healing Center in the 1980s before being bought out by an IT university. Lots of white and glass buildings with a chapel in the middle beside what looked like a rain garden. An antenna rested on the peak of the old chapel, which sat in the center of the five-building cluster that served 300 students a semester.

"They probably set up a dampening field," Cassidy murmured, scanning the area with field glasses. After a night under a tarp, they'd spent the day working their way up from the lake, before they'd finally reached their destination. They observed from far enough away that they didn't risk being overheard, but Geo knew the feeling that you needed to be quiet. Geo watched through his glasses.

"There's a motor pool. See the covered truck?" She shifted her glassing to where the truck passed into a garage created by tarps hung off the side of one of the buildings. "Could be anything in the trucks. Enough military vehicles though that you can bet all the services met up here. You ready for this?"

"Yes. What do we do with the gear that makes us look suspicious?"

"We stow it here then walk a half-click in that direction, so we look like we came by road."

They stowed the gear in two dry bags, one sized for her, and Geo concealed it while she gazed around to try and memorize the location.

The late-afternoon sun lowered into the trees as they walked up the road to the campus and Geo was hungry enough that he didn't need to fake it. Cassidy dragged one foot a little like they'd walked far too far. A soldier in disheveled fatigues straightened from a task spied them and spoke into a radio.

Here we go. No turning back now.

A moment later four soldiers greeted them in the road, their guns drawn but pointed toward the ground.

"Who are you? What are you doing here?"

Cassidy didn't need to fake fear. He smelled it on her.

"We came from Seattle." Geo played exactly what he was, so he didn't flinch from the guns, although Cassidy cringed enough for both of them. "I'm Geo. I'm with the Teams. I heard you might be looking for guys like me."

A tall blond soldier with brown eyes patted Geo down, finding his gun and knife and stripping off his pack. A sergeant came striding up.

"Take the girl and have Franky talk to her."

Cassidy grabbed for Geo's hand, looking like a terrified waif. Geo surely hoped she was acting. He knew this game. Divide and conquer. Find out how different their stories were. The blond guy prodded him in the kidney.

"Come with me," the sergeant ordered, and a bag went over Geo's head. He stumbled along for 642 steps, the last 200 up an incline. They removed the bag in a small windowless room with two chairs and a desk pushed up against one wall.

"What's your name?"

"George Tully. Geo. I was a Navy SEAL out of Whitby, got caught up in the Takedown."

"And where have you been since then?"

"Homeless camps mostly. Had to keep moving."

"You *heard* about us, huh? From who?"

"People. The refugees talk. Cassidy knew some people who said you were here. The Knights are looking hard for guys like me, so we decided to risk coming, see if you were real."

"So you're looking for a unit. Ain't got a lot of SEALs here."

"I don't have to work with my kind. I can be an asset to any group. These Knight fuckers need payback."

The door opened, allowing Geo the briefest glimpse of a glassed-in atrium lit by a brilliant sunset. The enlisted handed the sergeant Geo's identification which he'd put in the bottom of the pack, so it looked like he hid it.

"Who's the girl?"

"Cassidy. She was my brother's girlfriend."

"You two aren't keeping each other warm at night."

Geo had always been shy and awkward around girls and though he'd gotten over that in recent years, he felt his cheeks flush at the thought of holding a warm female body against his belly.

"It ain't like that."

"Sure, it ain't. What's your brother's name?"

"Jim. That's how we met."

"Where?"

"Wow, some hole in the wall bar near SU. Don't remember the name. I was a little drunk."

"Where's your brother?"

"Iraq, I think."

"The Takedown happens, and you head to rescue his girl?"

"Um, no. We just ran into each other at Pike's Market. There's a refugee camp there. We're just friends and two is better than one. We can watch each other's back. One can sleep while the other guards. That sort of thing."

"Hmm."

Geo's stomach growled. You couldn't fake hunger and the sergeant heard the proof.

"Take a load off. I'll be back in a little while."

Geo lowered himself onto the chair as the door closed behind the sergeant and then the lights went out.

Complicating Relationships

Columbus, Ohio

Perry joined them for dinner for the first time in two weeks. He looked haggard – dark circles under his eyes, cheeks hollow, and he needed a shave. They could hear Joseph snoring loudly in the bedroom.

"This is good, Julian." Perry moved the food around on his plate. He'd eaten a few bites. "Sorry, my appetite is a little weird."

"It's fine. Just glad to see you on your feet again."

"Long as I can sit down 30 seconds out of every minute. What's going on with us?"

Perry was the unacknowledged leader of their group. Julian realized he'd felt awkward in the position over the last week.

"The compound is in lockdown, the city will shoot people who try to travel, the highways to the west are clogged with a month of snow and not being plowed. The good news is SullCorp thinks they have enough food on hand to make it to spring."

Perry took a deep breath as if to say something, but then started coughing and couldn't stop. Andi brought him a glass of water.

"I'm not up for a jailbreak just yet and Joseph's not going anywhere for a while. How are you two feeling?"

"Fine so far." Perry looked at Andi, who shrugged.

"I had a cold a couple of weeks ago." She shrugged again.

"I need to crash. I'll take the couch if you two want to sleep in a bed."

"Sounds good." Julian exchanged a glance with Andi as Perry headed toward the couch. She wrapped the leftovers. Julian took a shower. He didn't know how he felt about sharing a bed with Andi. He was just sitting down on the bed when she came to the door.

"We can just sleep if you prefer." She closed the door behind her.

They lay there in the dark, staring at the ceiling. The wind whistled around the warehouse.

"Good night?" Andi seemed to hold her breath.

Julian rolled onto his side facing her, caressed her cheek.

"It complicates things."

"It doesn't have to. I promise I won't." Her eyes reflected some light from the window as she looked at him.

"I don't have any condoms."

"Modern birth control. I've got, uh, 18 months."

"It's not – I spent all that time in prison. I've never tested positive for anything, but there's a risk."

"Not if you've never tested positive. You were tested, yes?"

"Several times." He slid his fingers down her throat to settle his hand on one of her breasts. She wasn't wearing a bra under her t-shirt. "I just felt like I should tell you."

"Done. I'll take the risk. Bet starvation or marauders will get me before HIV anyway."

She rolled over and up, straddling him.

"Maybe we should discuss...."

She covered his mouth with hers and kissed away all his objections.

VIP Guests

Jericho Ghost Town

Grant, Emily, and Ami waited while April Halloran read through her notes. Her husband Brian had just explained that Dylan's right side was paralyzed. He had some slight movement, but no control. Brian would return the day after tomorrow to start physical therapy. April smiled tremulously. She seemed less resilient than her husband.

"It's called aphasia. I suppose you know that, Dr. Ceylon."

"Ami, please. It was Dr. Kletti's diagnosis. How severe is it?"

"Moderate Broca. He understands most of what is said so long as he can concentrate. He struggles to express his thoughts – to find words. He could match short sentences to photos, but he couldn't select words to describe photos, so I suspect writing is impaired and reading is probably slowed but intact."

"Can you recover from that?" Emily asked.

"Once, if, the encephalitis clears, he'll improve and I can help him learn ways to cope. Somewhat like Brian was explaining, the brain can rewire itself around damaged areas. He's only 19, so there's reason to hope for a substantial recovery if --."

The radio on Grant's belt squealed.

"I need you out here," Jim said. "Over."

"I gotta take this. Emily, Ami, you can explain it to me later."

They both nodded.

"Where are you? Over."

"Front gate. Damnedest thing I've ever seen. Uh, over."

Javi wore sunglasses even on this overcast day. Jim had an AR15 at the ready, pointed vaguely at the huge orange track-vehicle. When Ren Sullivan emailed them via a Knight channel last night, Grant hadn't been entirely certain what was going on was real, but here they were, and he recognized the richest man in America.

"Why are you bringing her here?" he asked after Sullivan explained who his passengers were.

"I can't risk anyone recognizing her and I can't take a Tucker Snow Cat through town without just about everybody seeing it. I've got enough food to pay their keep until the dust-off."

"How do you even know what's going on here?"

"You think I didn't know who bought this place? I'm not that stupid. I should have done something to stop you back when you were going after McAuliff, but my wife was dying, so I didn't want another battle to fight. This time, I figure you can work for the people instead of against them."

Grant sighed.

"I only have to take two people?"

"And food for four."

Grant asked him to get back into the vehicle and moved to confer with Jim and Javi.

"She's the daughter of the acting president," Jim pointed out.

"Allegedly," Javi countered. They both ran true to course. "You have no idea who she really is."

"Why would Ren Sullivan lie to me?"

"Maybe he's been duped."

"This is Warren Sullivan, one of the most astute businessmen of our time," Jim argued.

Okay, they weren't going to be any help and Javi returned from the town earlier today to report that Shane was injured. He'd live but would be down for several weeks. It was beginning to look like Patterson was right. The field of agents was almost deserted. Patterson had arranged a meeting with Josh Callahan later in the day. Until then, Grant alone could make these decisions.

"I'm going to let them stay. Jim – uh, no, Javi – could you ask Emily to make up the spare room just as soon as she's done with the doctors?"

Javi winced.

"You're right. All I can see is a big orange blob. I'll take care of that."

Jim waited for him to close the door behind him.

"I can't imagine what he's going through. Tough guy."

355

Grant wondered if Dylan would take his diagnosis and prognosis as well as Javi took his.

"Just back me up here. Stand there and pretend you're walking point."

"I've done this before, youngster." Jim jerked his head to indicate Grant should get on with it.

Eden Maracal and her boyfriend Michael shouldered their packs and followed Grant inside while the Tucker made a wide loop at the end of the road and headed back toward Old 24. Emily met them in the foyer.

"Welcome. Please hang your coats and take off your boots and I'll show you to your room. We only have one left. I hope that's okay."

"It's fine. We're --." Eden blushed.

"Okay, then." Emily probably didn't want to know.

"Where's Javi?"

"Ami asked him to go with her. Brian reported someone sick in the neighborhood. It looks like it might be related to Dylan's case."

Grant paused in following them up the stairs. Was it a good thing that there were other cases Ami could learn from or should he wish his son were the last of the affected? Either way, it seemed heartless to think so.

Hard News

Lufgren Farm

A mi had wondered about the yellow farmhouse a few times since moving into the neighborhood, but she'd been too busy to be friendly, even if she'd been inclined. Brian seemed to have made friends with the family that owned the farm, though the darker couple were the parents of the ill boy.

They'd drawn the curtains and only used the light from the hall to illuminate the room. The boy practically screamed when Ami peeled his eyelid back to check his pupillary response. While the mother explained that he'd taken ill Christmas Day, Ami tested his reflexes. The right leg lay completely flaccid and the boy didn't even wince at pinpricks. It hurt him when she moved his weakening left leg. He had significant foot drop, but he could still push against her hand. He could still use both hands and, although he had a hard time concentrating because of an ongoing migraine, he made sense when he spoke. She asked his parents to follow her downstairs. The mother said she would stay, and the blonde girl should know what's going on. Ami had previously met Keri Lufgren, who interpreted for the girl, who appeared to be deaf. Ami addressed her comments to the father.

"This is a form of encephalitis. We don't know very much about it. Your son is following the pattern of another young man we treated. I hate to bring bad news, but the paralysis eventually progressed to where he couldn't breathe, and he died of hypoxic asphyxiation." Both the father and the blonde girl's eyes widened. "The good news – perhaps, is that he is progressing more slowly. From what you've told me, anyway, it's nearly twice as long."

"He'll need a respirator?" Keri said. Ami realized she was interpreting for the girl.

"Likely, but we don't have any. We've tried to make the one we had work, but the Pulse fried it."

"What do we do?" the father asked. Keri's husband straightened from where he'd been leaning in the doorway to the kitchen.

"I have no idea," Ami admitted. "I wish I did."

Alex Lufgren was a big man and his blue eyes were sharp and intelligent.

"Is this like polio?" he asked.

"This version of it seems to follow a similar pattern except that feeling is lost."

"So, we don't have a respirator. What else would work?"

"Nothing. Intubating him and hand bagging him could support him for a few hours, but he might need days or weeks or the rest of his life. I'm sorry to deliver such news, and I hope the progress of this disease stalls before it gets to that point, but you need to know the eventual prognosis."

The blonde girl signed as if in protest, angry, and denying. Her brother didn't speak as he replied in sign. And then the father thanked Ami for stopping by and then she explained that if she could get blood from them all, it might move her a little closer to understanding this virus. Mark Ramirez was the first one she tested. The deaf girl signed something rude but let her take blood.

Pete settled quietly on his back while she drew his blood.

"Will this help?" he asked.

"I don't know."

"I'm going to die, aren't I?"

"I hope not. The other two patients are still alive."

"When my other leg started hurting, I knew." He looked toward his mother. "I'm sorry, Mom, I just want to not lie to myself."

Alice Ramirez fled the room. Ami thanked Pete for giving her what she needed and promised him she would try to unravel the mystery of this illness. She knew she probably wouldn't find it before he needed it, but she left him with hope as she found her way to where Javi waited by the kitchen door. He slipped an arm around her shoulders as they walked to the Trooper.

"It's not your fault," he assured her.

"I know. I can't save everyone – unless I can figure out this damned virus and I can't seem to do that." She heaved a deep breath and asked Javi to drive her home. "Maybe something in these samples will finally put me on the right path."

"There's the spirit, but you're going to need to drive. I probably shouldn't even have driven here and now that it's getting dark – yeah, nothing but grey."

She took the keys from him and let him sort out how to get himself into the car.

"You're going to figure it out."

"How do you know?"

"I have faith in you. So, let's head home."

Acceptance

Kenmore, Washington

Geo worked his tongue around the inside of his mouth to raise some spit. He needed water, but there hadn't been any in this small room when the lights went out, so he assumed there still was no water here. His training taught him to withstand all sorts of torture and going without food and water was basic BUDS training. He stayed in the chair and waited. Time passed, but there was no way to know how much. Thirsty, hungry and he needed to pee. A paradox. Had to be at least two hours, maybe as much as four. He rested in a light doze, listening for any noise in the hallway. When the door opened, he merely slid his butt back on the seat, so he was sitting up straight. He blinked as the lights came back on.

The sergeant leveled a direct gaze on him and started asking him the same questions from before. Geo answered them about the same, adding a few of the agreed-upon details, letting some others drop. Nobody told the same story twice in a row. The sergeant read through a spiral steno pad, frowning.

"Our goal in gathering here is to reestablish the rule of law and remove the usurpers in Seattle from power. How do you feel about that?"

"I became a Navy SEAL to uphold the US Constitution and defend the country against enemies foreign and domestic. The mercenaries in Seattle aren't part of the US government."

"So, you'd be willing to use your skills to attack them?"

Geo nodded.

"If there's a proper chain of command, yes." The sergeant's name patch read Yarnell. He shifted. That suggested a dubious chain of command. "It doesn't have to be SEAL command. I'm willing to work with any branch of the US military, but there needs to be someone higher than a sergeant giving the orders."

The sergeant stared at Geo, who thought he saw a twinkle.

"Come with me."

Geo stood and followed. The atrium lay in darkness, but the sergeant carried a lantern. Geo followed Yarnell down that incline, outside, across a paved area and into what the maps said was the campus administration building. Geo remembered dorm rooms occupied the upper floors. They took the stairs to the second floor where a large cafeteria served its intended purpose. Lanterns lit the space, although the kitchen, visible through the pass-through, had electric lights. A fir tree wrapped in ribbons and shiny things occupied a corner – a reminder that yesterday was Christmas. The sergeant led Geo to a table where Cassidy waited. She looked nervous, but then she winked surreptitiously.

"Thank God." She sounded as nervous as she looked, but he sensed she was a better actor than he was. "Are you okay?"

"Yeah. You?" She nodded. "What did they ask you?"

"Well, first they locked me in a windowless room for – I don't know. Then this female soldier came in and asked me a shit-ton of questions. How did we meet? How long we'd been traveling together? Where Jim is serving? Then they left me alone for a while and came back and asked the same questions again. And then they brought me here. Here." She offered a bottled water. The seal was still intact, so he cracked it and drank half.

An enlisted soldier approached them. Her name patch read Braxton. Her delicate bone structure might have been pretty under other circumstances, but she just looked spare in fatigues with straight dark hair that hadn't been styled. She said they could get food from the communal pot. There had to be about a hundred people here, representing all the forces, although Geo didn't see any he thought were SEAL. Geo had just about cleaned his bowl when a lieutenant called for everyone's attention.

"Our expertise grows. Geo Tully is a Navy SEAL who sought us out after seeing the Knights reign of terror in Seattle firsthand. We'll be working with him over the next few days to improve our plans to begin taking the fight to Seattle. As long as people seek the safety B&W is promising, they will support the monsters, but when they see that as false hope, they will remember the freedoms they are currently forsaking. Stand up, Geo, so people can see who you are."

Geo stood and the crowd clapped. As he sat down, the lieutenant introduced Cassidy.

"Who is the lieutenant?" Geo asked Braxton.

She smiled, gaze still on the lieutenant. Cassidy stood. A catcall from somewhere in the crowd elicited a few others. She sat down, meeting Geo's gaze. The story of Tailhook came to Geo's mind. He'd need to assert his dominance sooner rather than later. Maybe they needed to revise their bio to include some more personal attachment.

"Lt. Reed is Army out of Ft. Lewis. He's serving under Colonel McGowan at Provisional Base Alpha."

"He's the base commander here?"

"He is. McGowan is the regional commander."

"Is that as high as it goes?"

"For now. More military personnel find us every day, so it's likely someone of higher rank will join us soon. In the meantime, you go with the army you have."

"Of course. So, am I the only SEAL?"

"I don't think so. There's been a few show up. I'm not sure where they've been assigned. Provisional Base Alpha typically likes to talk with the Special Forces at some point."

"That's near here then?"

Braxton laughed. That wasn't for him to know yet.

Geo noted people watched them as they passed their table. Was the curiosity because they were new or because they weren't to be trusted?

"Is there a bathroom?" Geo asked Braxton.

She pointed to a door near the pass-through to the kitchen. Geo and Cassidy exchanged glances and then he headed that way. A single emergency light lit the interior room. Geo scanned the urinals and let the door close behind him. It felt good to relieve some pressure. When he returned to the table, Braxton offered to escort them to their quarters. She grabbed a lantern, told Geo to grab a second one and they took stairs to the fifth floor. A long corridor lit by emergency lights opened onto dorm rooms to either side.

"This is the only shower room. Men shower at night. Women shower in the morning. There's only hot water when they're preparing the meals, but you could probably get a shower now, Petty Officer. It'll still be warm...ish."

"Thank you." A little way down the corridor, she pushed open a door on the left.

"We're sharing a room?" Cassidy sounded a little concerned.

"You're partners, right?"

When Cassidy shot a glance his way, Geo nodded. He preferred it this way. It would worry him if Cassidy were on her own, especially considering that sexism appeared to be accepted.

"We've been sharing heat for a while now." Cassidy shrugged, smiling.

The dorm room had two single beds with a highboy dresser between them, closets at their feet, and a toilet and sink area. Their gear, including weapons, already rested on the blankets. Braxton said "good night".

"What do you think?" Cassidy asked as the door closed.

He held up a hand, shaking his head. He tried the knob. The door wasn't locked. He gestured her to follow him into the bathroom and he turned on the sink full blast. He leaned in to whisper in her ear.

"They could be bugging us. Go back into the main room. Sit on the bunk you want. I'll follow in a minute."

He washed his hands and shut off the water.

"Beats sleeping on a steam grate."

"It's not as wet," she agreed. "Do you trust these guys?"

"No further than you could throw me. But we'll see how things go." He picked up a towel from the stack on the foot of his bed. "I'm going to grab a shower. You sit guard. Wouldn't want anything disappearing while we're both out."

Geo showered alone, in lukewarm water, but there was soap. It only took the apocalypse to make soap seem a luxury. He needed time to sort through what they knew so far. All their stuff returned to them and they weren't locked in. It seemed he missed something. He put on his same dirty clothes and went back to relieve Cassidy who was in friendly conversation with Braxton in the hall. The floor had been deserted when they got here, but there were now doors propped as people got ready for bed.

Cassidy remarked that she was exhausted, then closed the door, jerking her head toward the sink room.

"I don't think there are any listening devices, but they might be cleverer than I think they are."

She shut off the sink and went back into the bedroom.

"Braxton's kind of chatty," she reported. If anyone was listening, them not talking would seem odd, after all. "Lt. Reed is the highest-ranking officer on base. That's what they call this anyway. He's got a lot of plans for bringing the Knights low."

"Good. Someone has to pay them back for what they did."

"Calm down. Jim would hate to see you like this." She leaned in and whispered into his ear. "PBA is northeast. She looks that way every time she references it."

He flashed her a thumbs-up sign and spoke in a normal voice.

"Yup. Radio girl, huh?"

"I told you about the DJ gigs I did."

"Yeah, I really probably wasn't listening. What was the name of the bar we met at? They kept asking me that question and I really couldn't remember."

"The Elbow Room."

"Ah! Yeah. Could barely turn around in that place on a Friday night."

"Yeah. Remember that guy who wanted to pick a fight with you because of the high and tight?"

"Navy swabbies. Idiot."

"Drunken idiot. Anyway, now that I've had a bit to think about it, I'm going to grab that shower."

"Don't take too long. I'm exhausted and fresh out of reading material. And the water won't be warm." He signaled she should look around.

She nodded, grabbed a towel, and went out the door. He checked the guns while he waited. Nothing seemed out of place and that worried him. He turned off the lantern and stared out the window at the foot of his bed. The campus was mostly dark. A few minutes later, quiet descended over the complex and Geo realized he could no longer hear the generator that supplied limited lights. Cassidy seemed to be gone longer than necessary, so he dozed sitting upright when she got back.

"The water was barely tolerable."

She leaned into his ear.

"Dorms this floor and the one above. There's security on the third floor. Not sure why." Then in a louder voice, she said "The lights, when they go out, even the emergency lights go down. Ever try to dress by Braille?"

"Great. These lanterns are solar battery, so best turn that off too. You should get some sleep. I'll take guard."

"I don't think you need to. I locked the door."

"What?"

"Yeah. Apparently, they allow that here. And I found these." She jingled the keys.

In the quiet dark, Geo pondered the significance. First, they weren't locked in and now they could keep people out. No doubt, the base command could override the locks, but to trust Geo and Cassidy on their first night here seemed naïve, which made Geo extremely nervous. One thing the

US military wasn't as trusting. He sat up listening to Cassidy breathe for a while, but eventually, as the building grew utterly quiet, he slid down under the covers and slept.

Change of Plans

December 29

Emmaus

Sharon McLaughlin navigated the narrow bumpy streets of Emmaus' eastern side, slewing into the Delaney driveway where Rob worked in the garage, spreading straw for the horses that were picketed alongside the driveway. He looked up as she approached the open doors.

"What brings you here, Sharon?" He had that judgy look like he wanted to ask about Danny. But Danny worked hard, dawn to dusk, and never complained. That should be enough to win Rob's confidence. Jacob saw him kill a man and he still knew the boy was redeemable. *Rob is a card-carrying judgmental stone-chucker, but he knows that about himself. He'll make the right decision in the end.*

"Need to modify my will, but Brandon didn't answer his door and the bank is all locked up. His house looks froze up."

"Cai's crew found him and his wife … yesterday."

Sharon took a deep breath, coughed, and sat down on a saddle over a sawhorse. It felt like she'd been kicked in the stomach.

"So much death." Rob nodded. "The flu?"

"Suicide. Their pantry was empty. Both were at least 30 pounds ligher than before the Bombs." That made sense. They were rich…in money…but nobody but farmers kept a fully stocked pantry these days. "They went out sharing a bottle of pills and a bottle of vodka. With no heat, it was probably the least painful choice."

"He graduated in our class."

Rob nodded, but he had nothing to say. Brandon and Maxine's children didn't live in Emmaus, so there probably wouldn't be a funeral. Everyone was too worn out for such niceties these days. How things had changed in just a month. After a minute, Sharon pulled an envelope out of her pocket.

"I'm wanting to swap heirs, make Shane an oversight, and let Danny earn the land over a 10-year period."

Rob scanned Sharon's handwritten two-page codicil. He didn't even blink that his son was being disinherited.

"You have a clear vision. Give Danny 10 years and he might be ready for such responsibility. And, Shane has enough farmland to worry about and zero skills to apply to them. I'll make sure it's done. You come all this way for that?"

"No, I come bearing gifts." Rob frowned. "I'm getting tired, out of breath. Don't think I'll make summer. I've got some quilts and pottery for you folks. Come help me."

Rob stabbed the pitchfork into a bail of straw and went to the truck to hoist the box out of the bed. Sharon carried a smaller box of preserves into the mudroom. Lugging that box had been easy last summer and now it made her arms quiver.

"Where's everybody?"

"Shane's sleeping – pretty much 20 hours a day right now. Cai's running the body squad. Marnie and Alicia are at the medical center. Not sure where Click is right now. Jill's here. She's probably --."

Jill came into the kitchen pulling off gloves and the scarf she'd wrapped around her lower face.

"Didn't know a broken leg was contagious?" Sharon remarked.

"Dislocated hip and I'm just being cautious with him because he's delicate right now. Catching the flu might well kill him."

Sharon nodded.

"So, I guess I can't see him?"

"That's fine. You just can't touch him, get within an arms' length. But why do you want to see Shane?"

Sharon shot a glance at Rob, who shrugged.

"It wasn't my story to tell."

Of course, it wasn't, which was what Sharon liked about Rob, but that meant she had to tell it herself.

"Is he clear-headed?"

"He's in and out. I just finished bathing him and he ordinarily needs a nap after that."

"Then, I'll write to him. I just don't want to let it all go unexplained."

Days didn't always go how you planned, so Sharon didn't fight against it. Just because she felt the Hound of Heaven on her heels didn't mean she didn't have time enough to let the man heal. Rob walked her to her truck.

"Sharon, I'm sorry we can't do more for you."

"I'm not. Ain't no use fussing over what we can't change and – it's been a good life. I had a dream the other day – EJ visited me. Haven't had one of those in decades. He said I know our daughter."

"You didn't say it was a girl before."

"Didn't know it was. I told you, they didn't let you know that back in my day. I don't know how I could know her. Her? I went to Wichita and the adoption was there too."

"How'd your parents arrange it?"

"Wow, it was a long time ago. I know Doc Hanson was involved with it. Pa told me Fes Sullivan was involved too."

"Fes? Why?"

"Not sure. Lottie mentioned it once. You know she gave a baby up for adoption a year before. Fes helped that time too."

"I didn't know that. Must have been before she fell in love with Ren."

"He was gone to war. It wasn't his. I don't know the whole story. The past is shrouded in fog."

"More like dust, but … yeah. You want me to see if Marnie has those records at the Medical Center?"

Sharon's heart fluttered. She'd buried that grief a long time ago, but …. She nodded, and then mounted her truck and drove away.

Fear

December 30

Dell hung the pitchfork up and headed toward the house. Geneva and Silver were supposed to shovel the yard down, and they were while having fun dumping shovel loads down each other's backs. Dell didn't scold them. Whatever worked to get the job done. Rafe and his family were doing the same thing over near the soddy. Eventually, the yard would be knocked down enough to walk – until the next storm.

Dell paused in the kitchen, pulling off his coat and gloves, hanging them to dry, draping his socks over the rail in front of the coal stove. The floorboards creaked above his head, so he went up to check on Leisha who was, of course, taking care of Kix. She talked to the boy, telling him what she was doing as she did it as if he could understand her. Dell hoped he could. Kix had no voluntary movement anywhere in his body.

"How's he doing today?" he asked.

"Fever's up. He's not making any noises at all today."

She washed the boy's arm, slowly relaxing it from its spastic posture. Only the right side drew up like that. The left side lay limp. Yesterday, Kix moaned like it hurt when she stretched his arm, but today – his vocal cords might be paralyzed too. When she was done with washing his arm, she closed his fingers around a section of wooden dowel so they wouldn't be fisted. The boy didn't seem to notice.

"What's the blood for?"

"Ami says he's anemic. She says fresh blood might help him overcome the illness."

"I was anemic once back in high school. I remember it made me tired."

"Yeah." Leisha placed her hand on Kix's forehead.

"I'll be back in a little while, Kix. I've got to get dinner started."

Nothing. Dell wasn't sure what he'd expected. It had been nearly a week. The kid might stay this way for the rest of his life.

When they got to the bottom of the stairs, Leisha turned into Dell's chest, weeping.

"I feel like I'm being punished for Mace," she admitted.

"Oh, darling, you know that isn't so. Kix was already sick. This encephalitis was going to do this regardless of what happened."

"He's my son and I want to help him."

"Of course, you do. There's not much we can do until the fever breaks. Just take care of his needs and pray."

"And if he never gets better?"

"Then we'll take care of him. He's our son. Darling, we're not giving up on him."

"A lot of the kids with polio never got better."

"Yeah, but a lot of them did."

They neither of them remembered polio, but that didn't stop them speculating.

"I'll get the coals going so you can get dinner done, then I'll go up and sit with him. It must be terrifying to him not to be able to move."

Leisha nodded, wiping her cheeks. There was so much to be done and so little time to do it. What would happen if any of the other kids got sick with this?

Disenthrallment

Kenmore, Washington

W e're getting ready to blow them off the map,"
Johnston said. There weren't a lot of National
Guardsmen at Kenmore and most of them had been
absorbed into the Army before the Takedown. Johnston still
wore his National Guard uniform. His buddy Manuelo was
Navy and wore his fatigues also. The majority of the
personnel at Camp Kenmore were Army and they all took
orders from Provisional Base Alpha and Colonel McGowan.
But where was PBA? Geo had yet to discover that
information and he thought it might matter. Northeast was a
large direction.

The Kenmore base denizens were true believers, Geo
decided. They honestly believed the Knights were trying to
overthrow the legitimate government of the United States.
It was as if they hadn't seen the American government
collapse after the terrorist attacks took out its central
control operations. Cassidy dropped hints about the people
she'd seen disappear when the Army was in charge of
Seattle. She described their justifications – these were
trouble-makers and terrorists. Her questions came back to

Geo as a warning to keep his woman in line. He assured Yarnell that Cassidy might have her doubts, but she would throw in with whoever kept her warm. She was his brother's girl after all, but they were sharing a room. Right? Wink!

Privately, Geo became more convinced of what he was doing. The military here didn't care about the people of Seattle. They hadn't cared when they were in charge of the city. The Knights maybe took advantage of the chaos after the Bombs, but they didn't cause it. Even the Kenmore true believers blamed North Korea and Iran. And, yet, they were determined to overthrow the Knights rather than try to work with them. They referenced freedom a lot as if the mark of the US military brought freedom. Did it matter whose boots were on your neck? The Knights seemed determined not to be overlords. They were okay with people acting as individuals.

Yes, he enjoyed being on a military compound where discipline was expected, and lines of command were clear. Almost every day he needed to remind himself this was not a normal way of doing things. Military discipline only worked because there was individual freedom in the surrounding society. When he'd been in Afghanistan, he'd seen a lot of abusive behavior in the name of imposing military discipline on the entire society. He needed to remember that, and the young mother and her children being taken into the command trailer at the Ballard Market. Usually, the Kenmore people reminded him. They killed any civilian who got close to the compound. Cassidy risked her life walking up to the compound with Geo, but because they'd assumed they were lovers, they'd allowed her to stay. Cassidy said there were other civilians here, but all of them were affiliated with soldiers in one way or another. She warned many of the women were being treated like prostitutes. Geo worried about her, but he also knew she might surprise anyone who didn't know she had military training and a gun hidden in her clothes.

The conference room gave a sparkling view of the lake from the third floor. Kenmore's campus comfortably looked out toward Seattle. They monitored radio transmissions and sent out scouting parties. The Knights, knowing something was coming, had stepped up border patrols and tightened security protocols. Geo and Cassidy had a deadline – 10 days and then bug-out. Together they were trying to gather as much information as possible. Geo felt the most important discoveries would be the location of Provision Base Alpha and the plans for the attacks on Seattle.

Lt. Reed leaned over a hand-drawn map spread across the table. Johnston put a finger on the map.

"The substation in Seattle Way is critical infrastructure for B&W to get the power back on in Seattle. Intel says it'll be up by Saturday."

"Are we going to take it out before then," Manuelo asked.

"The Knights aren't equipped to handle an attack by government-trained troops," Reed declared. Geo found that assessment naïve. Many of the Knights trained in the military before they either washed out or bugged out for better cash. Some of them served years before they retired. They knew military tactics. But they also knew how to win hearts and minds by feeding people and reestablishing power.

Listening to the discussion, Geo kept his face impassive, pretending to be in favor of their plans, but thinking about ways to improve them from a SEAL perspective. Of course, any improvements he suggested would be weaknesses to be exploited.

"There's a border patrol here." Johnston indicated a zone south of Seattle Way, near the end of the lake. He then traced up north. "We couldn't get into the area, but a month ago they had few if any actual troops around the substation. They seem to think people won't attack this infrastructure."

"Freedom is worth more than electricity," Reed said. Geo heard that dogmatic statement enough to begin to question it. The Knights weren't abusing people. They'd allowed a local online newspaper to post to electronic billboards so people would know what was going on. They allowed gatherings in parks and churches. They hadn't imposed their own version of martial law but were providing a rudimentary bus system and work for those who no longer had jobs. They were trying to get the power back on.

"We take out this substation and the southern half of the city no longer has an easy means to get power." Reed smiled.

"Let them get it up and running. Let people feel like their lives are getting better. And then end it for them. It'll be a lot sweeter for them when the government gets it up and running. It'll belong to them and not be subject to Wilson's rule."

"So, what's our plan?" Geo asked.

"Wednesday a week from now, we'll cross the lake by boat here." Johnston showed the route across the southern section of Lake Washington. "We'll break into five teams and take the substation at midnight using handheld rocket launchers."

Effective! Unless the Knights knew they were coming. They discussed some more details and then Reed asked Geo to walk out with him.

"Your girl, she's good with radios. My superiors don't like non-military on our bases. We try to keep them at a minimum. Would she be willing to take the oath?"

"You could just ask her," Geo replied.

"Her unit commander is planning to do that. I just figured she might listen to you better."

"We wouldn't want to be separated."

"Of course not. You're going on the raid, though."

"Yes, that seems right. I have a few ideas for strengthening the attack using SEAL techniques. I find it interesting that I'm the only one on base."

"Provisional Base Alpha is aware of your presence and will no doubt ask you to join a reassembled team when the time is right."

"Again, I'd want to take Cassidy with me. I owe it to my brother to keep her safe. Well, as safe as anyone is in this mess."

"Of course. There's another planning meeting tomorrow at 0800. I'll expect you there."

"Yes, sir."

They saluted and Geo crossed to the telemetry building where Cassidy spent her days. It was nearly lunch and they'd learned this was the best time to meet. She slipped out of the backdoor, scanning around her, ducking among parked trucks until she reached where he was crouching in a pod of trees.

"They're going after the Halls Lake Switching Center."

"No, the Seattle Way Substation."

They stared at one another.

"We maybe are being played." Geo shrugged.

"This was radio chatter. Provisional Base Alpha is coordinating the attack."

"Handheld rocket launchers."

"They were mentioned."

"Division of forces. When?"

"Next Wednesday."

"Hmm. I just listened to two hours of ranting about how people won't mind going through winter without electricity if the government restores it later."

"That might be true in Seattle. We probably won't freeze to death."

"Unless the flu really hits us. They're going to ask you to take the oath."

"Should I?"

"Yeah. But we're bugging out, probably tomorrow night."

"Good. I got a Sergeant Chacon sniffing up around me and if we stay much longer, I'm going to have to hurt him."

They grinned at one another. "I recorded the radio transmission."

"That'll be helpful. Cass – if anything goes wrong, grab the bugout bag and head to the canoe. Don't wait for me, coz I won't wait for you."

"That's so sweet. I know that. We better get to lunch before people wonder where we are."

She always said that. They emerged from the woods with her shirt slightly untucked, to maintain the illusion that they might be having sex. As they neared the slope onto the parking lot, the ground tremored and they paused, watching as a large truck braced by two MRAPs rumbled by.

"What is that?" she asked as he pulled her back into the shadow of a parked vehicle. She snuggled into his chest like they might start kissing. The truck pulled into a large tarp structure created off the side of the telemetry building.

"Something big. Tonight might be the night I need to go check it out."

"There's a file room in there that they seem to guard pretty tightly during the day. I got the code for the door this morning."

"How'd that happen?"

"Carelessness."

"Let's go."

They headed toward the headquarters building, holding hands.

Talking & Protein

Shane hummed with contentment as she fed him slivers of venison. He'd been too weak and hurt before to chew but today he seemed brighter, more energetic. He'd been awake a little earlier in the morning and now he seemed less tired this afternoon.

"Have I said, 'thank you'?"

"For?"

"Keeping your head out there?"

"Yes."

"And saving my life?"

"Yes."

"And venison?"

"You shot it."

"Yeah, but right now, if it were in the kitchen, I'd starve to death because I couldn't get to it."

"How's the pain?"

"Not so bad if I don't move or breathe deeply, but everything else is out of the question."

"Not talking or eating venison? Marnie says you need the protein."

"I didn't know talking provided protein."

He grinned at her. He still looked pretty battered, but his eyes twinkled.

"You are feeling better, aren't you?"

His gaze shifted. A naturally taciturn and private person, he didn't like sharing his feelings and she knew she pushed in where he probably didn't want company.

"Not sleeping makes a man grumpy."

"Right and your body is sort of demanding you sleep now, but I'm talking about your head."

"Yeah. I'm better." He sighed. "There was just uh, stuff that followed me from Miristan and – leaving Mike in Santa Fe triggered it. I'm better, but it's not over."

"No. We are the sum total of our pasts and it's going to always be a part of you."

His green eyes met her gaze. He looked immensely sad for a moment, then he blinked away the sadness and glanced at the bowl of venison.

"More, please?"

Changing the subject prevented him from spilling his guts, or reliving what was painful, or getting too emotionally intimate with Jazz. She fed him another bite of venison. He ate three more slivers and then yawned, wincing because it moved his ribs. Jazz helped him roll onto his left side and then just waited quietly until his breathing slowed. She prayed he would continue talking to Rob and was encouraged that he was reading the Bible. Would the depression return after he grew stronger? Or had he turned a corner and would get better now? She didn't know and could only pray for him.

Breathing

Columbus, Ohio

The SulllCorp hub had a well-equipped medical clinic, but when Joseph started having breathing difficulties, they needed to reach out to the Columbus hospitals for help. Katharine dissolved into a most-unKatharine-like puddle. Perry still couldn't sustain an upright position for more than 10 minutes and Andi barely knew Joseph and cared less. That left Julian to deal with the medical professionals. They met in the clinic where they were giving Joseph supplemental oxygen so he would no longer look blue.

"It's probably pneumonia," the physician's assistant said after listening to Joseph's lungs. "I'll show you how to deal with that." She looked at Carmen, the RN who headed the staff of two at the SullCorp clinic. "Antibiotics are in short supply and I don't know that it's bacterial, so we'll have to use physical means. This flu is probably a novel, but it doesn't seem to be that deadly, except a subset of patients develop pneumonia."

Julian wandered into the sitting area while they got a distressed Joseph into a prone position with his head down.

His breathing immediately eased. Carmen and Neisha joined Julian in the sitting area just as Fred Green arrived.

"You know who he is, right?"

"Of course. He's important to someone important so he's important to me." Neisha sounded insulted. "I think we got it early enough. The ones that die waited too long."

"What about the secondary effects we're hearing about?"

"There does seem to be something that follows some infections. It's like Guillain Barre Syndrome or some thought it might be vaccine-resistant polio. It appears to affect mostly younger people. He'd be the oldest patient I've seen."

"We're also hearing there's a deadlier version in the Southern states."

"It's rumored. Could just be stories magnified by retelling. I've not talked to anyone down South."

Fred and Julian exchanged glances and Fred nodded slightly.

"I'm unlocking the Internet and the rumors appear to be true. There's more going on down there than that, but perhaps you'd be willing to look over what we've heard so we can get a better picture of this disease."

"Not a virologist, but I can give an opinion. Dr. Khouri over at Methodist has been working on it. She might have a better idea of the broad scope of this disease than I would."

"Send her our way," Fred advised. "As we unlock more of the web we should be able to transmit this information to other labs."

"Excellent." Neisha turned to Carmen. "Monitor his fever and be prepared to suction him from time to time. I'll drop by tomorrow to check on his progress."

She shouldered her bag and looked at Fred once again.

"This flu – this version of it – isn't so deadly but be aware that the secondary effects sometimes include respiratory failure."

Fred nodded. Julian did too, though he wasn't sure why it mattered whether you died of pneumonia or respiratory failure. You turned blue regardless.

Back Doors

Jericho Ghost Town

I found them," Patterson reported as Ami followed Grant into the server room in the basement.

"Them?"

"Dylan's back doors to the Treasury Department."

"He was able to give you that?"

"No, he can't talk well enough for that and the more I pushed the more frustrated he got. That chick April said, 'maybe in a month.' I don't have a month, but I think I found them. Now I have to get through his password protection."

"Good luck with that. He was only a year in, and they were asking him to teach courses in encryption."

"The last day Dylan was functional, he gave me instructions so I could work on something that he'd unencrypted." Ami looked at Grant for permission to continue. He nodded. "I still have the codes he gave me."

"You can give them to Rod. He's working on deeper areas than before since I've admitted Dylan's not coming back anytime soon."

"I have them in my paperwork in the lab."

Ami left them to get what she needed. When she came back, they had their heads together discussing something in low terms.

"That's a firewall that you don't want to poke too often," Grant admitted. He straightened at Ami's entrance.

"Here you go. Can I catch a ride with you to the compound when you go? I want to get blood samples out there and Nick said it would be okay."

"Yeah. You won't be able to come back until morning though because that's when I come back."

"Understood. Is there a place where I can sleep?"

"Of course. It's a much bigger complex than meets the eye. I'm pulling stakes in an hour."

The term "pulling stakes" perplexed Ami for a moment and it must have shown.

"Old term for breaking down camp," Grant provided.

"Oh, yes, of course. American slang sometimes flies over my head. I'll go get my gear ready and find Javi, so he knows where I've gone."

"He was chopping wood, last I looked."

"Chopping – that man!"

Javi hadn't gone completely kamikaze. He wore chainsaw chaps to protect his legs and he never missed the log he was splitting. She paused just outside the door as he fumbled around to find the half-log he meant to split next. He narrowed his eyes and then flared them wide in an attempt to focus. With every loss of another section of vision, he took a few days to adapt. He'd function for a few days at that new reduced level and then he'd lose more vision. Sooner or later, that process would become futile.

"I can hear you breathing." He set the ax down and put the last two quarter-logs in the wheelbarrow, his breath fogging the air around him.

"You realize you might hurt yourself?"

"You realize I'm not a five-year-old? I'm not stupid." He fingered the chaps.

"That would turn an ax, not stop it from breaking your leg."

"How would you know? You've never chopped wood."

"Neither had you before we got here."

"City boy born and raised and proud of it, but I can adapt. What brings you out here into the cold?"

"I'm leaving for the militia compound. I won't be back until morning."

"Dang, I'll have to leave the door open to keep the room warm."

His hand settled on her shoulder. "You'll be back for New Year's Eve, though?"

"Yes. When is that?"

"Tomorrow."

"Then I'll definitely be here. I'll have blood samples to analyze. Are we planning something special? Fireworks or …?"

"I'll give you fireworks if that's what you require." He laid a kiss on her mouth. "You be careful over there. They may seem civilized, but they were plotting the overthrow of the government."

"Or the reformation of it." He shook his head at her. "I will be careful. I promise. You practicing what Brian suggested?"

"Yes. And I get my first Braille lesson from his wife this afternoon."

"You're all about learning skills."

"Those were not ones I wanted to learn, but want has nothing to do with it, so --." He shrugged. "I need to get back and don't you have gear to pack?"

They kissed once more and then he turned back to the wheelbarrow. A shiver ran down her spine as a gust of wind caught the trees and shook them like a giant walked near. No doubt it was her anxiety over how he would cope with the eventual loss of his sight that made her pause to memorize him hefting the wheelbarrow handles and trundling the load toward the back porch. She had lab gear to pack and shook herself firmly because she would see him tomorrow and life would go on.

While she packed her lab gear into the back of Patterson's truck, he came to her.

"I got a data packet from Santa Fe with your name on it."

"Dr. Perrin must be reaching out again. You got it ready for me or should I wait until I get back?"

"Here you go." He handed her a tablet with Dr. Perrin's email on it.

As a FEMA doctor, Dr. Perrin stood ground zero of the southern version of what he was calling the Lakeland Flu, after the lab he believed it had escaped from. While the flu in Emmaus was relatively mild, mostly killing people who were already vulnerable to hunger or weak from old age, the southern version was deadly. Alicia Sanchez proved you could survive it and that survival provided immunity. Dr. Perrin had promised he'd share information with her as he had it. Today's email, however, surprised her.

PERRIN - Your analysis of Alicia Sanchez's blood verifies that Lakeland North and Lakeland South are the different strains of flu. I believe the southern strain was weaponized before being released into the population.

Your information on the secondary encephalitis was quite informative. We've had a few cases appear as well. Our mortality rates from the first infection are high enough that no one really cares about the secondary infection. It looks a bit like polio or GBS. They've all died of respiratory failure or brain hemorrhage. I did notice a statistical anomaly. The sample size is too small to be definitive, but all confirmed patients of this encephalitis are males between 12 and 20. Have you had any female patients or outside of that range?

The situation here is becoming untenable. If I can find a working semi and driver, I might haul the trailer north come spring. Your work on this has been remarkable considering your resources. We could combine our expertise. If I live to spring, of course. That's a question here that is not easy to answer.

Another thing you might want to know – Shane Delaney is immune to the southern strain, suggesting he was possibly an asymptomatic carrier of the northern strain. He was no longer shedding virus when I took his blood, but you might want to do a thorough contact tracing with him. If we could trace this back to Patient Zero, we might learn valuable information on how to fight it.

Ami wished she had more time to give Dr. Perrin a more thorough report and to analyze the data he sent along with his email. He had so much better equipment than she did. Unfortunately, a large percentage of his patients died before he could learn much from them. Shane's blood had done nothing to knock back the virus load, so she'd assumed it wasn't worth following up on. She sent herself a note to follow-up soon and then sent a quick reply to Dr. Perrin.

CEYLON - No females and no one outside that age range, but the statistical sample is too small to conclude. I'll get back with you after I've analyzed your data and send you what I have. Winter here means things are very slow and hard to get around. The northern strain is still with us, but most people who die while having it were already compromised by the cold and lack of food. We've only had the one death from the secondary encephalitis, but we have a second patient with a similar pattern of symptom progression. I had to tell his family what the future might hold. In Egypt, we occasionally saw polio still and I imagine that's what doctors felt like when they saw similar progression. They at least had access to respirators.

She logged off her profile and gave the notebook back to Patterson, who said he'd be ready to go in five minutes. That curious chill ran down her back again as she shrugged back into her coat. Back in the Baltimore ER, her colleagues would tease her that she always knew when something bad was about to descend upon them. She had that feeling now as if something unseen had turned its eyes toward her and was now watching. Silly thoughts! Grant and Javi could handle anything. It was probably just her nerves concerning going to the militia compound. She didn't like to think Javi could turn her into a bigot, but nothing else was likely to happen on her trip besides meeting people who just thought the United States government needed reform.

Family Visit

Lufgren Farm

Alex smiled at Pete when he woke from his nap, putting his measuring tape in his back pocket.

"How are you feeling?"

"Headache's not so bad today." Pete could turn his head side to side without agony. He wanted to push himself up against the headboard, but he couldn't move or feel either of his legs anymore. He heard laugher float in from the hallway. Sounded like a bunch of people gathered in the living room.

"Who's here?"

"My cousins dropped by. You want to come down and join us?"

"I can't walk."

"You don't need to. You don't weigh more than a calf."

"I'm tired of lying here waiting for another body part to stop working."

"If the pain's stopped, that's maybe a good sign."

Pete nodded. Alex dressed him in pajama bottoms and a sweatshirt, then scooped him up. Pete felt strong, his arm around Alex's neck. He closed his eyes going down the stairs, afraid his brother-in-law would drop him.

Everyone seemed happy to see him as Alex settled him into a recliner. Nehemiah and his sisters Rachel and Leah brought pie. Their mother had the flu so they were technically in quarantine, but since Alex's household had already had it, they could visit. They were a family given to laughter, a lot like their father Micah who had been killed by the USDA in October.

For a few days, Poppy seemed at a loss, because Pete couldn't understand her sign when his head felt about to split open, but now she came to sit on the floor by his feet and ask him questions. He replied that his head didn't hurt as much, and he couldn't feel his legs. She looked sad but told him he'd improve now that he was starting to feel better. He hoped in her optimism.

He couldn't keep up with all the conversations because ASL wasn't his native language. He'd only learned it over the last three months. The fire crackled, warming the room. He accepted a cup of hot apple cider. His headache eased more. He could feel his back stretching as he rested in the recliner. His father Mark came over and asked him how he was doing.

"Fine, except for feeling slightly left out of the conversation."

"They don't mean to do that to us," Keri said, turning on the ottoman. "Just like when you speak Spanish with your parents around someone who took Spanish in high school. You don't mean to leave them out, right?"

Pete and Mark exchanged glances, then laughed. Sometimes they were just being unthinking and other times, they'd talk so fast they knew nobody save a native speaker could keep up. Alex told a story with bold gestures and facial expressions Pete never saw him use with hearing people. The Deaf Lufgrens laughed. Keri looked perplexed.

There was peach pie and another cup of cider. Pete knew he'd have to go to bed soon. His head felt heavy. He finished off the cup of cider and tried to put it on the side table. He tipped sideways, elbow landing on the arm of the recliner, the cup tumbling to the rug. Mark caught his shoulders, pushed him back into the recliner, picked up the cup. Frustrated Pete closed his eyes. Yesterday, he still had some sensation in his left leg and now … nothing. A headache swelled in the back of his neck. The room started to grow bright and loud.

"You need to go back to bed?" Alex asked, leaning over him. Pete nodded, wiping tears. Alex scooped him up and carried him up the stairs, Mark trailing behind them. Pete felt weak and exhausted and his neck started to stiffen again. Alex set him on the camp toilet they'd set up in the corner. Pete could still stay upright without someone holding him. While he waited for his bladder to release, nausea rolled over him. He told Mark he was going to puke and a bucket appeared. Cold shivered down his spine as the apple cider came back up. He could hear Keri and his mother Alice whispering not far away. His bladder finally leaked into the pot and Alex lifted him into bed. The house grew quiet and Poppy came to lay beside him. He slept and dreamed of running along a backroad, lost in the trees. He woke to Mrs. Delaney, Keri's mother, leaning over him.

"Why are you here?" he whispered. She looked at someone on the other side of the bed, but it hurt to roll his head that way. His mother put a cool hand on his forehead and looked him directly in the eye.

"The paralysis is ascending. She's showing us how to catheterize you."

Pete didn't know what that meant, but as he lay listening to what Mrs. Delaney said, he realized that he'd lost the ability to urinate. The lack of feeling had climbed above his hips. Hot tears spilled down his cheeks as his head throbbed in time with his heartbeat.

Sneaking

Kenmore, Washington

The building lay quiet as Geo picked the lock on a backdoor facing the woods. Commercial-grade, it wasn't the easiest job he'd ever undertaken, but eventually, the tumblers fell into place. He paused, waiting for a potential siren, but without power, the Army had opted not to bother with that security measure. Or guards. There didn't seem to be any guards.

He swept his flashlight along the corridor and then signaled Cassidy to follow him. Technically, he followed her because she knew where the file room was, but he was the one with infiltration skills, so she walked to his left and a little behind and he obeyed her gestures. The building echoed with empty. The file room was also locked, but that one fell into place much easier. He left the door ajar and listened to the hall while she scanned the file drawers. A good five minutes ticked off before she whispered, "found it" and he heard the drawer open.

He didn't like how long this was taking. What if someone knocked on their dorm door and they weren't there. He knew that wasn't likely. They weren't the "new" any longer. At least a dozen others had shown up since their arrival. Still, SEAL training taught you to have eyes in the back of your head, to anticipate what might go wrong with a plan. He expected the lights to come on at any moment.

"Geo, come here."

He eased the door closed and made his way to the second row of file cabinets. This one held large-format maps and designs. By their flashlights, they looked over what was there – a map of the Greater Seattle area. Geo's heart started thumping, looking at the markings on the map.

"They're not planning an armed assault on the substations. They're planning something larger."

"What would be larger?"

Geo shook his head. Far off in the building, he heard a door open and close. People talked. With exquisite control, Cassidy silently slid the drawer closed. A light shined under the file room door. Geo pulled Cassidy to the end of the stacks and they held their breaths. The guy with the keys whistled to himself. Geo drew out his knife. The door opened. The guy scanned the room with a headlamp, but the light never touched Geo or Cassidy. Turning in the other direction, the soldier never saw them as they slipped out the door behind him. As they moved along the corridors, Geo listened. Someone waited inside the door they'd come in. He signaled for Cassidy to follow him into the stairwell.

"What do we do?" she whispered.

"Basement level. Be ready to kill if you need to."

She nodded, her mouth set firmly, drawing out her gun and checking that it was cocked and locked. In another time, he might have admired her as more than a coworker. She reminded him of his sister.

The basement level was deserted, and they climbed steps at the far end. He signaled for her to be quiet as he stared at a large truck that they'd seen previously. He could hear guards talking outside the tarp tent. He lifted the edge of the cover on the back of the truck and shined his flashlight in there. Shit! That's what he was afraid of.

"What is it?" Cassidy barely whispered.

"Rocket launcher. Plans and means." He indicated the back of the tent. They listened as a guard walked by outside. Geo traced his movement with a finger. When he went around the corner, Geo let him go a bit further and then he lifted the tent bottom so they could both slip under. They crept up the stairs to the 4th floor and managed to slip into their room without detection.

"We need to get out of here," Geo told her, whispering in her ear.

"Not until we find a location for PBA. This is a multi-prong attack and PBA is coordinating. We need that information before we bugout."

She spoke the truth. They only had one shot at this.

"Okay, but we leave tomorrow night even if we don't have that intel. Agreed?"

She nodded. They didn't dress for bed tonight, but Geo laid down on his bunk. Sometime before dawn, she crept over and said, "I want to lie here."

He scooted over and let her join him and they lay the rest of the night in each other's arms.

Progress & Ending

Emmaus

Shane had had enough of lying in bed staring at the ceiling or the woodstove and expressed a requirement for a change of scenery. The day before New Year's Eve, he informed Rob that if he didn't help him move to the couch, he'd do it himself. You really couldn't blame him. He'd been lying in bed for a week. Brian had worked on his shoulder which was healing nicely, though still sore and weak. Marnie agreed his left ankle was, at worse, a simple fracture and probably just a bad sprain.

"You can put weight on it, so long as you're not walking, hopping, etc."

His worst injury was his hip and Clem said no weight-bearing for a while yet. To provide the change of scenery, Cai and Rob used a fireman's two-man chair-carry to get him from the mattress by the woodstove onto the couch. It clearly hurt, but Shane sucked it up, followed by a low-key celebration when he got there.

"Woohoo, a different view of the room and, look, back support." He gingerly shifted himself to sitting up against the arm, then carefully placing a pillow under his knees. His black eye was now a yellow smudge. "Cai, can you move that stack of books to the end-table?" At the risk of engendering opposition, nobody mentioned the Bible that was part of the stack or the notebook that was slowly being filled in.

Rob filled a water bottle and left a jar nearby.

"If you need something, yell. I'm scrubbing clothes."

"I'm good." Shane did seem to be mending. The crying jags lessened. Jill stopped the cannabis oil yesterday and Shane didn't seem to be in agony. He talked with Rob now.

"Dinner in about an hour," Cai announced.

"When was the last time any of us saw a clock that worked?" Shane asked.

Cai shrugged and moved into the kitchen. Rob followed him.

"When are we going to trust him to be alone?" Cai asked.

"Soon. He should at least be mobile before he's on his own. Brian's bringing a wheelchair tomorrow."

"It's snowing tomorrow." Cai supported his forecast by rubbing his left shoulder.

"How'd you hurt that anyway?"

"Adventures in Apocalypse World."

"I guess I don't need to ask more than that, do I?"

"Not really."

"And your wife can't fix it."

"She did, but it takes time to heal."

Rob moved into the well room where the clawfoot tub was also their laundry – a bucket of soapy water with a scrub board and two buckets of rinse. He aimed for clothes that didn't stink and didn't worry too much about the stains.

A knock on the back door made him wipe his hands and go to it. Ren Sullivan stood there, smiling. He looked thinner and older, about what Rob saw when he looked in a mirror.

"Ren? When did you --? How did you --?"

"Tucker Snowcat for the second one. Just got here last night. Where's my granddaughter?"

"Vance's. She couldn't stay in that big house alone."

"No, of course not. Did she have to be convinced or is she as wise as I think she is?" Rob held up two fingers and Allison's grandfather smiled proudly. "Vance's? Why there?"

"They needed help and she needed a place to stay."

"No sign of Joe and Katharine?"

"No. Have you had the flu yet?"

"Yes. Why?"

Rob briefly explained the situation at his house. Shane couldn't risk catching so much as a cold right now. Ren nodded sagely, but clearly, he had other priorities.

"And my brother?"

"Carl? Yeah – I saw him – Christmas Eve. He brought some canned goods for us."

"Good. Can you do me a favor? I've got to go see Allison, but I want to get these meds over to him." He held out a small box of blister packs. "These roads – somebody needs to get these things plowed."

That sounded so like Ren – just in town and already trying to organize people.

"Vin has been working on the road to Mara. Folks shovel out as they can. Not as necessary to plow when you're using horses."

"True. Maybe Vin will work a little faster for some food. I've got a truck-train following me. Food and fuel. Should be here today or tomorrow, weather permitting. Anyway, you will do it?"

"Sure. I need to leave the laundry to soak anyway."

"Make sure he knows I'm back and if he needs anything, I'll be in the groom's cottage up at the Shack."

"I'll tell him. He's been really worried that he would run out. Kept reminding me that his doses run out on January 3. This is timely."

"I knew I needed to be back by New Year's. Tried to be back by Christmas, but – blizzards overrule sentimentality. Maybe something to do with the bombs, but this is the worst winter in a long time."

"It has been." They hugged. "It's good to see you back, Ren."

"It's good to be back. Now I gotta go."

Rob told Cai he was going to Carl Sullivan's and donned his winter clothes. Macky picked his way through the snow-covered landscape – sunlight bouncing off white crystals and lighting the façade of houses, sparkling on the barren trees. Kids threw snowballs at one another across three yards, a testament to the resiliency of youth. Carl lived a few blocks over. On the outside, the house looked as neat as all the others around it. Ren saw to that. And twice a year until October, he'd forced Carl to submit to a cleaning crew in his house. Rob shuddered to think what it might be like now. A large pile of trash next to the garage warned him of what he might be facing.

Nobody answered his knock on the front door, so he wallowed around to the back where the door was unlocked. He pushed in, stepping over the last blizzard's snow accumulation.

"Carl, it's Rob Delaney."

His breath fogged and terror struck his heart. The kitchen looked pretty clean for Carl's house. No obvious health hazards, which was something of a miracle.

"Carl." No reply came. Rob went immediately to the radio room beside the kitchen because that was Carl's favorite place. The radio had been powered down and covered in plastic and an envelope with Rob's name scrawled on it sat atop one addressed to Ren and another addressed to Click Michaels.

Rob,

I figure you'll be the one to check on me. I'm sorry I couldn't make it neater. Don't blame yourself. This was always how it had to end since the day I went to Basic. And with your boy down – there's

417

nobody else here who'd help me do it and — really, I shouldn't ask anyone else. Killing innocents has consequences and I shouldn't ask people to violate their consciences. I'm not innocent, but you all like me, so it would hurt you to do what you needed to do. It's for the best. You can't have Crazy Carl running around un-medicated. It would make a bad situation worse. And that's not your fault. It's not anyone's fault. Not even mine. It's just what needs to happen. I stuck around a long time so Ren wouldn't feel bad about it, but he's not here, so it's not his fault either. You have been a good friend. Always treated me like I'm not crazy. Just so you know — when it comes to that burky bitch following Shane around — I'm not crazy. She's there and he needs your help. Hope the cannabis breaks down his walls. It's a good pain-reliever, but it always makes me confess shit I don't want to confess, and Shane really needs that.

Carl

The door to the basement loomed open and Rob steeled his backbone. He'd been in Vietnam when EJ hung himself, but Pa had told him about what it was like to walk in on his son hanging from the rafters of the garage – the creak of the rope over old wood, the smell of piss and shit. Carl had planned his suicide better – a wooden coffin lined with plastic and a razor blade – but he was just as dead with an iron tang to the usual stench.

For a long time, Rob just sat on the bottom step and cried, mourning for Carl, EJ, his uncle Lai and all the men who lost their hope in faraway lands to make a reputation for politicians who were now quite literally burned to ash. What the hell was wrong with a world of people who couldn't see that they should just leave the other guy – the other nation – alone? Let them be stupid. Let them kill one another so long as they kept it within their own borders. Let nation war against nation and third nations stay out of it. Stop sending young men to die or come back permanently wounded so the US government could notch another win on its belt. Hell, we weren't even winning wars anymore. The last US win was World War 2, before Rob was born.

An unexpected chortle broke from Rob's chest. There was no more USA. The government and its nasty interfering belt were burned to ash just like those politicians. Viewed that way, the apocalypse was not a curse. He needed to go find Ren, let him know, and then get on with life because that was the world they lived in after the well-earned reckoning. He suspected Carl would have agreed.

Blown

Kenmore, Washington

Geo bent over a railgun, cleaning the mechanisms. Beyond the tarp lay a typical Puget Sound December afternoon, grey and drizzly. Cassidy walked by. He nodded at her. Normally, she'd come over and pretend to snuggle, but her eyes shifted nervously. He wiped his hands and spoke to Manuelo who was cleaning another railgun.

"I need some more gun oil. I'll be right back." Manuelo nodded. He wasn't smart enough to wonder why Geo didn't just borrow his.

Geo exited the back of the work area, angling toward the supply trailer, slipping around the corner and into the woods. He wove his way through devil's club. Just as he neared their usual rendezvous spot, the loudspeakers crackled.

"Apprehend Cassidy Walden. She is wanted for questioning concerning classified documents and radio transmissions. Apprehend Cassidy Walden."

Geo was at their meetup point in less than a minute. Branches to the west bobbed whether from rain or the passage of a runner, he couldn't tell. He looked down to see a map lying on the ground. He picked it up to learn Provisional Base Alpha was located at Echo Lake. Tucking the map into an inside pocket, he crept west, crouching low. Behind him, the base mobilized and people shouted. When they realized he was missing, the loudspeakers announced they should be looking for him too. Although he could hear them, he was already out of sight of the campus. If they had found Cassidy, they'd not still be telling people to look for her. Reasonably, she got away after dropping the map. The soldiers at the base knew a trained Navy Seal was not going to break cover for a captured team member, so they weren't even going to try a ploy like that. He kept creeping through the brush, trying not to disturb the bushes and give away his position.

As he slunk through the forest, he occasionally saw brush movement ahead that gave him hope Cassidy hadn't been captured. Geo's SEAL training meant he could slither through the woods without detection. Cassidy flunked out of Basic training. The soldiers at the base might see those mistakes too and give them both away. He could care that she made it to safety, but the mission was primary. One of them needed to get across the lake to deliver the intelligence they'd gathered.

When Geo heard vehicles starting up at the base, he froze. He could almost see the position where they'd stashed the go-bags. He waited, listening for approach. When none came, he continued forward. The branches covering the bags had been flung aside and the smaller of the two bags was gone. Cassidy made it this far. Good girl. She wisely didn't wait for him, but hopefully headed for the canoe. He put the branches back in the same haphazard pattern they'd used in the first place. In case someone followed them, hopefully they wouldn't be alerted to their general direction of travel. Geo crouched there several minutes, rain running down his neck. He could see the road from the hollow and vehicles moved there. He didn't want a pack of wolves on his tail as he ran for the canoe, so he took his time settling the go-bag on his back, using the compass for a heading on the canoe.

When he couldn't see movement on the road, Geo slipped carefully through the devil's club, headed downhill. The joy of the Pacific Northwest rain forest was that rain covered your tracks quickly and the movement of branches could be mistaken for shedding rain. He hated devil's club and the bugs that bit you when you traveled through them. He'd have to lance boils when he got back to Seattle. He paused to listen. Rain and more rain, the drip-drip-drip of a million leaves laden with water. He could hear a heavy vehicle way up on the road, but he could see the road and doubted they could see him. There was a substantial tree canopy here that should cover any movement in the undergrowth. Geo started running downhill toward the lake, dodging trees, rocks and roots. Soon the sound of vehicles dropped entirely behind him. He settled into an easy lope, wondering when he would overtake Cassidy.

Return of Shane Delaney

Emmaus

So how do you feel?" Brian asked, gaze resting on Shane's face. Being moved hurt, but it didn't look like the pain subsided even after he'd had time to relax.

"It feels like all the weight of my body is right on my hip." Shane's teeth gritted against the pain, bracing his forearms lengthwise on the arms of the wheelchair to get some weight off his butt. His right shoulder still healed, so he couldn't lift himself for long.

"You want us to transfer you back?"

"Yes and no. I – ." He grimaced. "Can you just put me back on the couch so I can think clearly?"

Cai helped Brian shift Shane back to the couch. Pain sweat streaked his brother's forehead now. It pleased Cai that Brian waited. Shane liked things to be his own idea and, since chemical pain relief was in short supply, he needed to listen to his own body. Shane stared at the wheelchair.

"I don't think I can take anymore lying in one place all the time."

"Right. You're going stir crazy. That's understandable. Maybe you need a few more days, though."

Shane frowned at Brian's suggestion. They waited for him to accept that he just wasn't ready. While they waited, it occurred to Cai that maybe Shane wasn't getting restless so much as he worried about a return of the depression. Suicidal and stuck in bed would just feed on itself, wouldn't it?

"Would padding it help?" Jazz asked, coming from the dining room with a couple of chair cushions in hand. Brian tested it with a practiced hand, then handed it to Shane for the decision.

"How about a pillow instead?" Shane pointed to the stairs. "Keri gave me this memory foam thing a long time ago. I hated it, so I think I put it in my closet."

"I'll get it." Cai donned the headlamp they all carried in a pocket now since electric lights were a luxury. The second floor temperature hovered about 40 degrees. At night, it dropped to whatever the outside temperature was, often below zero. Shane's memory for memory foam proved correct. Cai stopped at the linen cabinet for a pillowcase. He remembered how their memory foam mattress topper made him sweat until Marnie covered it with a standard mattress topper. He found a quilted pillowcase. The pillow's length just filled the seat with some lap up the sides, which provided Shane's weak pelvic muscles with some needed support. It took one of the chair cushions behind Shane's back to make a tolerably comfortable position. Brian adjusted the right footrest to support Shane's injured leg.

"You sure about this?" he asked Shane.

"The discomfort isn't so bad now. No worse than sitting up in general."

Brian nodded.

"Don't be a tough guy. When you get tired, you need to say so they can take care of your needs, right?"

Shane's lips skinned back from his teeth in a wolf grimace. The Indian blood showed in his prominent canines as much as in his cheekbones.

"Much as I hate being dependent, I don't want to f – screw up my recovery, so I'll tell you." Shane gave Cai an almost apologetic smile. "Am I allowed to wheel this thing?"

"Uh, yeah." Shane clearly moved faster than Brian was used to in patients. "If it hurts your shoulder, you shouldn't use that arm. But for short distances, you could probably use your left foot and arm and get across the room. Just remember – if you're feeling sharp stabbing pains …."

"Probably shouldn't do it." Shane sighed. "I get it. If I hurt myself, I'm back in bed for however long."

"Exactly. I'll come back tomorrow to see how you're doing and, provided you're still on the mend, we can start range-of-motion exercises. I'll show Cai and Jazz how to do them so you can overdo and heal so much faster than you probably should in the absence of cortisol shots."

"Have you been talking up my pain tolerance, big brother?"

"I might have mentioned that you channel pain better than most, yeah. It was meant to be a compliment."

"I guess it's okay to be legendary." Shane grabbed the blanket off the couch to cover his legs. Dressing hurt, so he wore gooseflesh and a towel wrapped around his waist.

"I'll walk you out," Cai told Brian. In the mudroom, as Brian donned his jacket, he asked. "How is he, really?"

"This is uncharted territory. A hip reduction without an x-ray, no steroid treatment, etc. He seems to be healing. Don't let him sit up too long."

Cai wandered back to the living room where Shane was proving the theory that his shoulder was not ready for wheelchair maneuvering.

"Stop that! I thought you were finally learning."

"Learning is not the same as learned."

Cai sighed. Shane laughed, then shifted his weight like he might be in pain.

"Easy. You need to lie down?"

"Stop. Cai, really. I'm paying attention to what pain is telling me. I'm not trying to overcome it. I'm letting it put limits on me … for now. But I can't lie in bed any longer. I'm not cut out for that … and you know that."

Cai sighed again.

"I'm just looking out for you. You're my little brother and when we picked you up out of that frozen field – I thought you were dead. And, suddenly all those times we fought, all the disagreements …." Cai wiped away a tear.

Shane nodded.

"I'm sorry I have been such a difficult brother. And, yeah, I'm sorry I scared everybody last week."

"Were you …." Cai preferred denial, but Shane worried him. "What happened out there?"

Shane leaned back, shifting slightly.

"I'm not altogether sure. I remember I was sweating, trying to catch up to the deer. I remember taking the deer. Did Jazz get her rifle back?"

"Alex brought it back a few days ago along with everybody's skis. Don't change the subject."

"I kind of have to because what I remember of the rest of it doesn't make a lot of sense." Shane stared at the wall for a moment. "I don't know if I got hypothermic and started hallucinating or – Dad's theory – the deer's blood triggered the PTSD, which was already triggered, and I started hallucinating and took off all my clothes to hurt myself. Either way, I engaged in behavior that was pretty damned self-destructive. I'm sorry I scared you and I'm going to try not to do that again."

"You're actually apologizing?"

"I did try to do that when I first got back to town. So, can I just get a fresh start now?"

Shane looked used up and thin. His fingers twitched nervously in a thoroughly not-Shane way.

"I'll forgive you. That's not – are you okay?"

"I'm pretty beat up, but yeah, I'll heal."

"No. I mean your head."

Shane sighed, wincing slightly because of his ribs.

"I know Jazz and Dad think I tried to commit suicide." Shane scratched his chin. Jill shaved him yesterday and he already needed to shave again. "I'm feeling better. My head is better. I think it's going to take some time, but --." He yawned, bracing his ribs and wincing.

"Ready to go back to bed?" Cai asked.

Shane sighed.

"Unfortunately. Maybe I'll be able to join the festivities tonight – for about 15 minutes – but I need a nap now. This is going to be a longer winter than Pedaresh."

"You'll live."

"Yeah. And, contemplating my navel will hopefully get easier with practice. Might as well get me back to bed before I can't function."

The pain clearly cut right through him as Cai shifted him back to the couch. When he was settled, he looked up at Cai.

"Thank you."

"For?"

"Not pushing when I'm not sure. For caring about me all these years. And forgiving me when I asked instead of expecting me to earn it."

"You can't earn it. None of us can, even those of us who act like we did."

Shane laughed, holding his ribs. Then he yawned.

"Nap time. This is so not me."

"It's temporary. Yell if you need anything. I'm doing laundry."

"Glad to be missing out on that." Shane's murmur promised he'd be asleep any moment.

Cai's gaze drifted to the Bible and notebook on the end table. Curiosity pulled him along, but he knew better than to invade Shane's privacy.

Winnowing

Columbus, Ohio

Julian no longer kept the situation in the South secret since Connie insisted they needed to be honest. He'd felt nervous about revealing it, listening to a voice in the back of his head that this would set off a riot. Connie and Fred weren't the only black people working at SullCorp and what if they agreed with the Southerners? Connie insisted they wouldn't, but Julian still worried about it – until after he'd made the announcement. So many of them expressed sadness that black people would practice slavery. At least one of the node workers pointed out that Africans practice slavery now, so maybe they shouldn't be surprised. Overwhelmingly, the blacks were supportive. The whites were nervous. They'd faced so much animosity for so long, they weren't sure how to handle this bit of news.

It didn't take long for the Southern Situation to become a favorite research project. Every time someone was waiting for an algorithm to untangle an internet knot, they'd try to get some more information about the Situation.

Be careful what you wish for. Corey announced he'd found an advertisement for a livestream and thought they should watch it.

"It's called a Winnowing."

"That sounds ominous," Connie whispered. The empty microphone stand stood on a stage. A black man wearing Kenti cloth approached from the wings. He adjusted the microphone down a bit.

"Brothers and sisters, we are gathered here to release these folks into what they deserve. I ask the priests to come forward and stand next to the one you will release. The world is turning, brothers and sisters. The rightful heirs to the world rise now."

The camera cut to a large park where thousands of white men knelt, their hands behind their backs, tied to posts so they couldn't do much more than swivel their heads. Black men wearing black clothes approached them, machetes in hand.

"What we do is necessary to protect ourselves. Prepare."

The machetes came up.

"Ready."

The machetes cocked back. Some men wrapped two hands around the handles.

"Release."

At least 60% of the kneeling men lost their lives immediately. The remaining 40% weren't going to survive the wounds. Some of the wielders granted them mercy.

Some of them let them die bleeding and gasping for air over the next few minutes.

Nobody moved. They all stared at the overhead screen, shocked. The Kenti-clad man took the microphone with the scene behind him.

"Let me be clear. This winnowing was necessary to balance the scales but make no mistake – we will liberate the entire country."

The screen went black and nobody moved for several heartbeats, then Connie spoke for everyone in the room.

"I need to get home to my husband and kids."

Separated

Kenmore, Washington

Geo approached the lake with caution. There were no signs of pursuit here, but the open expanse of the lake meant exposure, which was dangerous. Paradoxically, SEALs considered water their natural element. Geo relished the water, knowing his pursuers were less able to follow him there. A long way to the south, he heard a motorboat start, then sputter to a halt. He worked his way through the underbrush until he was just above where they'd stashed the canoe.

He found one of the paddles first, paused, searching the underbrush with his eyes and ears. The rain caused the bushes to jigger and jump, collecting water and then shedding it in a noisy flood. He missed his short haircut now as water ran into his eyes.

He found the other paddle and did the stop-and-look-around routine again. It had taken him nearly an hour to make it here and he'd been easing around in these woods for twenty-four minutes with no sign of Cassidy. A lot could happen running through unfamiliar woods in the rain when you weren't a trained SEAL. She could have broken an ankle or run up on the stabby end of a branch right into her eye. She might have tripped and fallen down a ravine. Or been captured by the base. How long would a half-trained soldier hold out against torture before she told them exactly where to find Geo? Or maybe she'd just had to crouch in a stand of brush waiting for her pursuers to go around. He didn't know and that was always the risk in ops without overwatch or communication. He only knew what was going on with him. Cassidy was completely on her own.

Geo uncovered the canoe and stood there listening and watching. Devil's club rinsed water down his back as he stared through the trees toward the grey lake. The rain obscured everything more than a few feet in the woods, but he could see a few miles across the lake. The sun hid behind thick cloud cover, but he guessed sunset might be an hour away.

Thirty-two minutes and no sign of Cassidy. She wasn't a trained SEAL. They had been synchronizing watches, but there was no reason to believe she'd think of that while running through the woods. She might not think he'd be any faster getting to the lake than she was. From her perspective, getting here without attracting attention was far better than getting here fast.

Thirty-six minutes and no sign of Cassidy. He had to assume she'd been caught, injured or lost. Breaking his own rules only meant he risked getting caught too. The mission was more important than either one of them. He hadn't seen Cassidy in more than two hours. A lot of something bad could happen in that time.

Geo knew he couldn't stay here much longer. He'd heard a vehicle ten minutes ago, probably up on the park road which was way closer than he liked. The canoe stood ready, the paddles shipped. It had always been a long-shot that both of them would make it out alive. He'd just thought it would come down to a last stand, not this quiet wet beach and a decision to leave because he couldn't wait.

Geo grabbed the bow cross-brace and dragged the canoe down to the waterline. He scanned the tree line again. No sign of Cassidy. SEALS didn't do that no-man-left-behind thing. You did the best you could for your teammates, but when things went south, you cut your losses as needed and took the intel home.

He sighed and bent to push the canoe out into the lake. Water lapped up above his boots as he stepped into the floated canoe. A sharp report and something hit him in the back. He bent to grab one of the paddles and just kept going, face-first into the bottom of the canoe. He'd been creased with a bullet once in Kandahar and it had burned like fire, but it hadn't slowed him down much. Here there was no pain, but far far away, he thought he heard someone scream and then, he felt and knew nothing.

Watch Night

Emmaus

Jazz hadn't spent a New Year's watch night with the
Delaney family before. Keri invited her last year, but she'd
driven to Mara Wells to spend it with the family. Jim had
been gone to somewhere far and militaristic, but Geo had
been home. She missed them, but the Delaneys welcomed
her like a long-lost daughter. Maybe next year ... if .... Were
she and Michael the only ones left? Shane said Geo marked
himself safe when Facebook still existed. Jim was still
overseas. Her parents ... she didn't know and that continued
to worry her. But she was safe, and she couldn't look for
them until the weather broke.

New Year's watch night at the Delaneys' consisted of
hot buttered tea, buttered toast, mulled apple cider and
popcorn and an epic game of the Kingdom of Jeriko –
which was D&D using Jericho township as the map. Rob
assumed the role of dungeon master that had always been
Jacob's.

"Oh, I so miss your brownies," Rob mourned. "I can
smell the chocolate." He smiled fondly at his wife of 40
years.

"I tried getting chocolate or cocoa powder, but everybody is hoarding. No luck."

"This is just as good." Rob sipped some tea. "It's different, but variety is the spice of life."

"I was sort of hoping Shane would join us." Jill glanced toward the closed interior patio doors. They'd closed them so Shane wouldn't be disturbed by their revelry.

"His energy is limited." Cai rubbed Marnie's foot. "This afternoon maybe wiped him out."

"That hip's going to hurt for a long time." Marnie pulled one foot free to give her husband the other.

"Brian thinks Ric – Shane -- will be able to handle an aggressive stretching regime." Alicia arched her back, hands rubbing the small of it. At seven and a half months pregnant, everything ached.

The Latina woman surprised Jazz earlier in the day by asking if she'd ever assisted her mother, a well-known midwife in the area. She apprenticed with her mother for a year before deciding she'd rather be a teacher. Her mother's partner was in Mara Wells which might as well be on the far side of the moon now that winter blocked all the roads. Why Alicia would prefer a half-trained midwife over a doctor and a nurse mystified Jazz. She would need to solve that mystery before February.

"That might help." Marnie shrugged. "At this point, I can't do anything for him medically except let Brian experiment."

"Are we anywhere near midnight?" Cai cast a skeptical gaze at the cuckoo clock atop the china cabinet. When the

EMP took out all the accurate clocks, the century-old cuckoo hadn't been wound in a decade, so nobody was really certain of the time. The clock in the city hall tower was Emmaus Mean Time, but Rob had just sort of guessed with the cuckoo. You could hear the bell tones of the city hall tower on a clear winter night, but barely.

"We'll pretend that thing knows what time it is." Another 20 minutes.

"I'm taking the last of the cider into Shane unless someone objects." Jazz glanced around the group, but nobody did. Click shifted his feet so she could reach the kitchen.

"You read Carl's note to you yet?" Rob asked Click.

"Yeah. He left me his radio, the tower and – 'if my danged brother doesn't think he owns it' – his house. And he thanked me for helping clean his kitchen the other day. I swear, I had no idea that he was planning ...."

"Of course not." Cai, Jill and Rob spoke at the same time. "He was always at risk. There were several attempts over the years." Rob shrugged. "It's nobody's fault. Don't know why he'd make it about the meds and then decide to check out five days early."

Jazz stepped back into the dining room, worked around to the living room entrance, slid the interior French doors open just enough to let herself through. In the dim living room, she was surprised to see Shane sitting up on the couch, awkwardly maneuvering the wheelchair so he could transfer into it.

"You okay?"

"Yeah." The little bit of light that came through the doors showed the conflict in his expression. "I thought I'd try to join you."

"We're just about ready to start praying."

She expected him to decide he wasn't interested, but he pulled the near armrest off the wheelchair so he could slide across. Breathing heavily with pain, he didn't object when she settled a quilt over his bare legs.

"You need a push or you want to do this on your own?"

Shane tested his shoulder.

"I should do this on my own, so I know I chose it."

"This will be waiting for you when you get there."

She indicated the cup and he grinned, teeth flashing white in the low light. Everybody looked up as she came back into the dining room.

"He still conked out?" Cai indicated the cup. Jazz sighed in lieu of answering. If Shane changed his mind, he deserved the dignity of not disappointing them. She sat down in Alicia's seat. She must have quietly excused herself to the basement now that the praying would start. Click hadn't moved.

"So, I guess we should get started." Rob reached for the breadbasket where everyone had put their prayer requests. "Let's see what the first one --." He broke off as a section of bifold door moved aside and Shane pushed in. Eyebrows went up.

"We're just about to start praying." Marnie pulled her feet out of Cai's lap to sit up fully, maybe preparing to lecture Shane about unassisted transfers.

"I know." Jazz pulled a chair away from the table and he maneuvered up to it, then massaged his shoulder. "I think it's time I joined you guys – unless there's some objection."

Of course, no one objected. A couple of decades of Delaney watch night prayers preceded tonight. While they bowed their heads and the circle voiced the prayers in the basket, Jazz felt a chapped hand caress hers, shyly linking with her. She allowed him to pull her hand over onto his lap because she knew his shoulder was weak, even as she had the scary thought that he might have other plans for her hand. He didn't. He just held it on top of the quilt covering his legs. He didn't pray aloud, but whispered "Amen" a few times, and a couple of times she knew he wiped away tears with his free hand.

"Father, thank you for the extra place set at Your table tonight." Cai's whisper fell in the room like an arcane magical intonation. Shane's breathing stalled for just a second and then resumed. Somewhere far off they heard fireworks, probably leftover from someone's 4th of July or Labor Day celebration. Shane flinched and his hand almost twisted away from hers, but then his fingers tightened, though his breath came in gasps.

"It took years for me not to flinch over explosions." Rob sighed. He was the only one looking at Shane, though it was hard not to see his vulnerability. "Even when I'd do fireworks for you kids, I'd still wince." As if in agreement,

Glister growled, pushing up against Shane's leg, the pain distracting him from his fear. Cai ordered the Lab into the corner while Shane wiped perspiration off his forehead with trembling fingers.

"What are they celebrating?" Cai frowned in the direction of the explosions like he'd like to go out there and wield his deputy badge.

"Life." Shane whispered. All gazes turned toward him where previously they'd been trying to avoid embarrassing him. He glanced at Rob for verification. His father nodded. "Despite the crappy circumstances, we're alive and some people think artillery shells are a good way to celebrate. They don't even know that guys like Dad and I want to duck for the incoming."

"We are alive," Rob agreed. "And when Ren's trucks get here, we'll live a little longer. That's all we can really ask of God, that we have a chance to live a little longer and hope for a little better."

"Amen," Shane whispered, echoed by everyone else in the room. From his corner, Glister whined as if in protest.

Inside the Wire

Jericho Ghost Town

Joe Kelly paused to watch the fireworks. It looked like Liberty Trucking stocked up. Fireworks seemed an extravagance in a world where food was an issue, but he supposed there were no other uses for them. Their bright colors and multitudinous patterns pushed back a dark and lonely night, seeming to promise that the wizened corpse of the old year would give way to the hopeful infant of the new. Since his mother's death from the flu last week, Joe struggled to see the bright side, but he lifted his chin at the lights and promised his mother he'd go on.

When the fireworks stopped, he pulled his flashlight out of his inside pocket and crossed the bridge toward the Jericho Hotel. He hadn't been here in a while. There'd been too many other things to do, including helping Murphy and Cai Delaney train the new Volunteers organization to help him keep things calmer inside the wire. The turnout was not so great as Shane had managed for the Defense force, but he hoped it would be enough to keep neighbor from raiding neighbor. It had been at least two weeks since he'd been here and he couldn't hear water running under the bridge anymore. He wondered what that might mean for water in town. He'd have to ask Jace Welton next time he dropped by City Hall.

His flashlight picked up footprints in the snow on the other side of the bridge. They had to be fairly fresh since there'd been some snow yesterday morning. Beside Shane Delaney, who obviously hadn't been here in the last week, who else might be frequenting this property? You could reach the Delaney cabin on the other side of the lake off the Beulah Cemetery Road. The Lufgrens might fish the lake, but they'd access it from the back of their property, not through Shane's lot. He wondered if the B&B people might be coming over this way. Why would they? He shouldn't be so suspicious of strangers. It was small-town-minded and he didn't like that about himself.

The snow stacked up against the lower window covers of the hotel. Shane reported the building couldn't be broken into, not even by him since the Pulse fried the security system. The woodshed looked untouched, the door sealed shut by four feet of wind-blown snow. The last time Joe had been this way, the snow had only been two feet deep. Shane pumped the diesel tanks dry weeks ago to supply the medical center. What besides firewood was accessible and attractive? Maybe just someone out for a walk, but he still needed to check it out.

His beam passed over something dark in the snow. He swept back. A dark bit of cloth fluttered in a swirl of wind. Joe's heart stuttered in response and a yawning cavern opened in his gut. His feet dragged as he crossed the backyard. Against the old greenhouse, someone had tried to bury a man, but the ground was now frozen solid, so they'd settled for piling snow on top of him. The wind eroded the makeshift cover and now he stared sightless into the night sky.

Joe used his flashlight to scan the length of the body, what was visible. A shudder ran up his spine. More than the surprise of finding a dead body in the snow was the overwhelming recognition that someone had killed this stranger inside the wire.

The End

###

A Taste of "A Death in Jericho"

Marnie called in Amisi Ceylon and Nick Kletti as her coroner's inquest panel. The three of them stood on the far side of the body, wrapped in heavy jackets. Rob, Cai and Joe huddled in their own coats on the other side of the gurney. Marnie supposed the lack of heat in the building would keep the body fresh for a bit longer.

"To start – he's John Doe. He had no ID. So far, nobody has recognized him. He's a mixed-race male, approximately in his late 30s – Asian and black. Medium height, medium build – good musculature and he's been eating regularly, which makes him a unicorn." Her audience didn't laugh so she kept going. "He has several interesting scars – bullet and stab wounds and I'm going to guess that a parent used to use a cigarette as a punishment."

Cai winced. Joe signed heavily. Rob just waited for her to continue.

"He was rendered unconscious by blunt force trauma to the right parietal lobe and then he was smothered. I found pillow material in his airway. I've got Sharon McLaughlin trying to figure out what fabric it might be. It's possible that'll help."

Now Marnie glanced from Nick to Ami, inviting them to join the presentation.

451

"He would have died from the head injury," Nick explained. "There was penetration of bone fragments into the dura mater and subdural bleeding into the brain tissue. By the size of the hematoma, I would guess whoever struck him took up to an hour to decide if they should kill him for real or not, but he would have been disabled by that level of damage regardless of what followed."

Nick glanced at Ami.

"We're none the three of us a medical examiner or forensics expert, but I can tell you there were defensive and offensive wounds on his hands and forearms. He fought back. I think there might have been at least two assailants — one right-handed and the other left-handed."

"A lot of what might have been forensic evidence was destroyed by lying in the snow for a few days and the body freezing." Marnie just wanted to make that clear.

"Joe, you got anything?" Marnie figured the police chief should be entitled to a report.

"I don't think he was killed behind the hotel. I think he was killed somewhere else and then dumped there."

"That's consistent with the freezing pattern." Nick leaned against the counter. "I think he was dead when he was set outside."

"Anything else, Joe?"

"I didn't study for this. We always figured the state cops would take over if we found a dead body. Or the county sheriff."

"I understand. You're what we have, and Bart couldn't have done any better. Cai, you got anything?"

"Um, I'm completely new to this. The five minutes I spent in a criminal law class didn't prepare me for much, but – there are no labels in his clothes – not even his shoes. Along with the missing ID – I tried to fingerprint him, and I don't think freezing after death would remove the fingerprints entirely."

"I thought it was something akin to freezer burn," Ami announced. "What else could it be?"

"Some classes of criminals remove their fingerprints with acid." This came from Nick. Marnie assumed he'd learned that during his years in prison.

"It's like a Le Carre novel." Rob frowned at the sheet-covered body.

"There is that possibility, right?" Father stared at son a moment before Cai continued. "Shane's not the only one hiding secrets. No offense to you, Ami, but several of the people at the B&B are spooks, right?"

"I probably shouldn't confirm that, but I don't know this man and that means he's not from the B&B."

"Could there be others hiding somewhere else in the community?"

"Not to my knowledge and – well, frankly, the others speak rather freely in front of me and I think if there were another safe house here, they'd have let it slip by now."

Cai picked up the sheet to look at the man's face, setting the sheet back in its place, tongue playing with a chill blain on his own lip.

"I suggest I start interviewing everyone in the area. Joe and I can each work on it in the course of our duties and see what we find."

Rob nodded. Marnie shifted on her stool. It was metal. Who thought metal stools were a good idea? Sanitary, but they sucked the heat right out of a body … which was a terrible pun she'd love to share with her husband, except he had that Golden-Retriever-focused-on-a-duck look that meant he wouldn't get the joke.

"There is one possibility you might want to consider." This came from Nick. "Suppose this man came from outside the community."

"How would he get here?"

"Don't know for certain, but perhaps the same way I got here from the compound – snowmobile."

"But why would he be here?" Rob asked.

Nobody said anything for a fist of heart beats, then Cai spoke up.

"Spooks convention, maybe."

Other Lela Markham Titles

Other Great
Breakwater Harbor Books

http://www.breakwaterharborbooks.com/

Check out my fine fellow authors
at Breakwater Harbor Books

Fantasy, Science Fiction, Romance, Historical, Horror, Dark Paranormal, Crime Thriller, Women's Fiction, Psychological Fiction, Christian, Poetry, Wasabi Punk ....

The Immortality Game
Ted Cross

Moscow, 2138. With the world only beginning to recover from the complete societal collapse of the late 21st Century, Zoya scrapes by prepping corpses for funerals and dreams of saving enough money to have a child. When her brother forces her to bring him a mysterious package, she witnesses his murder and finds herself on the run from ruthless mobsters. Frantically trying to stay alive and save her loved ones, Zoya opens the package and discovers two unusual data cards, one that allows her to fight back against the mafia and another which may hold the key to everlasting life.

www.breakwaterharborbooks.com

Waste Energy Resources Company
werc-u.com

Want to know how to do it yourself? Bern is offering access to how-to videos for a $5 subscription at woodstove.locals.com, where you can help build a community around this innovative technology and learn how to turn your woodstove into a central heating unit.

Meet Lela Markham

Hi. I was raised in a house made of books in Alaska and told tales from the time I could talk. A teacher eventually made me write one of them down. I hated the exercise, but it was the spark that ignited a fire that has never gone out.

My daring husband, two fearless offspring and I live the adventure of a lifetime here on the Last Frontier where the midnight sun encourages wandering the wilderness and the long dark winters favor reading, writing and staring at the northern lights ... hence the moniker Aurorawatcher.

It's all about the aurora watching!

www.ingramcontent.com/pod-product-compliance
Lightning Source LLC
Chambersburg PA
CBHW031942260626
47157CB00017B/2025